Praise for Erin Dutton

Landing Zone

"Erin Dutton is great at writing relatable characters, and Kim and Lauren are no exception. These are two interesting, strong women who have a lot to figure out if they're going to be together, and I enjoyed joining them for their journey. The romance is also done well, giving that satisfying push and pull that often comes in enemies-to-lovers pairings."—*The Lesbian Review*

Planning for Love

"What a wonderful and fun read. This is the first book I have read by Erin Dutton and it certainly won't be the last. Great novel with a very intriguing story. The writing was very tight and the pace was perfect."—*Les Reveur*

"*Planning for Love* has an engaging style that kept me hooked from the first page to the last. While I can't really call it an enemies-to-lovers romance, there's definitely a hate-to-love aspect that's so well done that it's delicious…Erin Dutton knows what's up when it comes to writing romance, and she did a fabulous job with *Planning for Love*. It's sexy, sweet, and well worth checking out. I'll be reading this one again!"—*The Lesbian Review*

Capturing Forever

"While there is fire and passion,[*Capturing Forever*] is a thoughtful romance, well written and well paced, it brings to life the reality of adult experiences and the strength of family despite the mistakes we all make."—*Lesbian Reading* [illegible]

T0125688

"This story had so much dep[illegible] show how fragile relationships are and how they can be des[illegible] through careless words and stubbornness. The love scenes [illegible] k were beautiful and emotionally charged. They were about deep love and were so vital to the story. I want to go back and reread this book as I felt so invested in it and didn't want it to end."—*KittyKat Book Reviews*

"The book is written very well and will hold your attention from start to finish…I found myself cheering for their love to get back on track…This is one of those books I will reread someday, and that is how you really know that it is a book worth talking about." —*Amanda's Reviews*

Dutton "takes you deep into the heart of both these women…The story flows like a river, smooth on the surface, beneath, a current pulling you away."—*Lunar Rainbow Reviewz*

Officer Down

"This book is a true romance…I liked seeing the characters grow, expand their horizons, and become, in Olivia's case, the woman she so desperately wants to be."—*Prism Book Alliance*

"One of my favorite things about the story was the attention that was put into the details of each woman's work environment and what their respective tasks entailed…The story was fast-paced and I enjoyed reading about how the relationship between Olivia and Hillary developed from being work acquaintances to much more."—*Bookaholism.com*

For the Love of Cake

"Thoroughly enjoyable reading. If you like a good romance this will hit the buttons, and if you like reality cooking shows you will have a double winner. As many others will probably say—it has hot women and cake, what else could it possibly need?"—*Curve Magazine*

"In Dutton's highly entertaining contemporary, well-drawn characters Shannon Hayes and Maya Vaughn discover romance behind reality TV…Dutton's love story never loses momentum." —*Publishers Weekly*

Point of Ignition

"Erin Dutton has given her fans another fast-paced story of fire, with both buildings and emotions burning hotly. *Point of Ignition* is a story told well that will touch its readers."—*Just About Write*

"Erin Dutton has written more than seven lesbian romance titles for Bold Strokes Books, and boy can she write."—*The Bright List*

Designed for Love

"*Designed for Love* is…rich in love, romance, and sex. Dutton gives her readers a roller coaster ride filled with sexual thrills and chills. *Designed for Love* is the perfect book to curl up with on a cold winter's day."—*Just About Write*

A Place to Rest

"If you like romances with characters who could live next door to you and the element of family interaction and dynamics, *A Place to Rest* is for you. It's charming, moving, and emotionally satisfying."—*The Lesbian Review*

Fully Involved

"Dutton literally fills the pages with smoke as she vividly describes the scene. She is equally skilled at showing her readers Reid's feelings of guilt and rage at the loss of her best friend. *Fully Involved* explores the emotional depths of these two very different women. Each woman struggles with loss, change, and the magnetic attraction they have for each other. Their relationship sizzles, flames, and ignites with a page-turning intensity. This is an exciting read about two very intriguing women."—*Just About Write*

"Dutton's studied evocation of the macho world of firefighting gives the story extra oomph—and happily ever after is what a good romance is all about, right?"—*Q Syndicate*

Sequestered Hearts

"*Sequestered Hearts* is packed with raw emotion, but filled with tender moments too. The author writes with sophistication that one would expect from a veteran author…A romance is about more than just plot and character development. It's about passion, physical intimacy, and connection between the characters. The reader should have a visceral reaction to what is going on within the pages for the novel to succeed. Dutton's words match perfectly with the emotion she has created. *Sequestered Hearts* is one book that cannot be overlooked. It is romance at its finest."—*L-word Literature.com*

"*Sequestered Hearts* by first time novelist Erin Dutton is everything a romance should be. It is teeming with longing, heartbreak, and of course, love…as pure romances go, it is one of the best in print today."—*Just About Write*

By the Author

Sequestered Hearts

Fully Involved

A Place to Rest

Designed for Love

Point of Ignition

A Perfect Match

Reluctant Hope

More than Friends

For the Love of Cake

Officer Down

Capturing Forever

Planning for Love

Landing Zone

Wavering Convictions

Visit us at www.boldstrokesbooks.com

Wavering Convictions

by

Erin Dutton

2019

WAVERING CONVICTIONS

© 2019 By Erin Dutton. All Rights Reserved.

ISBN 13: 978-1-63555-403-8

This Trade Paperback Original Is Published By
Bold Strokes Books, Inc.
P.O. Box 249
Valley Falls, NY 12185

First Edition: June 2019

THIS IS A WORK OF FICTION. NAMES, CHARACTERS, PLACES, AND INCIDENTS ARE THE PRODUCT OF THE AUTHOR'S IMAGINATION OR ARE USED FICTITIOUSLY. ANY RESEMBLANCE TO ACTUAL PERSONS, LIVING OR DEAD, BUSINESS ESTABLISHMENTS, EVENTS, OR LOCALES IS ENTIRELY COINCIDENTAL.

THIS BOOK, OR PARTS THEREOF, MAY NOT BE REPRODUCED IN ANY FORM WITHOUT PERMISSION.

Credits
Editor: Shelley Thrasher
Production Design: Stacia Seaman
Cover Design by Jeanine Henning

Acknowledgments

Once more I have to thank Radclyffe and Sandy and all of the staff at BSB that get it done every time. Over twelve years of events, workshops, conferences, and working with my editor, Shelley Thrasher, my craft has grown and changed. Here's hoping for twelve more years.

Special thanks to the readers with whom I am delighted to share each book. Many of you have reached out on Facebook, personally and in various groups, and have, in turn, shared your lives with me. And I thank you. It's awesome to get feedback on my books. But I especially enjoy finding people that I share common interests with, as well as those who introduce me to new ideas.

Thank you to the readers who spend their valuable free time from the real world to travel and visit with us at the various events, whether just for a day for a Pride festival or taking a longer trip to Women's Week, GCLS, and other gatherings. I hope these events are just as fun for you as they are for me.

And finally, to my wife, who is always willing to talk story or read pages and offer feedback. And who takes care of everything around the house during that last month before my deadline, while I'm catching up from my procrastination and grinding out the final chapters. I love you, Christina.

For my family—who have never wavered
in their love and support of me.

Prologue

"How late do you plan to stay?"

Maggie Davidson glanced up from her desk. Her boss and close friend, Inga, leaned against the edge of her cubicle divider. She already wore her jacket and carried her large leather shoulder bag. Before she left each evening, she often took a lap around the main section of the office, where her four records clerks labored in a quad of cubicles. Often, Maggie was the last one left working.

"I want to finish this request and email it before I go." She hated leaving in the middle of a project. Then, the next day, she would spend the first fifteen minutes reviewing everything to remind herself where she'd left off. If she took that extra time today, she could complete her work and start fresh on a new request tomorrow.

"You work too hard. And you make the rest of us look bad." Inga grinned and winked. "Luckily, I mitigate that fact by taking credit when our department exceeds our productivity goal."

"Have a good night." Maggie turned back to her computer screen as Inga continued down the hall.

The automatic lock clicked behind Inga, and the office fell quiet. Maggie picked up her phone and set it to stream through the Bluetooth speaker on her desk. Easy-listening music drowned out the clicking of her keyboard. A phone rang somewhere else in the office, then stopped.

Ten minutes later, having reached a satisfactory stopping point, Maggie packed her leather tote and slung it over her shoulder. After a short elevator ride, she said good-bye to the night security guard on her way out of the building. He grumbled his response. She'd thought he was crotchety because he was stuck working overnights. But Inga said he had enough seniority to work the day shift if he chose to. So maybe grouchy was just his natural state.

Since she'd barely glanced at the window all day, the smattering of rain as she stepped outside caught her off guard. She dug in her bag, then popped open her umbrella. Now, in addition to rush-hour traffic and the usual Friday-evening influx of people headed into downtown for dinner and night life, she'd have to deal with slick roads and bad drivers.

As she walked two blocks to the parking garage where she paid a monthly fee, she passed only a couple of people. She leaned her umbrella to one side, and they tilted theirs to the other to make room on the sidewalk as they met. Before she entered the darkened structure, she fished her keys out of her bag. She lowered her umbrella and tucked her key ring in her closed fist, leaving one key sticking out between her fingers. Her father had given her those instructions when she'd moved to the "big city" over a decade ago. For a man who'd never left the rural north-Georgia town where he grew up, Nashville was very metropolitan.

She took the stairs down one level, then found her car, two rows over, halfway across the cavernous garage. She'd taken a long lunch for a dentist appointment, and when she returned, she'd had to park farther away than usual. Luckily, Inga was flexible regarding their schedule. Tomorrow, Maggie would work through her lunch to make up the work she'd missed. She began making a mental to-do list for the next day.

She heard several heavy footfalls behind her, and then a deep voice said, "Give me your bag."

Maggie turned, certain she'd misheard. "What?"

A man stood a couple of feet from her. He wore a black

hooded sweatshirt and a menacing snarl, but she couldn't stop staring at the gun he held. Her stomach swirled with nausea, her arms felt weak, and she couldn't catch her breath.

"Just hand it over, lady. I don't want to hurt you." He took several steps closer, thrusting the gun in her direction, and Maggie shrank back against her car.

She fumbled behind her for the door handle. If she could just get inside, she'd have a chance to get away. Her keys. The angled edge of the one key dug into her fingers as she'd clutched it tightly. Her father had told her to grasp it this way—to punch with it. She lashed out, simultaneously trying to connect with some part of his body while also bracing for the gunshot. He yelped as her fist glanced off his shoulder. Before she could act on his distraction, he swung his free hand out and caught her wrist.

"I said, I don't want to hurt you. But I will." He squeezed her wrist, hard, then twisted it away from her, forcing her to contort to ease the pain. He pushed her back against the car, using his body to pin her there. When he shoved the barrel of the gun under her chin, she froze. His eyes shifted over her face erratically for a second, and she thought she felt a tremor in his hand where it held hers.

She'd barely registered that he'd released her wrist before he grasped the strap of her purse where it lay against her shoulder. As he wrenched it from her, he staggered back several steps. She jerked forward, stumbling to her hands and knees. Her keys clattered across the concrete and under a nearby car. He mumbled something, but she couldn't make it out over the pounding of her own heart.

By the time she raised her head, he was running away. She leaned back on her heels, still too shocked to try to stand. The sound of footsteps sent a renewed wave of panic through her. Was he coming back? What would he want from her now? As a figure rounded the corner, Maggie's fear eased. The sensible shoes of an older woman clacked against the concrete as she hurried over to

Maggie. When she drew close, she slowed and hesitantly reached out as if to touch Maggie's shoulder.

"Honey? Are you okay? Did you take a fall?"

"No. I—I need to call the police." She braced a hand against her car and forced herself to her feet. "But he—my purse. My phone."

"Okay. Where's your purse?" The woman looked around for it.

"He took it."

The woman nodded and fished in her own shoulder bag for her phone. While the woman recited the address and a confused account about finding Maggie on the floor of the garage to the 9-1-1 operator, Maggie stared into her car, wishing she could sit down. But she'd have to crawl under that other car for her keys to unlock it.

"Well, I don't know. She's kind of out of it, but she doesn't have her purse or anything," the woman said into the phone. "No. I don't see any injuries." Then to Maggie, she said, "They want to know were you robbed or attacked or something?"

"Robbed. A man. Black sweatshirt." She frantically searched her mind for some other piece of his description but couldn't see anything except the gun. The police would come, but they would never find him. How many men were running around in a black sweatshirt?

Chapter One

Less than a week later, Maggie's stomach wavered as she guided her car down the ramp leading to the underground parking garage. The shadow from the concrete roof overhead ominously crawled across her windshield toward her. She glanced in her rearview mirror. The driver in the car behind her appeared impatient to get inside, and suddenly, she didn't want to enter at all. But she couldn't very well throw her car into reverse, and she was even less likely to get out and ask him to move so she could escape. So she forged ahead, trying to ignore the darkness traveling over her steering wheel and up her arms and the dread that seeped in with every fading inch of sunlight.

Inside, she rolled her window down only long enough to grab the ticket stub that would both activate the mechanical arm allowing her entrance and later calculate her charges as she exited. She found a spot as close to the elevators as she could, circling down several ramps into the abyss as she passed open spots at the far end of each level. She backed into the space. When she shifted into Park, the automatic unlock of the doors startled her. She jammed her finger down on the button, relocking them, then cursed under her breath as she startled herself.

"Get a grip, Maggie."

She sat there with her hand on the door handle, staring through the glass vestibule that separated those waiting for the elevator from the rest of the garage. A crowd had already gathered, and Maggie stayed safely ensconced in her Prius while the elevator doors opened. Once the passengers disappeared inside and the doors closed, she quickly exited and hurried over to press the call button once more. Maybe the next car would arrive before any other riders did, but with only two elevators, the chances were low.

The slam of a vehicle door echoed from the far end of the garage. Her palms grew damp, and she clenched them into fists. The sharp sound of approaching footsteps indicated some type of hard-soled shoe.

"It's okay. Hard soles—maybe a dress shoe or a woman in heels," she whispered. They weren't the heavy footfalls of a large man's boot. Despite her own reassurances, she felt light-headed, and her breathing quickened. Fear brought a sour taste to her mouth as she remembered staring down at a pair of dusty brown work boots and praying she wasn't about to die. Five days had been enough time for details of the robbery to begin coming back to her, but not enough to dull the edge of terror.

Fighting panic, she glanced at the stairwell. Did the unknown spiral upward hold less danger than being trapped in a tiny box with a stranger? She dashed through the door before said stranger came into sight and climbed the stairs as quickly as she could manage in her own flats. These days she dressed with consideration to how fast she could flee if she needed to.

By the time she reached the top, her calves burned, and she struggled to catch her breath. The stairs ended in a small vestibule that opened to the courtyard outside city hall, across the street from the courthouse. The tension in her chest lessened. She crossed the street, sucking in as much fresh air as she could.

She stepped inside the front door and stopped immediately, stuck in some kind of line that snaked out into the vestibule between the inner and outer doors. She rose on her toes to see over the people in front of her, and luckily none of them were much taller than her own five feet seven inches. The crowd spilled back from three metal detectors manned by uniformed security guards.

The line inched forward until it was finally her turn. Then the guard ordered her to drop her purse into a bin and empty the pockets of her dress slacks, waving her through the metal detector. As she exited the other side and waited to gather her belongings, another guard passed a wand over the front of a man holding his wallet in one hand and his belt in the other. Maggie hadn't set off any alarms and was allowed to reclaim her purse and progress into the lobby toward a bank of six elevators, three on each side of the space.

The crowd in the lobby was not nearly as organized as the lines out front. Here, in fact, she couldn't detect any order to the horde. Some people huddled close to one of the elevators, obviously having chosen to hedge their bet on that one being next. Others hung back in the center area, the tension in their posture indicating they were ready to shove forward toward the first doors to open.

Maggie chose an elevator on the end and tried to make her own place in line, not interested in cutting ahead of someone else just to get into one of the tiny boxes. But most of those around her didn't share her respect for order. A rotund man practically rested against her right shoulder. When someone pressed into her back, she tried to shuffle forward a step, but she had no escape. The stinging scent of too much cheap cologne mixed with body odor turned her stomach. Pretending to rub her face, she breathed shallowly into her cupped hand.

She missed the first time the closest elevator opened. The

car filled quickly with those in front of her and a few who crowded past her. The next time the doors opened, she shuffled forward with the surge of people. She tried to work her way to the back but ended up trapped in the middle. Hunching her shoulders inward, she attempted to lessen her footprint in the already small space. The woman standing close on her left reeked of stale cigarette smoke. She was too skinny in a seemingly unhealthy way, and her skin appeared paper-thin. When she buried her fingers in her messy ponytail and dug at her scalp, Maggie fervently wished she had imagined the dusting of flakes floating in the air. If she could have shifted to the left, she would have. But two men occupied that space.

One, wearing a pair of khakis and an ill-fitting plaid shirt, kept tugging at his tie. The other was dressed in a sharp suit, with a bright-blue shirt and a boldly patterned contrasting tie. The way he leaned close and spoke quietly to the other man hinted that he might be the man's attorney.

Why wasn't this elevator moving? Every time the doors started to close, someone in the large crowd still waiting for the next car would push the button, causing her elevator door to open again. The first two times, someone new tried to squeeze in. By the third time, she was ready to scream at them to wait until her car left to push the button again. Surely elevator programming couldn't be that difficult to figure out. The man behind her shifted and brushed against her.

"No," she murmured, then repeated it more loudly as panic surged up in her throat. She didn't even excuse herself as she shoved between the woman and child in front of her and stumbled back into the lobby before the doors closed once more.

Ignoring the exasperated looks from the people she pinballed against, she forced her way through the crowd until she reached the security check-in area again.

"Ma'am." One of the guards approached her. "Are you okay?" His hand hovered around his waist. Was she about to get hit with a Taser? She couldn't blame him for being suspicious. "Ma'am?"

"Yes. Claustrophobic." She didn't look up to see if he accepted her explanation before she hurried past him toward the nearest restroom. She would make herself presentable, grab a coffee from the shop adjacent to the lobby, then try the elevators again.

❖

Ally Becker shuffled along in a cafeteria-style line, selecting a small coffee and a plain bagel with cream cheese. She'd arrived at the courthouse over an hour early for her brother's hearing. His lawyer had warned her that she'd face a bit of a madhouse getting up to the courtroom. Apparently, all the judges liked to start their mornings at the same time, regardless of whether they presided over a docket or a criminal trial. She'd seen the mass of people waiting for the elevators and opted to take her chances that the crowd might thin a bit before his preliminary hearing started.

She settled at one of only a few remaining tables and pulled out her phone to check her email. Soon, she found the crowds milling about outside the café more interesting than anything on her screen. So her attention was on the entrance when a frazzled-looking woman walked in.

Ally didn't know the difference between custom and just well-tailored when it came to women's dress clothes. But either way, the woman's black pant suit fit her perfectly. Thick, light-brown curls floated around her head, defying gravity, in a short bob that just grazed her ears.

Her put-together appearance warred with the furtive,

almost fearful way she glanced around the café. Ally felt her discomfort from across the room. Realizing she was staring, she feigned interest once more in her phone screen. But she remained aware of the woman as she rushed through the serving line, then found herself standing in the middle of the crowded space.

Ally didn't see any free tables. So before someone could vacate one and steal away her excuse, she made eye contact with the woman. "I've got an extra seat, if you don't mind sharing." With her foot, she pushed out the empty chair across the table from her.

For a moment she thought the woman would refuse. She seemed to search the café for another available place.

"Look, it's either me or that guy over there." She tried to inject some levity into her voice as she tilted her head toward a grumpy-looking elderly man with a newspaper spread out on the small round table. The corners draped over the edges like some sort of disposable tablecloth.

The woman nodded and lowered herself tentatively onto the chair opposite Ally. She set her drink and napkin-wrapped-muffin as close to her edge of the table as she could without losing them to the floor. Ally moved her own coffee closer to her, making room, but the woman didn't adjust her snack.

"I'm Ally."

"Maggie." When Maggie scowled, Ally began to lose patience. She'd only been trying to be nice, and this woman was acting as if she couldn't be bothered to do the same. Ally held up her hands, palms out.

"Okay. We don't have to be cordial. I just thought since we were sharing a table—"

Maggie's face flushed. "I'm sorry for being rude. I—I'm not comfortable being here."

"In a coffee shop?"

"No. The courthouse."

"So you're not a lawyer? I wasn't sure, since you're wearing a suit and all."

"No. I'm not."

"So why are you here? If it's okay to ask."

"I'd actually rather not talk about it."

"If you're being charged with something, I'll try not to judge." She tried for a joke, but it fell as flat as Maggie's expression. "Well, then I'll tell you why I'm here. I'm clearly not a lawyer either." She gestured to her best navy slacks and button-down shirt. While her outfit was presentable, no one would mistake her for someone as white-collar as an attorney. "My brother has a preliminary hearing today."

"Oh." Maggie stared at her untouched muffin. "I'm sorry. I'm not really sure what to say to that."

"You don't have to say anything. He—uh—he has a drug problem. Now that I think about it, I'm not really in the mood to talk much about that either." She didn't know why she'd said anything to begin with. Her brother's addiction embarrassed her and made her ashamed that he'd reached the point he had. "Let's talk about something else. What do you do for a living, Maggie?"

"That's not an interesting topic either. I'm a public-records clerk for the city."

"Well, no—that's—"

"It's boring."

"It's not." Ally didn't think most would find her career interesting either.

"It pays the bills. And I love the people I work with. They're a great group and have been very understanding this past week when I haven't been able to be there." She rolled one hand in a gesture that Ally assumed meant she hadn't been there because of whatever brought her to court and therefore she likely didn't want to talk about it. "What do you do?"

"Carpentry. I recently started my own business, making furniture. But I supplement that job by working for a company that frames houses for new construction." Until six months ago, she'd worked on a crew with her brother. Even before his recent legal troubles, their employer had given him his last "one more chance" to get his act together. His losing his job had been the kick in the pants she'd needed as well. She decided to stop saying she'd concentrate on furniture-making "someday" and start putting her focus there. She still did framing in spurts to pay her bills, but now she contracted with the company by the job, when *she* needed to work. She was on a project now that would end in a couple of weeks.

"Carpentry, wow. I've always wished I was good with my hands."

Ally smiled and glanced down at Maggie's hands, which were wrapped around her coffee cup. They were small and looked soft, her medium-length nails well-shaped and painted a neutral shade.

"Sorry. I—I didn't mean that like it sounded." Maggie avoided eye contact. "My father was handy. He could fix anything. I've often wished I'd paid more attention instead of taking him for granted."

Ally nodded, picking up on Maggie's use of the past tense. "When did he pass?"

"About five years ago now."

"I'm sorry." She felt strange expressing sympathy for five-year-old grief but didn't know what else to say. Ally often got uncomfortable with anything more than light social conversation. On the job site, her crew didn't have time for small talk. And she rarely spent time with anyone other than her two best friends outside of work.

"It's okay. It's been a long time. I mean, it's never really the same, but it becomes the new normal, you know."

Ally's own father had run off when she was just four years old. Her mother had met and married Carey's father and given birth to Carey within a year. They'd divorced when Ally was in high school. He'd been a decent stepfather, but never close enough that Ally missed him after he left. He barely bothered to keep in touch with Carey, so Ally had never been surprised that he didn't maintain a relationship with her.

Maggie still looked sad, and Ally wanted to reach across the table and touch her arm. But she didn't think Maggie would welcome the gesture. "What about you? I know you're here for your brother. But is anyone else in your family coming? Are you close?"

"My mother is at home. She says she can't stand to see him in court. And my father is—not in the picture."

"I'm sorry." Maggie's *sorry* sounded sincere and warm and brought a lump of emotion to Ally's throat that she hadn't felt in years.

Ally swallowed, then rolled her eyes. "This isn't an appropriate getting-to-know-you conversation with a stranger."

Maggie smiled. "Is that what we're doing? Getting to know each other?"

"Yes."

"We were." Maggie glanced at her watch, then stood and gathered her trash. "But now I should probably head up. It looks like the crowd has dispersed at the elevator."

"Oh, right." When Maggie stood, Ally did, too.

"Thanks for sharing your table."

While Ally was working up the nerve to ask for her number, Maggie left the café and headed for the bank of elevators. She sighed and dropped back into her chair. Bringing her empty coffee cup to her lips, she pretended she was finishing the drink rather than watching Maggie until she disappeared inside one of the elevators.

❖

Maggie got off at the fourth floor and followed the signs for courtroom 4B, one of the general-sessions courtrooms. She stopped as soon as she stepped inside, overwhelmed and wishing she'd taken her boss Inga up on her offer to accompany her.

"Keep it moving, lady. We all gotta sit down, too."

She stepped aside to allow the four people behind her to pass, and they moved down the aisle and into a row of church-pew-like benches. Over half the seats were full already. Should she sit on a specific side? She scanned the people around her, then silently berated herself for trying to figure out which ones looked like the perpetrators of crime. She'd spoken with someone from the district attorney's office on the phone, but she had no idea what he looked like. He sounded young, but any one of the men in suits gathered around the two tables facing the judge could fit that description.

She'd just decided to move to the left when a woman carrying a clipboard approached. "Are you a witness in a case today?"

"Yes. Maggie Davidson."

"Who's the defendant?"

She cleared her throat. "Um—his last name is Rowe."

The woman made a mark next to Maggie's name. "Hold on. I think General Miller wants to talk to you."

"General?"

"Right. Sorry. In court the assistant district attorney general is addressed as general."

The woman turned and pushed through the swinging gate in the low railing that divided the front of the courtroom from the gallery. Bending, she spoke quietly to a dark-haired man seated at the table on the left. He turned to look at her over his shoulder as the woman gestured to where she still stood awkwardly in the aisle. The woman motioned Maggie closer, and she approached the rail.

"This is General Ralph Miller. He's handling the preliminary hearing for your case."

"Maggie Davidson." She stuck her hand out. "So you're the prosecutor on the case."

"No. Not exactly. I work here in general-sessions court. Our goal today would be to show the judge we have probable cause to get the case bound over to the grand jury. After Mr. Rowe is indicted, if the case goes to trial, another ADA will be assigned." He glanced at the judge's bench, then at a gathering of men and women in suits hovering nearby. "I'm sorry. I don't have time to go into all of that right now. But if you'll call our office later, someone can explain the process. In fact, I spoke with Mr. Rowe's attorney a few minutes ago, and he plans to ask for this hearing to be reset so he can have more time to prepare."

"So I'll have to come back to court?" She just wanted all this to be over. She'd fought her anxiety to get here, and now she'd have to do it again.

"Probably. Have a seat and wait for the judge to call the docket. When we get to Rowe, he'll assign another date on his calendar, probably sometime later this week or next." Without waiting for a response, he turned away and waved over one of the suited men nearby.

Clearly having been dismissed, Maggie looked around for the woman who'd helped her before, but she'd moved on and was now huddled in conversation with another woman and her teenager. Maggie found an empty space on a bench in the second row from the back.

A few minutes later, Ally eased through the doors, along with a tall, lanky, suited man. He angled his head as she spoke quietly to him. He murmured an answer, then pointed toward a seat on the opposite side of the aisle from Maggie. He continued to the front of the courtroom and joined several men and women at the table opposite the ADA.

Maggie considered moving to sit closer to Ally. Their chat downstairs had provided the closest thing to a distraction that Maggie had experienced in days. For the duration of a cup of coffee, Maggie had imagined she could be a functioning member of society again. Once more, she could be the kind of woman who spoke to an attractive stranger—maybe even flirted, instead of worrying about hidden danger.

She'd had game before—had never had a problem approaching someone, giving out her number, and leaving with a date. And Ally was exactly the kind of woman she went for. She was beautiful and strong. Openness and welcome warmed her dark-brown eyes. The cleft in her chin begged for Maggie's finger to stroke it. Maggie had entered that café completely closed off, and Ally had coaxed her out. She'd gotten more conversation from Maggie than anyone had since the robbery.

When the judge came out, Maggie stood because everyone else did. She sat at the judge's command. She tried to follow along as a court employee read off a list of names, and after each one, an attorney called out whether the parties were present. While she'd expected the prosecutors to be assigned to many cases today, she was surprised to find that some of the defense attorneys represented multiple defendants. The man she'd seen with Ally answered for at least seven cases, and she wondered how he could keep them all straight. She soon figured out that they were public defenders, assigned to represent those who couldn't afford an attorney.

Sometimes, the attorneys spent several minutes talking about motions and plea agreements. Though she had trouble keeping up with what was going on in each case, she stared at the front of the room.

Only a week ago, she'd been the kind of person who enjoyed people-watching while in a crowd. And she had a feeling last-week-Maggie might have liked to try to figure out the stories of the diverse group of people around her. But present-Maggie could focus only on the fact that half of these people were likely accused of a crime, and the other half were victims—like her. She didn't know which made her more uncomfortable.

Chapter Two

Hearing the clerk call Carey's name sent Ally's heart racing. She'd tried to act calm while on the phone with her mother yesterday, assuring her that she'd go to court so Carey would see a friendly face. But now, she was unexpectedly nervous about seeing him led out in an orange jumpsuit like the defendants before him. Since his arrest, he'd been in jail for five days already.

His public defender had advised them to leave him there until after his preliminary hearing. Though the suggestion sounded harsh to Ally, he wanted Carey to detox in jail. He planned to suggest that Carey go to a recovery house upon his release. He would participate in rehab while there and be closely monitored. His previous attempt at rehab hadn't stuck, but at least this way he wouldn't be staying at their mother's house. She coddled him and looked the other way when he was obviously using.

Carey's attorney addressed the judge, and he seemed to be asking for another court date. Was this for the criminal trial? She'd thought that would be months away. Earlier, she'd tried to follow along when he explained the process and thought that, after this hearing, the case would go to the grand jury for indictment. So why was the judge now talking about an opening on his calendar on Friday? Before Ally could figure out what had happened, the clerk had called another name, and Carey's attorney slung his messenger bag over his shoulder. Ally hated that he carried the olive-drab bag that looked more suited for an undergrad. Wasn't a reputable attorney supposed to own a nice briefcase or something?

What had happened? Ally hurried to catch up with him as he pushed through the divider and strode toward the back of the courtroom.

"Mr. Baez," she called as he cleared the doors into the hallway. He stopped and turned. "Why didn't my brother go before the judge?"

"Ms. Becker." He glanced around, then took her elbow and guided her out of the way of the doors, almost into the corner of the large hallway. "I didn't have time to tell you before the docket started. Carey has been ill, and he's in extremely poor spirits today."

Ally shook her head. "He's in poor spirits? He's in jail. Isn't he supposed to be in a bit of a bad mood? You're going to leave him there for four more days because he's a little down?"

"This judge isn't known for sympathizing with addicts who commit felonies. We need Carey on his best behavior if we're going to get him out and transferred to the recovery program."

Did some judges sympathize with criminal addicts? How could they get Carey's case assigned to one of them? Ally shoved her hand into the front of her hair in frustration. She'd worried about how they would pay for treatment. But Mr. Baez had said he would help Carey apply for assistance. She wished she didn't have to deal with all of this on her own.

"I'd hoped to convince him to agree to a plea deal. But he's not interested. When I spoke with him earlier, he was combative and not receptive to treatment."

"Not receptive—tell him he doesn't have a choice." What was the plan if he wasn't any more cooperative in four days? Would this guy leave Carey in jail indefinitely? He seemed unprepared for anything except Carey pleading guilty. And why not? In the short time she'd sat in the courtroom, Ally had heard several attorneys advise the judge that they'd worked out a deal with the prosecutor. That seemed to be all the defense attorneys were interested in: negotiate a deal, collect your fees, and move on to the next client.

"But he does, Ms. Becker. And he has to make his own decision, or his getting treatment is a waste of time and money."

"What are we talking about here?" Ally barked, then seeing several heads turn around her, she pitched her voice lower. "He's probably going to prison. If primetime television is to be believed, he'll be able to get drugs in there anyway."

"Ms. Becker, the hearing has been reset for Friday. Try not to get ahead of yourself in predicting the outcome of a trial that we're still months away from. Let's take this step by step." His voice carried a warning, but Ally didn't know if it was truly about her presumptive conclusions. Maybe he wanted to convey that she shouldn't imply Carey was guilty where she could be overheard.

"Mr. Baez—"

"Please, call me Jorge."

"I'm sorry. I'm feeling a little lost here. Nothing we've done so far to try to help Carey has worked. That's one reason I can't exactly summon any optimism right now."

"I know it's frustrating, but you need to trust that my job is to represent Carey's best interests and to think long-term about all possible outcomes for these charges."

Frustrating didn't even cover her emotions. As children she and Carey had been close. Their mother described five-year-old Ally creeping into Carey's room to sleep on the floor next to his crib. The chasm in their relationship had begun only in recent years, following Carey's injury on a job site and subsequent slide into an addiction to painkillers.

"You don't need to come to court Friday. If I'm able to get him released to the recovery house, he'll need to go right away."

She shook her head. "I'll be here. My mother will want it that way."

"Okay, then. Please, let me know if I can do anything for either of you before then." His words sounded sincere, though he'd already traveled several steps down the hallway away from her as he spoke.

She replayed their conversation while she rode down in the elevator, trying to align what had happened today against the legal timeline he'd explained when they'd spoken on the phone a couple of days ago. These were just preliminary hearings. His case would most likely be bound over to the grand jury, and Jorge seemed certain they would indict him. The criminal trial would be set months away. In the meantime, she had to worry about Carey getting clean and staying that way. She wanted all of this to be over, or better yet, to wake up and find it had all been a dream.

She stepped out of the lobby, breathing easier. On a good day, she didn't like to be inside. She was happiest building furniture in her garage or raising walls and building trusses. Today, the courthouse air had felt especially stifling.

She started across the expanse of landscaped concrete outside the courthouse, intent on getting as far away as she could. She almost missed Maggie lingering near a large planter, while on the phone. Giving her privacy, Ally kept walking, but Maggie finished her call just as Ally reached her. Maggie glanced up, and Ally stopped abruptly, inelegantly caught between hurrying by and exchanging pleasantries.

"Hey. I was just asking my boss if she wanted me to pick up some lunch on my way to the office."

Ally wanted to ask Maggie if *she* could take her to lunch. She glanced at her watch and amended, a late lunch. Anything to spend more time with her. But her mother was expecting her at home, and Maggie apparently needed to get to work. Maggie fiddled with her keys, and Ally latched on to a reason to grab a few extra minutes.

"Did you park in the garage across the street?"

"Yes." Maggie glanced in that direction, and though they couldn't see the entrance from where they stood, apprehension filtered across her expression.

"Me too. Can I walk you to your car?" She flushed at the awkwardness in her words. She felt like a teenager asking a girl to the dance. Could Maggie tell what an idiot she was?

"Sure." Was that relief on her face?

"Yeah? Okay." Ally fought the urge to poke out her elbow for Maggie to take. She didn't even know Maggie's whole story, but Maggie brought out a protective instinct in her. She waited until Maggie started forward, then moved beside her. As she let Maggie go in front, she touched her hand to her back. Maggie flinched, and Ally dropped her arm back to her side.

"Everything go okay in there?" Maggie tilted her head toward the building they'd just left.

She shrugged. "I don't really understand all the legal stuff."

"Isn't that what your brother's lawyer is for?"

"I guess so. It would help if I trusted him, instead of feeling he's just another overworked government cog." They paused at the end of the sidewalk, waiting for the light to change.

"Ah, a public defender."

"Yep."

"Well, speaking as a government cog myself, I can confirm that we're exhausted, under-appreciated, and underpaid. But that doesn't mean we aren't trying to do a good job." The light changed, and Maggie didn't wait for Ally as she proceeded into the crosswalk.

Ally grimaced and followed. "I'm sorry. I didn't mean to imply—"

"Yes, you did."

"Okay. I did."

"And that's all right. Your brother's future is in his hands, after all. Clearly, he means a lot to you."

Their sleeves brushed as their arms swung at their sides, but despite Maggie's earlier reaction, Ally didn't step away. In fact, she wanted to move closer. Maggie was a few inches shorter, so her shoulder would fit right under Ally's arm. She imagined their hips bumping together lightly as they walked. But, of course, she and Maggie didn't know each other well enough for such intimacy.

"He's my half brother. He was only ten when his dad and my mom divorced. He had a tough time after that, and I kinda knew what it was like to not have a dad, so I tried to take care of him."

"Your father…" Maggie let the question hang in the air, but Ally knew what she was asking.

"He took off. I haven't seen or heard from him in thirty-five years."

"That's rough."

"Stairs or elevator?" Ally seized the chance to change the subject as they approached the entrance to the underground garage.

Maggie glanced between the elevators and the entrance to the stairs. She didn't look happy about either option. "Stairs are fine. What floor are you on?"

"The second." They entered the stairwell, walking down side by side.

"I'm on the third." Maggie seemed bothered that they weren't on the same floor.

Footsteps below them indicated someone on the way up, so Ally slowed and moved behind Maggie to make room. Had she not been looking directly down at Maggie, she might not have noticed the way her shoulders stiffened and how she shifted closer to the wall as soon as the man came into view. When Ally put her behavior together with her obvious nervousness at the top of the stairs, her conclusions made her sick to her stomach.

Maggie had never said what she was doing at the courthouse. But, for some reason, Ally didn't think she was a defendant in a case. Something criminal had happened to Maggie—something that had rattled her enough to scare her in what should be a relatively safe situation. The man nodded at them as he passed, and Ally gave an answering lift of her chin. She wanted to reach out to Maggie—just a reassuring touch on the back or shoulder, but Maggie had already communicated that her touch wasn't welcome, and she seemed to be in an even more heightened state of anxiety now.

Maggie paused on the next landing and turned toward Ally. "This is you."

"I'll go down with you, then come back up."

"You don't have to—"

"I said I'd walk you to your car. You're not getting rid of me that easily." Ally gestured toward the stairs.

Maggie shrugged and headed for the next flight. As she turned away, relief flashed across her expression. Ally jogged a couple of steps to catch up and fell in beside her again. They exited the stairwell on the next floor, and Maggie led them to her car. She pulled out her key fob, unlocked her car, and turned toward Ally.

"Thanks for walking me down." She pulled open the door, clearly dismissing Ally.

"Would you like to get coffee sometime?" Ally blurted.

Maggie tilted her head slightly. "I thought we already did."

Ally recalled their shared table in the café. Why did that seem like so long ago? "While I'm still flattered that you chose me over newspaper guy, maybe this time we could sit together on purpose." She saw the rejection Maggie was constructing, even before she finished speaking.

"You seem very nice and all, but I'm not really looking to get involved with anyone right now."

Ally smiled and held her hands up, palms out. "Whoa. Me either. It's a friendly cup of coffee. Possibly a scone or some comparable pastry. And maybe we can talk about what we *are* looking for." She couldn't resist the hint of flirtation, though she knew she would probably scare Maggie off.

"Thanks, but—"

"Don't say no. Not yet. Just say 'we'll see' and take my

number. If you decide not to call me, well, I'll find a way to go on. But if you need someone to talk to or want to share a meal or something, you'll have it."

"Ally—"

"Please." She didn't know why it mattered so much. Something about Maggie's obvious fear in the stairwell earlier made her want to make sure Maggie had someone to call when things got dark.

Maggie sighed. "You're not going to leave me alone until I do, are you?"

Ally shrugged and shook her head.

Maggie took out her phone, unlocked it, and handed it over. Ally typed in her number and handed it back, resisting her urge to text herself from Maggie's phone so she'd have hers as well. After all, she didn't want to be tagged as a stalker.

❖

"Ma, I'm here," Ally called as she pushed through the door to her mother's ground-level apartment.

"Did you get my cigarettes?" Shirley Rowe barely glanced away from the television in front of her.

Ally rolled her eyes as she deposited the three plastic grocery bags hooked over her hand onto the table in the small area that passed for a dining room. The surface of the table was covered with stuff and hadn't been used for dining in months. Shirley ate her meals sitting in the same chair she currently occupied. Ally drew a carton of cigarettes out of one of the bags and placed it on the side table next to Shirley, being careful not to spill the coffee that had probably gone cold hours ago. Ally hated cold coffee, but it still had to taste better than the cigarettes Shirley smoked back-to-back all day long.

"You should quit." Ally didn't bother trying to inject sincerity into her suggestion. She'd given up hoping years ago that Shirley would quit smoking. Ally's grandfather, Shirley's father, had died from lung cancer, but that hadn't slowed Shirley's pack-a-day habit.

"Did you go to court?"

"Yes, Ma." She perched on the edge of the sofa in order to avoid immersing herself in the stale odors that permeated the fabric—smoke, greasy food, and the stuffiness of lack of cleaning and poor ventilation. Growing up, Ally had hated the smell she knew clung to her clothes when she went to school each day. In middle school, she'd secretly splashed herself with her stepfather's cologne to cover the odor. One day, she'd grossly over-doused, and her teacher held her over at lunch hour to talk to her. Ally finally broke down and explained. Even at ten years old, Ally had realized Miss Warren struggled with the cloying scent, but she pulled Ally into a tight hug anyway. Miss Warren had taken a small bottle of perfume from her purse and given it to Ally, with instructions to put on only one spray at a time so as not to overwhelm the senses.

"Did you see him?" Shirley ripped open one end of the carton and removed a pack.

"No. They didn't bring him out. Jorge asked for a new court date."

"Who the hell is Jorge?"

"Mr. Baez. His attorney." Ally cringed at her mother's distasteful expression and braced herself for the bigoted comment likely to follow. She wouldn't have faith in Carey's *Hispanic* attorney. Ally would have to bite her tongue not to point out that Jorge Baez was a lawyer and had made more of himself than either she or Carey had. "Jorge is optimistic that he can get him in that program I told you about."

Shirley waved a hand dismissively. "He doesn't need that. I don't understand why he can't just come and stay with me. I'll make him stop taking those pills."

Ally glanced into the U-shaped kitchen that opened to the rest of the apartment at the three liquor bottles lined up next to the toaster. Shirley liked her Tito's and hated to run out. Ally didn't have to wonder where Carey's addictive tendency came from.

"This is what's best for him." She wouldn't let Shirley see the doubts she'd expressed to Jorge. "Do you want me to put these groceries away?" Ally stood and picked up the bags, then headed for the kitchen without waiting. The answer didn't matter. She knew her mother's expectations.

"I don't want to trouble you."

"It's no trouble."

She filled the freezer and the canned-goods cabinet. After her mother's stroke four years ago, she'd tried to buy her mother produce and lean meats, encouraging healthier eating. But the next week, she wound up throwing away the soft and soggy vegetables and expired meats. At least the frozen dinners wouldn't spoil when her mother ignored them in favor of random meals like a can of beans or a bag of tortilla chips and a jar of processed cheese dip.

Shirley had been lucky to not have lasting effects from the stroke. However, her doctor had warned that if she didn't change her ways, a second stroke was much more likely.

"Do you want to stay for dinner?" Shirley meant, did Ally want to make her dinner? She'd had a long day and just wanted to go home, eat a bowl of soup, and go to bed.

"Sure. I can do that. Spaghetti okay?"

Without waiting for an answer, she pulled a box of pasta and a jar of tomato sauce out of the cabinet. At least Shirley wasn't picky when someone else was cooking. From the spice rack, Ally grabbed garlic powder, onion powder, and red-pepper flakes. She could handle a jarred sauce if she doctored it up a bit. As she fixed the food, she prepped herself for an evening eating off a plate in her lap while Shirley zoned out to the latest episode of whatever procedural crime drama she was hooked on now. Maybe it would be that one with the hot, lesbian detective her friend Kathi was always raving about.

Chapter Three

"How are you doing?" Inga dropped into the chair next to Maggie's desk.

"Busy." Maggie didn't look away from her computer screen.

"Maggie."

"I'm fine."

Inga covered Maggie's arm, stopping her mid-type. "How are you really?"

Maggie sighed and sat back, using the motion to politely ease her arm away from Inga. She'd never been a very tactile person, but she'd become less so since the robbery.

"I just need to keep working. You know, to keep my mind off things."

"Sure. That makes sense. How did things go in court yesterday? I'm sorry I missed you when you got back, but my meetings ran crazy long." Inga either didn't get the hint that she didn't want to talk or chose to ignore it.

Maggie considered telling her about meeting Ally, just to keep from talking about why she really was there. Inga would love to hear that Maggie was attracted to someone. And she couldn't deny she was—attracted. Ally was sexy and confident. She'd surprised Maggie with her chivalry when she insisted on walking her to her car.

But she didn't have much additional information about the case anyway. And she needed to let Inga know about the new court date. "The case was continued until Friday. The DA said I don't have to go if you can't spare me."

"Nonsense. Do whatever you need to do. We can manage. Especially on a Friday. Did you see him at all?"

"Inga—"

"I'm sorry. I've just never known anyone who's been through anything like this."

"Yeah, well, much as I love being a novelty for you—"

"Maggie, you know that's not what I mean. I want to support you. You've been so different since this happened, and I don't know what you need."

She wanted to shout that of course she was different. Who wouldn't be? She could tell Inga to just leave her the hell alone. Or perhaps more satisfying, she could stand up and storm out. Instead, she just shrugged and said, "How could you, when I don't even know."

Inga seemed hurt that Maggie hadn't come up with some suggestion of how she could miraculously make things better. She stood and hovered near Maggie's desk. "Let me know if I can do anything."

Maggie nodded, lacking the energy for anything more. When she heard the door close, indicating that Inga had retreated to her office, she slumped in her chair, letting her head rest on the back. Alone, she couldn't hold back the tears that filled her eyes. She swallowed a sob, refusing to completely lose it while at the office. She would wait until she got home and then would curl into a ball in the center of her bed and cry herself to sleep.

❖

"Becker, give us a hand with this," the site foreman, Reuben, called.

Ally abandoned the section of wall she was framing and took a spot on a wall that was ready to go up. She and three other guys muscled it up and held it until it had been secured in place.

"Thanks." Reuben walked with her as she returned to her framing. "How's Carey doing?"

"He's in jail. How do you think?" she snapped, then sighed and rubbed the back of her neck. "Sorry. It's pretty rough right now."

"I didn't want to fire him. We need all the hands we can get."

"I know." She grimaced, knowing he wouldn't like what she was about to say. "I need to come in late Friday, too. His case got pushed. I should be able to make it here by afternoon."

"I've already stretched us thin by letting you off yesterday. I have to be able to count on y'all to meet our deadlines."

"From what his attorney says, this should be it for a while. I'll work extra hard in the afternoon." She didn't need the lecture again. If they fell behind, the whole job was off. The guys responsible for the plumbing, electrical, Sheetrock, and flooring all relied on carpentry to get the walls and trusses up.

"You could make it up to me by signing on for the next couple of houses." Reuben didn't like the deal she'd worked out with their boss. He preferred to have more control over his crew. But with the current housing growth, the company had more work than they did crews to handle it.

"Sorry, man. I've got plans for the summer." In three weeks, she'd be done with this particular job. After living frugally for almost a year, she'd saved up enough to take some time off and focus on her furniture. She patted his shoulder. "I should get back to work. Our foreman's kind of a hard-ass."

She didn't wait for his response before she returned to her section of framing. Ally and five other guys made up one of three crews the company employed. They were spread out over three different homes in the same subdivision, a new development of small cottage-style homes.

The only other two women in the company were on a job site down the street from her. Ally had dated one of them. But she and Kathi had been better off as friends. And their status was cemented once Dani was assigned to Kathi's crew. Kathi and

Dani had been inseparable ever since, and Ally kept them both as good friends.

She slipped a wireless earbud into her right ear and started her favorite playlist. To be safe, she left the other ear open so she could stay aware of the job site around her. The other guys talked and joked while they worked. Ally used to enjoy her work, when Carey worked alongside her. Reuben had done what he had to when he fired Carey. Ally didn't blame him. But building houses had never been her passion. And not being able to help Carey figure things out had soured her on the work even further. But until her hobby/business took off, she was stuck in these subdivisions framing cookie-cutter boxes for middle-class families.

By lunchtime, they'd finished the exterior walls and were ready to move on to the roof trusses. She removed her earbud, not risking her safety as they climbed in elevation. The afternoon sun came out, and the weather warmed enough for her to shed the sweatshirt she'd worn against the cool, early spring morning.

Shortly before six, she headed for her truck. After she unlocked the toolbox in the back of her truck and dropped her tool bag inside it, her phone buzzed in her pocket, and she pulled it out. Kathi and Dani wanted her to meet them for a drink. She begged off, citing exhaustion, then had to promise they would hook up that weekend. Though she wouldn't admit it to them, their concern for her wasn't misplaced. Between Carey, her mother, and work, she often didn't know how she held it together.

Dani insisted she needed to get out there and date. But at the end of the day, she didn't have enough energy left for a relationship. She couldn't give sufficient time to another person. If asked, she would deny that her mind had wandered to Maggie several times today. She'd tried to picture Maggie at work. She had described a desk job. Did she have an office? Or did she spend her day in a cubicle? Maggie had looked great in that suit, but maybe she didn't dress that way every day. Surely an office job for the city didn't require anything more formal than business casual. Somehow, she suspected Maggie would take care with her appearance.

She'd wondered if she would run into her again someday. Or if Maggie would ever decide to use the number she'd pretty much forced on her.

She drained the excess water from her small cooler, then placed it in the bed of her truck. She didn't need to spend any of her precious time thinking about Maggie, because she'd lay odds that Maggie wasn't thinking of her.

Maggie checked her locks, the knob, the deadbolt, and the security bar lock she'd insisted her landlord install this week. He'd made her pay for it, but she didn't care. Though she lived on the second floor, she tested the windows, imagining a shadowy figure leaning a tall ladder against the wall beneath her window before forcing his way in. *That's just stupid, Maggie.* Like any thief would pass up the ground-floor apartments and go to the trouble of toting around a large ladder to break into her place.

Fighting her urge to recheck the locks, she brushed her teeth and washed her face. Then she put on her favorite nightshirt and crawled into bed. The switch she'd left on in the adjoining bathroom spilled light into the bedroom. She'd been leaving the television on in her bedroom, to avoid hearing the night sounds in her apartment, real and imagined. But the noise of the TV only disturbed her already restless sleep, so she graduated to just the bathroom light to chase away the shadows.

She stuck her arm out and grabbed her phone off the nightstand, then tugged the covers back up around her shoulders. Every night seemed to get worse. At first she'd relived the robbery in vivid detail whenever she closed her eyes. After that, her dreams grew muddier and gave way to full-on insomnia. She'd been surviving on scattered sleep that probably didn't amount to a couple of hours a night.

She'd climbed into bed early, hoping to find some rest. Tomorrow morning, she needed to be in court again. But after a mindless hour on Facebook and playing word games on her tablet, she was still not tired. She considered turning on music, but every sound seemed amplified tonight. Her looming attendance in court tomorrow no doubt had her more keyed up than usual. Judging by the clomping noises from above, her upstairs neighbor hadn't retired for the evening yet.

Hunkering down in the dim light, she scrolled through her contacts. Inga would pretend Maggie hadn't awakened her. But since she'd adopted an infant, Inga slept when the baby did. Inga would listen patiently while Maggie skirted the real problem. She couldn't bring herself to talk in detail about the robbery, afraid doing so gave the incident more power. But she also felt like she was being a bit of a baby. She should be able to move past this.

With a swipe of her finger, she rolled past Inga's number. Her mother would listen and—she quickly calculated the time difference—it was still a decent hour to call her in Indiana. She'd phoned her the day after the incident but hadn't let on how scared she'd been. She didn't mention the gun, and her mother had assumed she was referring to a purse-snatching. Letting on now that she was traumatized felt silly.

Scrolling back, she considered and rejected several other friends. They'd all expressed concern when they first heard what happened, but had quickly moved on and clearly expected her to do the same. She paused when she reached the *B*'s. Ally Becker. Ally had forced her to take her number. Sure, she probably meant in case she reconsidered a date. But since that wasn't happening, couldn't Maggie call just to talk? If Ally didn't seem receptive, she had nothing to lose. She might never see her again anyway. Before she could rationalize too much, she pressed the Call button.

"Shit." She almost hung up, but the call had gone through. Her number would appear on Ally's caller ID, and she didn't want that embarrassing moment when Ally called her back.

"Hello?" Ally's low, soft voice vibrated in her ear, clearly questioning who would call her after nine o'clock, not terribly late, but certainly past the acceptable telemarketer threshold.

"I'm sorry for calling at this hour."

"No problem. Who is this?"

"Maggie Davidson. We—um, we met at the courthouse earlier this week."

"Yes. Of course. How are you, Maggie?"

"This is stupid. Not you. Me. I shouldn't have called."

Ally was quiet for several seconds. Did she want to agree? Maggie didn't know her well enough to picture her expression. "Why did you?"

Maggie didn't hear judgment in her words, only gentle curiosity. Should she make up something and hurry off the phone? She didn't want to.

"I wanted to talk. To someone. I mean, I have other people I can talk to. I'm not some lonely, pathetic woman with no one to—" Miraculously, she found a way to stop her rambling.

"I can talk. Or, rather, I can listen. If that's what you need." Ally didn't address the rest of her bumbling. "What's going on?"

"I'm nervous about all this court stuff. This will probably sound dumb, but I haven't discussed what happened to me with anyone. Except the police and that guy from the DA's office, of course. And I thought, since you're a relative stranger who isn't connected to the case, maybe I could—"

"Tell me." Ally's smooth alto made her feel like she could say anything.

"Yeah?"

"Yes."

"Okay." Maggie activated the speakerphone, because having Ally's voice that close to her suddenly felt intimate. She set the phone on the bed beside her and rolled to her back, talking more to her ceiling than to Ally. "I was late leaving work that night. The parking garage was more empty than usual."

She laid out the timeline of events, struggling to keep her tone emotionless so Ally wouldn't know she was trembling from the inside out. She didn't need to close her eyes to recall the details. In fact, she was afraid to.

"The gun—it was silver, and—I don't know why this is so hard. I'm going to have to say all this in court eventually." She took a deep breath and began again. She stuttered through the timeline, glossing over the fear and skimming the part where he put the gun in her face. She finally ended with the Good Samaritan who'd called the police for her.

"Maggie. I'm so sorry." Ally sounded devastated. She cleared her throat. "I'm sorry you had to go through that. He didn't—this guy didn't hurt you—physically, I mean, did he?"

"A few bruises, but I'm okay." The mottled discoloration around her wrist had just recently faded. No one at work had questioned why she didn't take off her long-sleeved sweater even while inside the office. Her knees had ached where she'd fallen on them for a couple of days afterward, but she owed some of that to the fact that her body didn't bounce back like it had when she was younger.

She thought Ally whispered something, but she couldn't hear her through the slight distortion of the speakerphone. "What?"

"Oh—uh, I said, thank God. That you weren't injured." Ally drew in a breath so deep Maggie heard it through the phone.

"I'm sorry to dump this on you. The prosecutor says I shouldn't have to testify in General Sessions Court tomorrow, so I have lots of time to get used to telling my story before the criminal trial. But it helped to say it all aloud, you know."

"Absolutely. I'm glad I could be here for you." Did Ally sound more impersonal now, as if placating a stranger? Maybe. But they were strangers, weren't they?

"I'm sorry for dumping my sob story on you. I'm usually a

strong person. But this whole thing shook me." Maggie rubbed three fingers against her forehead and down between her eyes. The strain of holding back her emotions while she talked had started a headache there.

"That's understandable. What can I do to help?"

"You've already helped. Thank you."

"Do you want to talk some more about it?"

All that remained was to work through her feelings of insecurity, and she didn't need to lay all her weaknesses out for Ally right now. "I don't think so."

"Should I let you get some sleep, then?"

Maggie scoffed. "Not likely."

"Bad dreams?"

"Some."

"Okay, then. We'll stay on the phone as long as you need."

"That could be all night." Maggie laced her words with a chuckle, but she only half joked.

"I'm here for as long as you need."

"Why?"

"What?"

Maggie rolled to her stomach and stared at the phone as if she could see Ally's expression. She could recall Ally's face, her warm eyes, and the way she'd eased Maggie's discomfort in the café. But picturing them in the café didn't relax Maggie. "Where are you now?"

"At home."

"Describe it to me." Maggie thought Ally might not play along, so she rushed to explain. "I want to picture you there, so I'll feel better about being this vulnerable."

"I like you vulnerable."

"Well, I don't. Distract me and tell me about your place."

"It's a ranch-style home in Madison. I know it's not trendy, but I'm an almost-forty lesbian, so I've reached the age where I don't have to care what's in or not."

"We can tackle that statement later."

Ally's laugh sounded lighter than Maggie expected, and she tried to remember if she'd heard it before.

"Back to the house. I bought it two years ago, and it's about halfway renovated. I work on it in spurts, so I'm waiting for inspiration to strike before I tear apart another room."

"What room are you in right now?"

"I—uh, I'm in my bedroom." Ally cleared her throat. "The master bed and bath were my first reno project. It's my sanctuary. I've got a king bed with the best mattress I could afford, because my old body is starting to resent all my physical labor."

"Mine protests all the sitting I do." Maggie didn't have an eye for decorating. She'd never changed the plain beige walls in her one-bedroom apartment. When she'd first moved in six months ago, her heart crushed from a breakup, she hadn't wanted to make it feel like home.

"I did the bathroom in cool colors—white, light blue, and shades of gray. My bedroom is done in medium shades of the same colors. I like things that feel airy. Sometimes too much warmth can make a room seem heavy."

While Ally described the room around her, Maggie imagined her there. She didn't ask what Ally was wearing. That would maybe cross a line. But she pictured her lounging in bed in comfortable sweatpants and a soft cotton T-shirt.

"Where did you live before you bought the house?"

"With my partner and her son. We split up and she kept our condo."

"Oh, I'm sorry. How long were you together?" Maggie asked.

"Four years."

"I recently went through a breakup, too. Though I can imagine yours was more complicated, with a child involved. The house we lived in was hers. So we only had to decide who would keep the cat."

"Her son was seventeen when we got together. He and I

weren't close. He never liked me. And now, at twenty-one, he won't leave the nest. Honestly, that part of the separation was a bit of a relief. What about you? Did you get the cat?"

"No."

"I'm sorry."

"Don't be. The little monster always loved her more anyway. He'd wait for me to walk by, then attack my calves with his razor claws."

Ally chuckled.

"It's not funny. I couldn't even wear shorts in my own house." This only made Ally laugh harder.

They talked until Maggie's eyes grew heavy, and even then, she didn't want to hang up. She thanked Ally for distracting her. Ally's soft "good night" was the last thing she remembered as she drifted off.

Chapter Four

Friday morning, Maggie pulled into the courthouse parking garage with a sense of déjà vu and the same foreboding shadow she'd had earlier in the week. This time she didn't even pretend that she could brave the garage elevator. She hurried up the stairs behind a young couple, telling herself she was safe because anyone watching might think she was with them.

At the security checkpoint, she filled the plastic bin with her belongings and passed through the metal detector without incident. She debated a cup of coffee in the café, but it wouldn't be the same without Ally. So she continued to the elevators.

Outside the courtroom, she unexpectedly caught sight of Ally down the hall with the attorney she'd seen her with Tuesday. She wanted a moment to thank her for last night. No amount of extra makeup this morning could hide the evidence of her lack of sleep. But at least instead of restless dreams, she had pleasant conversation to blame. She didn't want to interrupt what was probably a private conference, so she headed for the restroom instead.

While she was still in the stall, she heard the door open and the sound of footsteps on tile. A phone rang and a woman answered it. Maggie had never understood why people talked on the phone in the restroom. More than once, she'd heard someone have an entire conversation while in the stall next to her.

"Mom, I can't really talk right now. I'm about to go into court." The same voice Maggie had listened to for hours the night before echoed through the room. Maybe she would get a few minutes to talk to Ally before entering the courtroom.

"What more do you want from me? I'm being as supportive as I can. But if he did something wrong—no, I know he's my brother."

Maggie flushed the toilet, then cringed at the sound that no doubt carried through Ally's phone call. But why should Maggie be embarrassed? Ally was the one having a phone conversation in a bathroom. She straightened her clothes and had her hand on the door when Ally spoke again.

"I have to go. Yes, I'll tell Carey you love him, if I even get to talk to him."

Did she say Carey? Suddenly, the coincidental timing of their court dates made far too much sense. The courtroom had been filled with people who weren't there for Maggie's case, and she'd just assumed Ally was one of them. Her head felt heavy and she became nauseated. She walked out of the stall as Ally disconnected the call, turned toward her, and jerked to a stop.

"Hey, Maggie. I didn't know you were in here."

"No." She barely got the word out past the sharp taste of bile in her throat. She hesitated, uncertain if she should run back into the stall and wait for Ally to leave.

When Ally reached for her shoulders, she flinched. Carey Rowe's face flashed through her mind, as she'd seen it that night—darkened by shadows.

"Maggie."

She leaned against the wall next to the paper-towel dispenser and forced herself to stare at Ally until her features came into focus. Maybe she had this wrong. Ally didn't look anything like Carey Rowe. "Who is Carey?"

"My brother."

"Your last name is Becker." She cleared her throat when her words came out as if through gravel. Had she imagined the moment's hesitation before Ally spoke, as if Ally already knew the distress her words would cause?

"He's my half brother." Ally nodded slowly, her expression flooded with sympathy that Maggie did not want to see. "Carey Rowe is my half brother."

"No." Maggie turned to face the row of sinks and braced her hands against the counter. She met Ally's eyes in the mirror, but having the reflection between them did nothing to dull the spike of pain driving into her gut. Ally *had* known before Maggie said anything. She'd already been aware that her brother was the man who robbed Maggie. "When did you know?"

"I promise you, when we met, I didn't realize you were the woman who—"

"When?"

Ally closed her eyes, and when she reopened them, she stared at the counter beside Maggie instead of meeting her gaze. "While we were on the phone last night."

"And you didn't think you should tell me?"

"I planned to—I would have."

Everything they'd talked about—all the personal details Maggie had shared—she'd given freely to the sister of the man who robbed her. She was still processing this realization when Ally's words from earlier replayed in her head. Anger crashed into her anguish like the tide colliding with jagged rocks on the shore. "You said *if*."

"What?"

"On the phone just now. *If* he did something wrong."

"I—"

"You don't believe it was him? Or you don't even believe it really happened to me?" She didn't wait for an answer to either question before shoving off the wall and glancing at the door, her escape route.

"No. I—that was my mother on the phone and—God, Maggie, I don't know what to say."

"You don't have to say anything more." She hurried from

the restroom, down the hall, and into the courtroom. She'd rather flee the building entirely. But at least inside the courtroom, Ally wouldn't be able to talk to her.

This time she slid onto the most crowded bench she could find so Ally couldn't sit near her. Nausea still churned in her stomach, and the buzz of conversation going on around her grated on her building headache. Ally. The woman she'd connected with in the café less than a week ago, the woman who'd offered her more comfort than anyone else had, was also the sister of her attacker. No matter how many times she laid out the details, she couldn't reconcile that relationship in her mind.

When the judge entered the courtroom, she barely managed to get to her feet. The chatter of the gallery had ceased, but she still couldn't follow the proceedings around her. She didn't look for Ally but stared ahead at the wall behind the judge instead. The clerk read the docket, which the ADA had told her was like a roll call to check the status of each case. Any pleas or continuances that could be quickly disposed of were handled during this phase. The attorneys for the rest of the defendants indicated they were ready to proceed with a hearing, including the man Maggie now knew to be Carey Rowe's representation.

Maggie glanced across the aisle. Ally sat over there, in the row ahead of Maggie's, staring back at her. Maggie fixed her expression into what she hoped was one of indifference instead of the confusion roiling inside her, then looked away, once more toward the judge's bench. On the phone last night, she'd tried endless times to imagine Ally's face while she spoke. Were her lips curled upward when she chuckled gently in response to something Maggie said? Did she narrow her eyes slightly as she tried to recall a detail in a story she'd told? Would her eyes warm as she expressed sympathy for what Maggie had been through? Now, Maggie wished she hadn't noticed that Ally's eyes telegraphed her every emotion. Or that right now, they were filled with grief, worry, and sorrow.

❖

"Do you understand that by entering a guilty plea you are waiving your right to a trial?"

The handcuffed man in the orange jumpsuit with DCSO emblazoned on the back glanced at his lawyer, then back at the judge. "Yes, Your Honor."

The defendant, who had assaulted someone with a knife during a Lyft ride, stared at his feet while the judge informed him regarding his plea. Ally had heard his attorney stress that he'd *allegedly* committed assault. But the prosecutor didn't appear to harbor any doubt about his guilt, and Ally's gut agreed.

The judge multitasked while he spoke, robotically, as if he'd recited these instructions many times before. He passed file folders and papers back and forth with his clerk, stopping occasionally to sign one of them.

Ally had already studied every inch of wood molding around the judge's desk, the witness box, and the low divider behind the attorney worktables, as well as each gold and glass light fixture. She couldn't find a scrap of sympathy for this man who got drunk, then started an argument with his Lyft driver, which had escalated into a physical altercation. What kind of guy pulled a knife on a man who'd tried to provide a sober ride home? She guessed somewhere in the galley, the driver waited his turn to testify if needed, but the defense attorney had negotiated a plea deal for his unfortunate client. Apparently, his charge of aggravated assault would be reduced to simple assault. From what Ally gathered, the lower, misdemeanor charge would garner him eleven months and twenty-nine days in jail. But lucky him, he'd get credit for the time he'd already spent locked up waiting for this hearing.

Ally couldn't imagine making a mistake that would ruin her life like that. But then, Carey had done exactly that, and they were raised together—same nature, same nurture. So she couldn't be that far removed from the kind of person who was capable of such a misstep.

The reminder that this guy wasn't that different than her own brother forced her to look more closely at him. Thirtyish, white, with sandy-blond hair that didn't seem to have been washed lately. This guy didn't look like a scary dude. Yet, based on her thoughts moments ago, if Ally sat on his jury, she'd have locked him up for the felony.

She'd judged this guy so quickly. Granted, he'd pled guilty. Though she didn't have much legal knowledge, Ally figured pleas weren't always about facts or character, but rather what the ADA could make a jury believe. All of this made her very nervous for Carey. He wasn't a bad guy. And she still couldn't get her head around what he'd done. *Allegedly.* She had even less doubt about Carey's guilt. And he still had to face a jury of his peers. She glanced around. If his peers were anything like her, he didn't stand a chance.

She believed Maggie. Despite being unable to reassure her earlier while in the restroom, she somehow knew Maggie's account of the incident would prove accurate. Her brother *was* capable of such an act, even if out of desperation. He'd been stealing from her and their mother for months before his arrest. She'd even started manufacturing reasons why they should meet in public, to keep from having to let him inside her house.

She'd heard the anguish in Maggie's voice while they were on the phone. She'd known Maggie for a matter of hours. Why did she so easily take her at her word?

Across the aisle, Maggie's gaze flitted around the front of the courtroom, and her brow furrowed as if she had trouble following the action. Ally had zoned out a time or two herself. Why did she have to sit here through the whole docket? She'd rather have come in just when Carey's name was called. There had to be a better way than to have a courtroom full of people who weren't related to a case bear witness to each defendant's fate.

Ally's stomach clenched as Carey was led into the courtroom

in an orange jumpsuit and directed to stand next to Jorge. She hadn't seen him in several weeks, even before his arrest. He'd grown noticeably thinner since she last ran into him at their mother's house. His perpetual five-o'clock shadow had turned into scruff. He usually kept his hair, the same almost-black shade as hers, cut short, but it too had gone shaggy. She made a mental note to talk to Jorge about getting him to clean up before his next court appearance.

She wanted to catch his eyes, to let him know that she was there, but he stared at the table in front of him. Given the spiral he'd been on lately, she should have expected this day would come. But knowing he was in trouble hadn't prepared her for seeing him this way.

"Mr. Rowe, how do you plead?"

"Not guilty." Hearing Carey deliver the words clearly and without hesitation should have eased Ally's mind. But she knew what a good liar Carey had become. He'd lied just as smoothly when confronted with irrefutable evidence that he'd stolen from his own family to buy drugs.

The ADA called a police officer to the witness stand. He described being dispatched to the parking garage to find a distraught Maggie along with the woman who'd made the 9-1-1 call. Next, the detective who arrested Carey swore an oath and stepped into the witness box. He explained how a citizen had found Maggie's purse dumped in an alley nearby. A fingerprint, later determined to be Carey's, was found on the purse strap. When the same detective took Carey into custody, he had the gun, which fit the description Maggie gave, still on his person.

The prosecutor didn't call any more witnesses. Jorge had warned her that the ADA would present only enough evidence to get Carey's case bound over to the grand jury, so that he wouldn't reveal everything he had to Jorge until the discovery phase of the trial.

When it was Jorge's turn, he questioned the witnesses as to the timeline of events. But he'd already told Ally that the robbery report and arrest were likely enough for the judge to send the case to grand jury. He focused instead on making sure Carey would go to the recovery house, and then, if he was indicted, he would fight the charges at trial.

As Jorge expected, the judge determined that the state had met the burden of proof for probable cause. After a short bond discussion, during which the ADA agreed to a lowered bond if Carey was released to the rehab program under strict supervision, the judge instructed his clerk to set a status court date, in sixty days, to assess Carey's compliance with his bond conditions.

The clerk gathered some paperwork and passed it through the court officer to Carey's attorney. Carey signed, agreeing to his bond. Jorge had helped Ally contact a bond agent who was prepared to make the arrangements. When a deputy led Carey back through a door off the side of the courtroom, Ally glimpsed a cell with several other jump-suited men all awaiting their fate.

The clerk called another name, and Ally stood and met Jorge's eyes. He'd told her Carey would be taken back through the sheriff's department holding area before being released. Jorge would drive him to rehab himself and said she could talk to him for a few minutes before they left. He'd told her to wait outside. As she turned toward the door, she saw Maggie slip out of the courtroom and rushed to catch up to her.

❖

"Maggie."

Maggie heard Ally calling her name, but she kept moving. She had to get out of this building. When every muscle in her body screamed to run, she'd forced herself to sit through Rowe's hearing. She'd kept her eyes on his back, as if daring him to turn and look at her, but he never did. She both wanted to see his face and dreaded it at the same time, as if testing herself. Would the rage simmering in her swell up and fill her? Or would her nausea eclipse it? She never answered those questions, and now she gave in to the need to flee.

"Maggie, please, wait."

Ally sounded like she was gaining ground, but Maggie didn't turn around to look. She arrived at the bank of elevators and stepped inside one, thankful to find it empty. Now if only the doors would close before—

"Maggie, I know you heard me." Ally slid between the doors just as they closed.

Refusing to feel trapped, Maggie forced herself to look at Ally's face. Her stomach twisted when she realized she was searching Ally's features again for a resemblance to Carey Rowe. She gasped and turned away.

"Please, let me—" When Ally moved toward her, Maggie jerked back and pressed tightly to the elevator wall. "I'm sorry."

Ally's apology ignited Maggie's anger. She refused to let one more member of this family make her feel like a victim. "For what? What are you sorry for?" She spun and took two steps, backing Ally up to the opposite wall. Ally's eyes moved over her face, then dropped to her mouth, and Maggie hated that her body reacted even when she was so mad. If she surged forward, only a few more inches, she could kiss Ally. She stepped back, reclaiming her side of the small space. Her ping-ponging emotions left her struggling to speak, and Ally took advantage of the silence.

"I'm sorry I didn't tell you as soon as I figured it out. I was shocked. I finally meet someone I—who I can—that I like talking to and—"

"Yet, the one thing you should have talked to me about—"

"Should have? Do you have any idea how torn I was? You and I, we just met, and he's my brother. I can't just forget that fact."

"And I can't forget that he put a gun in my face. Do you know how that feels? Of course not. How could you?" She shook her head, trying to free the memory before the fear could take hold. "I don't know why I thought we could be friends."

"We can."

"No. I can't look at you without thinking about what he did."

"I'm not him."

The elevator doors opened on the ground floor, and Maggie practically ran out. Ally would be right behind her, but this time she refused to stop. Ally had nothing more to say that she wanted to hear.

As she exited the elevator vestibule and strode across the lobby, she almost swooned with relief at seeing a friendly face. Detective Charlie Bell had responded to her robbery call.

"Detective Bell," she called, hoping the detective would remember her. She felt Ally pause behind her.

"Hey, Maggie."

Detective Bell had been a calming presence when Maggie couldn't answer the myriad of questions the uniformed officers had fired at her. The same steady energy emanated from her now, as she moved confidently to Maggie's side.

Either Maggie's distress showed on her face, or Detective Bell's investigative instincts were picking something up. She glanced between Maggie and Ally. "Everything okay here?"

"Everything's fine, Detective." She'd asked Maggie to call her Charlie, while taking her statement, but Maggie used the title for Ally's benefit now. "I'm on my way out."

"Maggie—" Ally started to speak but stopped when Maggie glared at her.

"I'm headed out myself," Charlie said, even though she'd just entered the lobby from the front door. "I'll walk with you."

As they strode away, Maggie felt Charlie's protective hand against her back. She imagined plenty of women felt comforted by Charlie's strong yet gentle demeanor after a trauma, as she had been. But she couldn't help wishing the pressure on her back came from Ally's hand. Angry at her traitorous emotions, she resisted the urge to look over her shoulder at Ally.

"Are you sure you're okay? I felt some serious tension between you two." Charlie held the door open and waited for her to walk out ahead of her.

Maggie nodded. "I'll be fine from here. I don't want to make you late for court." She chanced a glance back when they got outside, but Ally hadn't followed.

The first time they'd met, Charlie had been dressed in a fitted, navy button-down tucked in to black jeans. Her gun had rested in a leather holster on her hip, and Maggie had stared at it for several seconds, thinking how much less threatening it appeared than the robber's. At that point she hadn't known his name. Maybe the badge secured on her belt next to the holster made the gun feel safer somehow.

Today, Charlie had dressed up. Her dark pantsuit flared at the waist and over her full hips. Her badge and gun weren't visible, but Maggie imagined she'd fastened them to her waistband, under the jacket. A small plastic ID card with her picture and the police-department seal had been clipped to the hem of her blazer. Her hair, pulled back into a severe bun, put off a "don't mess with me" vibe that probably benefitted her as a police officer.

"I've got time. My docket doesn't start for another thirty minutes." Charlie led her to a small bench in the shadow of the building, and they sat. "Were you up in general-sessions?"

"Yes."

"How'd that go?"

She shrugged. "It was all a little confusing. But basically, he gets out of jail and goes to some kind of halfway house or something."

Charlie nodded. "The attorneys made a bond agreement." She touched Maggie's shoulder. "He still has to stay away from you while he's awaiting trial. He can't contact you, not even through someone else. Do you still have my card?"

"I don't know." She remembered taking the card from Charlie that night. But since she didn't have her purse, she couldn't recall where she'd put it.

Charlie slipped a silver case out of her jacket pocket and removed a card. When she handed it to Maggie, she held on to it until Maggie met her eyes. "If you have any trouble, you call me. If it's an emergency, call 9-1-1. Okay?"

"Yes." She didn't think Carey Rowe would bother her. But she couldn't really be sure, could she? Was she projecting the gentle interactions she'd had with Ally onto her brother as well?

Chapter Five

Ally stood next to Jorge's Honda Accord in the sheriff's department parking lot and stared through the passenger window. Carey slumped there sullenly, refusing to look at her. He'd rolled down the window and rested his arm along the top of the door. She'd walked the block to the building located behind the courthouse where Jorge said he would bring Carey out after his release had been processed.

"Mom said to tell you she loves you," Ally said.

Carey scowled.

"You should call her when you get settled." She glanced at Jorge. "Will he be able to call?"

Jorge nodded. "The recovery house will have a phone he can use any time before curfew. But he'll be staying busy with his treatment, meetings, and house chores. He's also required to secure a full-time job within fourteen days of admission. They can help him with that." He gave Carey a meaningful look, as if to remind him that he should use all the resources at his disposal. "After he's got everything sorted, you and your mother can visit."

"We can?"

Carey glanced at her as if surprised that she'd visit him, and for a moment she saw a hint of her younger brother. She touched his arm and bent to look in the window, waiting for him to meet her eyes.

"Let us know when you're ready for us to come see you."

He swallowed and nodded.

"Carey, I—" She didn't know what to say. She felt ripped apart inside right now, but he didn't look like he cared. This was her baby brother. While growing up, so often it felt like he and she against their mother. She'd watched out for him. Hell, sometimes she spent as much time raising him as Shirley did.

He looked at Jorge. "Can we go?"

Jorge glanced at Ally, and she offered no resistance. He gave her a supportive nod, then circled the car. "Call me if you have any questions."

She watched Jorge pull out of the lot and disappear down the street before she headed back to the other side of the courthouse, where her car was still in the garage. The overcast skies kept the late-spring morning cool enough for a comfortable walk, even in her khakis and button-down shirt.

Her phone rang, and she glanced at the display, then sent Shirley's call to voice mail. She paused and stepped to the edge of the sidewalk to send a text, telling Shirley that Carey was okay and that she'd call her later to fill her in. She needed to get to work, and if she spoke to Shirley, she'd get talked into stopping by her place. Reuben would be pissed if she didn't get there soon.

In her car, she pulled out of the lot and took a quick right without waiting for the light, despite the sign that read No Turn on Red. As she came up behind a small sedan in the left lane, she moved right to zip around it. She loved the pep in the V6 of her compact SUV and drove with the confidence of steering a tank.

She had little patience for people who drove like they had all day to get where they were headed. If that was the case, the driver should at least get in the right lane and leave the fast lane open for Ally. She glanced at the clock on the dash. She had time to grab a fast-food lunch and eat in the car on her way to the job site. Cutting down a side street provided the perfect shortcut into the drive-through of her favorite burger place.

How was she going to put this morning aside and concentrate

on work? She'd gone to court both looking forward to seeing Maggie and dreading how to tell her who Carey was. She'd expected that to be difficult. Even Maggie's unwillingness to talk didn't surprise her. But when they'd exited the elevator and run into that overprotective woman, Maggie seemed to have welcomed her presence. When Maggie had called her "detective," Ally had nearly nodded in agreement. That made sense. The tall, gorgeous stranger looked much more the hero/knight type than Ally did. Nobody had ever appealed to her for rescue. Nobody but Carey, and look how well she'd handled that.

She'd let Maggie walk away with that woman, knowing if she ever saw her again it would likely be at Carey's criminal trial. And she hadn't had time to gather herself before seeing Carey off. The place he was heading was called the New Life House. Did she have to be an addict to qualify for a new life?

❖

"Are you fucking kidding me?" Kathi stared at Ally, her beer bottle frozen halfway to her mouth.

"I wish I were." Ally tipped up her own drink, a peach hard cider. After work, Ally had accepted Kathi and Dani's invitation to drinks and snacks. She hadn't hung out with them in a while, and she'd thought she could avoid dwelling on her crazy day. But here she was, after a drink and a half, already wading all the way in.

Dani set a plate of nachos down on the kitchen table between them. "Language, honey. The kids are in the other room."

Dani's two toddlers chattered away in the playroom. They were so cute when they played together. Dani said when they got quiet, that's when she needed to worry.

"So you had a first date with the lady Carey robbed?" Kathi lowered her naturally boisterous voice.

"It wasn't a date."

Kathi wrinkled her nose in disagreement. "It kinda was."

"It was coffee and there were no other tables. Whatever. I didn't know who she was at the time."

"And you think he did it—what she says?"

"It's not really for her to say." Dani settled into the chair next to Kathi and rested her hand on Kathi's forearm. "This woman will get her day in court."

"Well, it's not really her, though. It's the state—right?" Ally said, then feeling disloyal, she hurried on. "The prosecutor feels like there's a case, based on their evidence. So it's really up to them—and now the grand jury."

"Right, but she's the one accusing him."

"She's—I mean—" She gave up on sorting out why putting all the responsibility on Maggie bothered her.

"Mama, Junie hid my Batman." Five-year-old Grayson ran into the room and climbed onto Kathi's lap. "Can I stay in here with you?"

Kathi swept her hand over his corn-silk hair and hugged him close. With his fair complexion and freckles, and his blue eyes, he was the image of Dani. Some people assumed Dani was gentle and sensitive, but her backbone and aversion to taking anyone's shit were legendary. And like her, Grayson was deceptively strong, both physically and emotionally. Except when someone hid his favorite Batman action figure.

"June," Dani called.

"I didn't do anything, Mommy." June's sweet voice carried from the other room.

"Get your butt in here."

June peeked around the corner of the doorjamb. Her dark hair and mischievous eyes would make her irresistible someday. Dani said she looked like the dude they had picked out of the sperm bank's catalog. Both kids had the same father. When they decided in their late thirties to become parents, they wanted their kids to share that connection. Only a year apart, they were very close.

"Over here." Dani pointed to the spot in front of her, and June inched into place. Dani bent and met June's eyes. "Where is Batman?"

"On a date." To her credit, June delivered the explanation with a solemn expression. Ally barely contained her snicker.

"A date?"

June nodded.

"I have to know. Who's he on a date with?" Ally asked.

"Rapunzel."

"Oh, damn. I was hoping she'd say Robin."

"Ally said damn." Grayson turned his sweet face up to Kathi's, clearly wanting some type of repercussions for Ally.

"Grayson said damn," Ally shot back with a grin.

"You gotta put a quarter in the jar." Grayson jabbed his finger toward the mason jar on the kitchen counter.

"Oh, yeah. Where's your quarter?"

"Okay. Enough. Everyone." Dani held up her hands and garnered both kids' attention. "Ally, put a quarter in the jar."

"What? I don't—" She caught Dani's stern look and stopped. Kathi's expression indicated she had Dani's back on this one. Ally huffed and dug into her pocket. "Who even has quarters anymore," she mumbled as she pulled out several folded bills. She separated one dollar from the others. While crossing the room, she made a show of flapping the bill in the air. "I'll tell you what, kid," she pointed at Grayson, "I'll pay mine, cover yours, and spot you two more."

After she shoved the money into the jar, she gave Dani a smug look.

"June, go get Batman," Dani said.

June pouted as she left the room, but when she came back, she held the action figure in one hand and Rapunzel in the other. Ally bit her lip while June handed him to Grayson.

"Now, go play. Because it's ten minutes to bedtime. Unless you want to go now."

They'd left the room before she finished speaking.

"Did you see? Rapunzel wore her best dress," Ally said when she was sure they were both out of earshot.

Kathi chuckled. "I bet she was going to let down her hair for him tonight."

"Yeah, but Dani's codpiece blocked him."

Even Dani's stern look wasn't enough to stop their laughter.

❖

Maggie knocked on Inga's door Sunday morning armed with a bag of her favorite bagels. When Inga answered the door with the baby cradled in her arms, Maggie cooed as she walked inside.

"We were up half the night. She just went back to sleep," Inga whispered. She nodded at the bakery bag. "Please, tell me you got the house-made cranberry cream cheese."

Maggie grinned and nodded.

"Let me go see if I can put her down without another tantrum." She disappeared down the hallway toward the bedrooms.

As soon as Maggie entered the kitchen, she abandoned the bagels in favor of the aroma emanating from the coffeemaker. Inga's favorite blend was heavenly. Maggie had just added creamer to her mug when Inga returned.

"You know, you just ruin my expensive coffee. If you're going to do that to it, you might as well drink that common brew they serve at the bagel shop."

Maggie handed Inga a cup of black coffee, then returned to stirring hers. "If you really felt that way, you wouldn't keep my creamer stocked in your fridge." She sipped experimentally, hoping the rich coffee and caramel flavor would deliver the caffeine she desperately needed to get through the rest of the day.

"Where's Kevin? There's a bagel in there for him, too."

"He's playing golf. I couldn't handle two whiny babies today." Inga dug a bagel out of the bag and slathered it with cream cheese. "Actually, he's been very good with her this week. And his brother is in town, so I practically pushed him out the door."

They settled on the couch, and Maggie laughed at the look of relief on Inga's face. Inga tilted her head against the back of the cushion and shut her eyes. Maggie sipped her coffee, letting her have this moment of silence. But she didn't close her eyes. Instead, she scanned the room, taking comfort in the familiarity of Inga's living room. In the twelve years they'd been working together, they'd spent plenty of nights in this room up late talking over too much wine.

"How are you, Maggie?"

"I'm good. Don't worry."

She raised her head and touched Maggie's arm. "You like to think you're stronger than the rest of us. But I'm here for you."

"I know."

"I realize I've been all about myself lately—"

"Taking care of your family isn't selfish."

"My point is that I may be beyond exhausted and completely distracted by that adorable little girl. But if you need something—"

"I know." She covered Inga's hand and squeezed. Maybe she should share a little bit of what she was dealing with. Talking with Ally had helped. But now just thinking about Ally made her sick with anger.

"Are you sleeping okay?"

"Occasionally."

"Have you considered getting a gun?" Inga held up one hand as if to stave off Maggie's protest. "I know it's a very Republican thing for me to suggest. I got one to keep in the house when Kevin started traveling for work and was surprised how much safer I felt."

"I don't know that I could even look at a gun right now." The thought made her stomach churn.

"That's totally understandable."

"I just wish this court stuff was behind me." Then she

wouldn't have to worry about running into Ally again. And she wouldn't have to examine why the idea of never seeing her again left her feeling sad and a little empty.

"Is there any indication that he'll plead guilty?"

"Not so far."

Inga sighed. "Why can't people take responsibility for what they've done?"

"From what I understand, he has some kind of drug problem. One of the conditions of his bail is that he has to get treatment."

"What kind of drugs?"

Had Ally said? No, but she hadn't really given her a chance to explain once she knew who Carey was. "I have no idea."

"It doesn't matter anyway. Addiction doesn't excuse being violent against another person."

Maggie agreed. She didn't understand how Ally could come to court in support of him. Maggie didn't have any siblings, so maybe she couldn't comprehend Ally's loyalty. She tried to imagine how she'd feel if one of her parents had done something criminal, but she just couldn't picture either of them in that place. They weren't the kind of people who could commit a white-collar crime, let alone something so personally violating as robbery. Had Ally ever felt that way about Carey, or had he always been troubled?

Chapter Six

Ally pulled her SUV into the parking lot of New Life House and chose a spot close to the building. She'd expected an institutional building, similar to any other generic health-care facility, not the large, renovated, two-story Victorian house before her. The lot beside the house had been cleared and paved for parking, but otherwise, the house fit right in with the rest of the nearby homes. The modern wood sign in the yard, identifying the business, also departed from the period of the home. The house needed a new coat of bold, blue paint and some freshening of the white trim. Otherwise, from the street, it appeared to be in good repair.

Shirley got out of the car and smoothed her hands over her hips, either out of nervousness or a desire to eliminate the wrinkles from her dress. When Ally had picked her up, she'd come out of the house wearing her Sunday best, though Ally couldn't remember the last time she'd gone to church. She wanted to ask who Shirley was trying to impress with her flowered dress and beige flats. Carey wouldn't notice. And she doubted anyone else here would care what she wore.

As they climbed the steps onto the wide front porch, Ally's foot wiggled on a loose board. At the door, a gap showed where the wide concrete porch had settled and tilted away from the structure. Ally glanced at the doorbell. Should they ring? Or did they just enter as if this were a business? She was saved from deciding when the door opened and a large man filled the doorway. He easily topped six feet. A polo with a New Life House logo stretched over his rounded belly. His gray sweatpants negated any professionalism he'd gained with the polo.

"Can I help you?" His voice was deep but warm, rather than intimidating.

"We're here to see Carey Rowe." When Carey had called to invite them to visit, she'd made sure he'd had whatever permission he needed. He'd been there for two weeks and insisted he was ready for visitors.

"Certainly, come in. I'm John. I work and live here with the guys." He stepped back to usher them inside. "I'm the bad guy who makes sure they do their chores and attend their meetings."

The foyer opened up on both sides with large, square archways. To the left was a dining room with a long table and eight chairs. On the right, two couches, a chair, and a coffee table had been crammed into a living room built to accommodate only half as much. Five guys filled the furniture, including Carey.

"Rowe, you've got visitors."

Carey levered himself off the couch and crossed to them. His athletic shorts and T-shirt appeared to be the unofficial uniform of the place, judging by the other men in the room. As soon as he was in touching distance, Shirley pulled him into a hug.

"John, this is my ma, and that's my sister, Ally." Carey extricated himself and gave Ally a nod. They'd never been huggers. "Let me show you around."

He led them into the large kitchen, with two refrigerators. A handwritten sign on the front of each designated them as "house food" and "personal food." The one for personal food went on to instruct the residents to store their items on their designated shelf and not to consume items off another resident's. A dry-erase board, with chores listed next to each man's name, hung on one wall. Carey had dish duty today.

"You saw the living room. That's where we hang out and

watch movies and stuff. We all have bedrooms upstairs, but visitors are restricted to the first floor."

Shirley looked like she wanted to argue, but Ally didn't care about seeing his room anyway. She'd seen several cleaning chores on the chart, but the place still smelled faintly sour and stuffy. Was that just the product of this many adults living in one house, or was it a man thing?

"There's a visiting room over here." He led them to a room in the back of the house, then pulled closed a set of pocket doors. "We don't have much privacy around here."

"That's probably on purpose," Ally said. She wandered around the room, studying the detailed wood moldings and built-in bookshelves. In the home's heyday, this room would have been the library. A few shelves were stocked with recovery-related books that looked to be geared toward helping family members cope with their loved one's disease.

Shirley gave Ally a sour look, then enveloped Carey in another hug. He rolled his eyes at Ally over her shoulder. When Shirley pulled back, she kept hold of his upper arms.

"You look good, honey."

"You don't have to lie to me. My room is tiny, but it does have a mirror."

Aside from a haircut and a shave, he didn't look much different than he did when Ally saw him at the courthouse, minus the orange jumpsuit. His eyes did look clearer, but the years and his rough living had started to line his face.

"Sit down. Tell me what's been going on out there in the world."

The furniture in this room fit much better in the space, though it was clearly chosen for short-term visits, not comfort. Carey sat on the boxy couch and Shirley followed, sitting close enough to grasp his hand. That left Ally in a patterned chair that looked like it had outlasted its usefulness. When she perched on the edge of the seat, it shifted beneath her in that not-quite-stable way that old furniture does. She tuned out Shirley's chitchat. She doubted Carey cared about the gossip from Shirley's circle of friends either, but he endured it more patiently than she expected.

Carey talked about the group therapy he had to attend, as well as individual sessions with a drug counselor, and his household chores. One of the employees had helped him get a job cleaning at an office complex at night. But he didn't like his boss, so he wasn't sure it was going to last.

"He's such a dick. He made sure I knew that he knew I have charges pending. And he acts like he has to watch me so much closer than the rest of his staff. Like I'm going to steal the paper clips to sell for drugs or something."

"Has your lawyer visited?" Shirley asked.

"Once. But he didn't have any new information. I'm stuck here until I complete this program."

"Meanwhile, you have this court case hanging over you." Shirley rubbed his arm as if he were the one who needed comfort, but she looked more upset than he did. "I don't understand how that woman can just say you did something and ruin your life over it."

"Maggie." Ally had stayed quiet while they both acted like the course of events that led him here were no big deal, but she wouldn't let Shirley blame Carey's "ruined" life on Maggie.

"What?"

"The woman he terrorized in order to feed his addiction—her name is Maggie."

He rolled his eyes. "Whatever. How do you even know that?" She was saved from answering truthfully as he continued to talk. "Oh, right, you were in court during my hearing. Anyway, I'm sure she's talked the ADA into trying to throw the book at me."

"As I'm sure Jorge told you, her testimony isn't the only evidence against you."

"I've met tons of guys in jail who did worse, and they're cutting deals with the prosecutor for probation. They don't even have to do more jail time."

She doubted the prosecutors were doling out light sentences

for felonies. But given his downplaying the seriousness of his own crime, she didn't know what these other guys might be charged with. "Didn't they offer you a plea deal?"

"Yeah. But I have to go to prison for three years. No thanks. I'll take my chances in court."

"Carey, they caught you with a gun on you. You're probably going to prison either way."

"One of the guys in here says if they can't prove I did anything to that woman with that gun, at worst, they have me for carrying without a license."

"So you're getting your legal advice from addicts now? What were you doing with a gun anyway?"

He looked away and cracked his knuckles, a tell he'd had since they were kids. He was keeping something from her.

"Where did you get it?"

He shrugged, but the tension in his posture belied the nonchalance he clearly faked. "It was your dad's."

Ally surged out of the wobbly chair and stared at him. Rage flooded her, numbing her extremities and accelerating her heart rate. Her father hadn't left many possessions behind when he abandoned them, but his gun was one of few Ally had managed to ferret away for herself.

When Shirley went on a bender, she hauled out the battered cardboard box that held his belongings and railed against Ally's father while pulling individual items out of the box and throwing them away. By the time Ally was a teenager, the contents had dwindled. She'd saved a photo of his parents, a broken watch with a leather band, and the Smith & Wesson .38 Special. She'd hidden them in a shoebox in the top of her bedroom closet and shared her secret only with Carey. She'd left the box there in the years after she moved out, hidden at her mother's house, because she didn't want a gun in her own.

He'd used her father's gun, the gun she was responsible for, to get what he wanted from Maggie. She pressed her hand to her stomach, fighting nausea. What if he'd wanted something more than just Maggie's purse? What if she hadn't given him the purse? How would she live with herself if he'd shot Maggie with her father's gun—her gun.

"Why did you take it?"

"It wasn't even loaded. I was going to pawn it."

She searched his expression for an ounce of self-satisfaction to fuel her anger. But his face was surprisingly blank, as if he felt nothing. Maybe that was worse.

"Why didn't you?"

"I was on my way there. And I thought that if I pawned it, I might get only a little bit of money. But if I held on to it, I could use it to get more." His eyes shifted back and forth between them as if imploring Shirley to help him. But she appeared too shocked to come to his aid. He'd stopped just short of admitting that he'd followed through on that idea, but he'd erased any trace of doubt Ally had clung to.

To Carey, more money equaled more drugs. Ally didn't want to own a gun. In fact, she didn't even have any ammunition for it. But she'd never been able to get rid of it. Carey's need for drugs had driven him to the point where her only connection to her father meant so little to him and, by extension, she meant so little.

"I have to go." She backed up a step, nearly tripping over that stupid chair. She stumbled around it and yanked open the pocket doors. The few occupants of the living room looked up at the clatter of the doors, but she stomped through without explanation.

She made it to the driver's seat of her car before the first tear spilled down her face. She started the ignition, debating whether to wait for Shirley or let her figure out her own way home. Or, better still, let Carey be responsible for her for once. She'd just put the car in gear when Shirley came out of the front door.

As soon as Shirley got in the car, Ally took her foot off the brake and backed out of the parking spot.

"Why would you pick a fight with him like that? You know

he's having a difficult time right now." Shirley spun in her seat, and even without looking, Ally could feel her glaring at her.

"Ma, shit. You couldn't let me get a block down the road before you started in on me."

"He needs your understanding right now."

"What he needs is not to be coddled." She didn't bother voicing her other question. *What about what I need?* She squeezed the steering wheel as hard as she could. Despite the many angry thoughts swirling in her head, she'd get nowhere airing them.

Maybe she shouldn't care about her father's belongings. After all, he'd left them and never looked back. He obviously hadn't harbored any sentimental feelings all these years. For whatever reason, the contents of that shoebox meant something to her. And Carey had known that. His lack of respect for her father didn't surprise her. After all, they'd grown up hearing Shirley say how worthless he was. But even after everything he'd done to them, Carey's level of disrespect toward her shook her.

❖

"Do you want a drink? I just made my second pot of coffee for the day," Kathi asked as she pulled another mug from the cabinet.

"Do you have anything stronger?" Ally had come straight to Kathi and Dani's after dropping Shirley off at home. She must really have pissed Shirley off, because she didn't even try to get her to come inside.

Kathi nodded and put the mug back. "Vodka or rum?"

"Rum and Coke."

"Can do. I think I'll join you. While I make them, do you want to tell me what's going on?"

"Ma and I visited Carey today."

"Ah, that bad?" Kathi slid a glass across the counter.

"Worse." Ally took a big swallow of her drink while waving

her other hand in irritation. "As usual, mama's boy can do no wrong." Kathi had gone heavy on the rum, and the burn made her voice come out a little rough. "He's almost certainly going to serve time for aggravated robbery, and *I'm* the one who's not being supportive. Everyone involved is at fault except him."

"So why does that have you so worked up today?" Kathi braced one hand against the counter and leaned forward, looking irritatingly more relaxed than Ally felt.

"What do you mean?"

"You said, this is as usual. But I haven't seen you this upset before. What's different?"

"He's sitting there in that fucking recovery house blaming Maggie and talking about the advice he's getting from the other junkies there."

"Maggie?"

"Yes." Ally picked up her glass and headed for the back door. "I need some air."

Kathi followed her onto the deck. Ally strode to the other end, a half dozen steps, then spun around and came back. Why couldn't they have a bigger deck? She needed more pacing room. Kathi had settled onto one of the chaise lounges, and Ally set her drink on the side table, then flopped down onto the one beside her.

"Maggie?" Kathi repeated more softly.

"I told you about her. From the coffee shop."

"Yeah. I know. But this sounds personal."

"Of course it is. Carey needs to take responsibility for the mess he's made of his life."

"I mean, it sounds like you're feeling personal about Maggie."

She glared at Kathi, but Kathi didn't blink. She was one half of the couple that could get away with being brutally frank with Ally. "You're missing the point."

"I don't think I am. Al, don't you think this could get a little complicated?"

"There is no *this*. I had coffee with her, that's it. And—we talked on the phone that one night. Then I saw her the next day, and she found out who I was. But that's all. I haven't heard from her in the two weeks since." She lay back on the lounge and stared at the sky, picturing Maggie's face. She'd thought of her often in the last weeks. Maggie hadn't answered when she'd tried to call, and her apology text had gone unanswered as well.

"Okay, first, you've been holding out on us. Let's start with the phone chat."

"It's no big deal. She needed a distraction from life. Who hasn't felt like that?"

"So she called you?"

"Yeah. But this was before we knew how we were—well, connected. I actually figured it out during that conversation."

"I'm guessing you didn't tell her right away."

"How do you tell someone something like that?" She sat up and turned sideways, then rested her elbows on her knees. She finished her drink.

"Refill?"

"Yes, please."

"Be right back." Kathi took both of their glasses inside.

Ally dropped her head into her hands. She'd known Carey had problems. He'd seemed in so much pain after his back injury that she'd thought the pain pills were a godsend. But he never stopped taking them, even when the doctor wouldn't prescribe them any longer. She hadn't realized how out of control he'd gotten, though, until she caught him stealing money from her wallet. She'd all but cut him off, and then she found out he'd been arrested.

Truthfully, she'd worried more about Maggie than she had Carey these past two weeks. What was that about?

"Where did you leave things with Maggie?" Kathi handed over a fresh drink. She'd carried the bottles of rum and Coke between one arm and her body, and now set them on the side table.

"She wants nothing to do with me."

"And that bugs the shit out of you."

"No."

"It certainly does."

"Sure. But why?" The rum was starting to do its job. Her head felt light and heavy at the same time.

"Because you're a caretaker."

She didn't like hearing her concern for Maggie reduced to a character trait. She'd felt something for her. The huskiness in Maggie's voice as they'd spoken on the phone had pulled out an echoing warmth within her. Maggie had even laughed a little, and Ally could listen to that sound over and over again.

"I liked her. Before I knew who she was. More than I have anyone in a long time."

"Hey, I know we've been after you to get back out there. But this wasn't exactly what I had in mind."

Ally laughed. "Does that mean you don't think we should all double-date?"

They'd worked through half the bottle of rum by the time Dani came home from her book club. She found them draped bonelessly across the chaise lounges like melted cheese.

"What's going on out here?"

"Take my glass." Kathi waved her hand at the side table between them. "You can still catch up."

Dani bent and kissed Kathi's mouth, then pushed on one of her legs. "Scoot." When Kathi moved her legs, Dani perched on the end of her lounge. She filled half a glass with rum and added a splash of Coke. "What are we drinking to?"

"Please, let me tell her." Kathi grinned.

"Go ahead. I'll just lie here and sober up." Ally rolled to her side and pulled her knees up toward her chest. She got tipsy on just a couple of drinks, but she always sobered up quickly once she stopped drinking.

"You know I hate that you can do that." Kathi scowled at her, then launched into a recap of what had happened since her first meeting with Maggie and an abbreviated timeline of their interactions. Ally closed her eyes and listened to their conversation. Kathi told the story in her usual no-nonsense tone, studiously ignoring all of Dani's attempts to lead her on a tangent.

"Wow," Dani said when Kathi had finished.

"Yeah." Ally sat up, her head clearer.

"I mean, what are the chances the first woman you really connect with in forever is part of Carey's case?"

"Yep. This is all so horrible. I'm still wrapping my head around my little brother going to prison. I don't need this, too."

"It sounds like you're sure he's guilty."

"He's stolen from his own family. Is this really a leap?"

"Armed robbery? Yes. I think it is."

"He all but told me he did it. He admitting to having my father's gun. And that instead of pawning it, he decided to put it to good use. What does that sound like to you?"

Dani refilled her glass and held out the bottle, but Ally waved her away. "What are you going to do about Maggie?"

She shrugged. "Nothing. She didn't answer my call or text. Jorge says the criminal trial won't be for months yet. So I won't have to deal with the awkwardness."

"And you won't have to face your emotions."

"My emotions?" She surged to her feet and stomped to the railing once more. "Why don't you have a bigger deck?" She descended the steps and strode across the lawn, calling back over her shoulder, "Between Ma and Carey, when do I have time for *my* emotions?"

When Ally spun around, Dani was standing at the railing. "You still think you should be able to metabolize your feelings as quickly as you do alcohol."

"Dani." Kathi's voice carried a warning.

"She needs to hear this."

Kathi gave Dani a look that even Ally could tell was meant to shut her up.

"It's okay, Kathi." Ally made eye contact with Dani. "Let me have it."

Sympathy softened Dani's eyes. "I realize your situation with your family is tough. I can't begin to understand how it feels for you to be in the middle of all that drama. But at some point, it's on you to make time to keep yourself healthy."

"I'm sure that's real fucking easy for you to say. Sitting here with your perfect wife and two kids. When have you ever had to worry about anything more than what to make for dinner?" In her peripheral vision she registered Kathi's stricken expression. They'd been frank with each other before, but she'd never injected this venom into her words.

Suddenly, she needed to be as far away from this reminder of what she didn't have as she could get. As she passed through the door to the house, she heard Kathi call out to her.

"What the hell, Al?"

"Let her go." Dani's calm demeanor churned up Ally's anger like silt in a riverbed, clouding her ability to think clearly. But it seemed her angry barb hadn't even grazed Dani.

Once in her car, she didn't uncurl her fisted grip on the wheel until she'd nearly arrived home. She grumbled to herself and wove between cars on the interstate while she replayed the conversation in her mind.

She was jealous of Kathi and Dani's relationship. That she could admit in the confines of her vehicle. No—more accurately, envious. She loved them both and wished only the best for them, together and separately. When she heard them commiserating over something one of the kids had done, or complaining about work, she often wondered if she would ever have someone in that way. A woman to come home to, who would listen when things with her mother got to be too much and she needed to vent. And for whom she could do the same. Usually, before she sank too deeply into that hole, she would give herself a lecture on feeling sorry for herself and push those thoughts out of her mind.

Chapter Seven

Maggie stood in front of a long glass case, staring at a row of guns in varying sizes and shapes. The two employees behind the counter were busy with other customers, so she had time to calm the nerves doing somersaults in her belly. The taller of the two employees, a man, wore a black T-shirt bearing the shop logo tucked into blue jeans. At his waist, a gun rested in a holster attached to his belt. Maggie moved toward the other end of the shop to keep herself from staring at the weapon, carried so openly. Maybe this was a bad idea. Inga had said she felt safer with a gun in the house, but all Maggie felt right now was nervous. She didn't think the mere presence of one could make her feel more secure.

The female employee seemed less intimidating. She was about Maggie's height, five foot five or so. Her brown hair was pulled back in a ponytail. Behind black-rimmed glasses, her eyes smiled as she interacted with two customers. Her red polo had "Beretta" over the left breast, and Maggie didn't see any evidence of a pistol on her. Maggie lingered at her end of the store, hoping she would finish with her customer first.

She'd purposely avoided the many pawnshops that advertised gun sales and had conducted an internet search for reputable stores. Through a little research she found that many gun shops had a target range on the property as well. They all seemed to offer some level of instruction, gun rentals, and gunsmith services as well. Muted popping noises vibrated beneath the floor, indicating the range here was located on a lower level. Was that safe? Surely they took precautions against bullets coming up through the floor.

Several racks on the back wall held long guns, but Maggie concentrated on the handguns in the cases. The larger ones appeared very military in nature, in varying combinations of black, gray, or tan. She found a collection of smaller guns, obviously geared toward women, but none of the teal, pink, or purple mostly plastic ones appealed to her either.

"Can I help you?" Maggie nearly sighed in relief at the feminine voice.

"I—I might be interested in buying a gun."

"Sure. What kind are you looking for?" The woman smiled warmly.

"I don't know anything about them."

"Okay. I can help you figure that out. Are you looking for a handgun?" She swept a hand over the glass case between them. "Rifle? Shotgun?" She indicated a row on the wall behind her. Maggie recognized the hunting rifles and thought she could distinguish the shotguns, but some of the others seemed much too aggressive for any citizen to own.

"A handgun, I would think."

"You've got two basic kinds here." She moved back to the low case between them. "Revolvers or semiautomatic pistols. Each has benefits and drawbacks. Then, of course, you'll find some variations with each of those, but this is your first decision."

She tried to follow along as the saleswoman explained the differences in the two types of handguns. The semiautomatics were intimidating, black and bulky. But the revolvers reminded her too much of the gun Carey Rowe had pointed at her. Just looking at it lying innocuously in the case made the back of her neck itch uncomfortably.

"Do you see any you'd like to look at?"

She pointed to the least scary one she could find—a more compact model, silver on top with a black handle.

"Beretta Pico. Good choice." She pointed at her chest. "I'm obviously a fan." When she took it out of the case and started to hand it to her, Maggie took a step back.

"I don't really know how—I've never—"

The woman turned it over and indicated the empty slot in the bottom of the handle. "It's not loaded. See here. The magazine isn't in it." She flipped it back up and pointed to the piece of red plastic wedged into a mechanism on the top. "And we use these in the slide so you can see there's nothing in the chamber." Maggie's confusion must have shown in her expression. The woman smiled. "Okay. Back it up a little. This is a semiautomatic pistol. The slide here on the top contains the mechanism that reloads the chamber after you fire it. Here in the side is where the empty shell ejects after the round is fired."

She talked about trigger pull and safeties, but at some point she lost Maggie again. Maybe this was a bad idea. Yet she only had to think about Cary Rowe's low growl to become once more saturated with fear. And she imagined any number of other guys were out there just like him—desperate enough to victimize someone else.

The saleswoman took a business card off a tray on the counter and handed it to her. "We have a range downstairs and offer a couple of different training options for novices if you're interested. Anything from an hour of private instruction on safety and operation of a firearm, up to the handgun-carry-permit class."

"Carry permit?"

She nodded. "Do you want to carry it on you or in a purse? Or is this just for home protection?"

She clutched her bag more tightly to her chest. "I suppose I'd like to have it with me."

"Then you'll need a permit. Call our training coordinator. She can set you up with a class date." She gave her a sympathetic look. "She even offers some classes for women only, if you'd be more comfortable with that."

She nodded. "Thank you."

The saleswoman laid the gun on the counter and met Maggie's eyes. "You have some options as far as carrying. Some women use a purse or bag. That's okay, unless your purse is stolen. And if I need to draw quickly, I'd prefer not to fumble in mine. So I carry on my person at all times."

Maggie glanced at her waist, still seeing no discernible bulge under her fitted polo. The woman chuckled.

"You won't see it." She stashed the gun back in the locked case, then circled out from behind the counter and walked to the corner of the shop where accessories hung on several displays. Maggie tracked her, paying close attention, but she still couldn't find any evidence of a gun.

She brought a package back to the counter and opened it. "This is called the flashbang holster. You carry it under your bra band. It attaches with this snap to your bra." She got the compact gun back out and popped the small plastic retainer out of the slide. Then she clipped it into the molded shape of the holster. She held it flat against her, just under her breasts, with the gun's handle centered over her breastbone. "If you get in trouble, you just reach under your shirt and—" With the holster still braced in her left hand to show the placement, she grasped the handle with her right and pulled the gun down and free of the holster.

"That's impressive—and a little scary. It's safe to have it there, near your…" She waved in the area of her own chest.

The saleswoman smiled. "You're not going to shoot your boob off. The holster has a trigger guard. But if you have zero experience with guns, you should learn how to handle them safely. I'd recommend the private instruction. It's not expensive for just an hour, and we can cover everything you need to know in that time."

"Would I get all that in the permit class?"

"In theory, yes. But a dozen other students will be in the class, with varying degrees of experience. And the instructors cover what's needed to get you through the written test and shooting proficiently enough to get your permit. You don't have to be a sharpshooter to pass. If you ever need to use your carry weapon, it's most likely going to be at fairly close range, so accuracy isn't usually an issue."

"Why is that?"

"If you can run, that should always be your first option before pulling a gun. We aren't trying to make vigilantes of you. This is self-defense only. They'll go through all that in class."

"What's the waiting period to buy one?"

"Tennessee doesn't have one. Every state's different. But here, we'd run a criminal-background check on you. It's pretty quick."

"Oh, so you can get one the same day."

"Sure. Some paperwork's involved. But we can get you out of here in less than thirty minutes."

Thirty minutes from deciding to buy to holding a gun in her hand? Was that safe? Could someone decide on the spur of the moment, perhaps in anger, to buy a gun, and it was that easy? The background check was supposed to make her feel better. But what if that was how Carey Rowe got a gun? Thinking about being on the receiving end of that transaction made her queasy.

"I don't think I'll purchase anything today. You've given me a lot to think about."

"Understandable. Here's my card, too. But if you come back and I'm not here, any of the guys can help you. They're all pretty good at helping out even the most novice gun handler."

"Thank you."

As Maggie approached the door, she moved aside to let two men enter before she stepped out. They both carried small black bags, and one had glasses with yellow-tinted lenses pushed up on his forehead. They headed immediately for a counter where a row of targets hung on the wall. As Maggie pushed through the door to exit, she heard one of them ask for two lanes in the range.

❖

Ally carefully lowered her large miter saw as the blade worked through the four-by-four post that would eventually make up one of the thick legs of a custom dining table. Next, using the table saw, she would notch an inch out of the end all the way around to create a two-inch tab that could be fitted into the perpendicular support.

She released the trigger on the saw, and as the high-pitched whine wound down, someone called her name. She set the piece of wood aside, took off her safety glasses, and turned. As she scrubbed a hand through her hair, sawdust rained down.

"Can we talk?" Dani stood just outside the open overhead door.

Ally glanced at the old analog clock on the garage wall. "Shouldn't you be at church with the family?"

"Kathi took the kids without me. She said I had something more important to do."

"More important than church?" Ally covered her mouth in mock horror.

"I know. I was shocked, too."

"Come on in." Ally grabbed two folding camp chairs from a tall cabinet against the wall. She slung one open and swept a hand over it. "Have a seat." She set up the other one for herself, then went over to the fridge she kept stocked with cold drinks. "Water?"

"No thanks."

"Beer?" she asked with a wink.

"Before noon on Sunday?"

"I won't tell if you don't." She teasingly held out a bottle of Dani's favorite brew, and Dani shook her head. Ally grabbed herself a bottled water, then settled next to Dani. She cracked open the seal, and they sat silently while she took a long drink.

"What are you working on?"

"Dining-room table. It's a wedding gift for a friend's son."

"Nice. If I haven't told you, I'm so impressed with what you can do out here." Dani smiled softly.

"And here I thought you kept that bedroom suite I made you just to be polite." She'd spent months on the headboard, dresser, and nightstand in a modern rustic style that fit Dani and Kathi's decor. She sighed. "I owe you an apology."

Dani chuckled. "Sounds like it hurts you to say that. Thank you. But that's not why I'm here."

"Then why?"

"I've never told you this. In fact, I've only ever shared what I'm about to say with Kathi. My mother had a drinking problem." She rolled her eyes toward the ceiling. "Not had—has. My mother is a recovering alcoholic. When I was a kid, I used to stay with my grandmother when things got really bad. After my grandmother passed, my aunt and her family took me in a couple of times, too."

"But I've met your mom. She's great." Dani's mother came to all the kids' birthday parties and brought gifts and a homemade side dish.

"Yeah, she is. Now. She's been sober since I was in my early twenties. A few years earlier and she might not have skipped my high school graduation."

"Damn, Dani. I'm sorry."

Dani shrugged. "It is what it is. I'm not telling you this for sympathy, but to let you know that I get what you're going through. I don't want you to ignore your own feelings and needs and end up like my mom or—"

"Anyone in my family?"

"See, you can say that. If I said it—"

"I shouldn't have snapped at you." She slid her bottled water into the cup holder in the camp chair and shifted to face Dani. "But you're right. At some point I have to stop taking care of Mom and Carey at the expense of myself."

"But you don't have to do it alone. Kathi and I think of you as family, and I hope you feel the same way."

"I do. But sometimes it's hard to talk to you guys about relationship stuff—or my lack thereof, I guess. You two have it all figured out. And look at me. I finally feel a spark with someone, and it's the most inappropriate woman I could find."

"Kathi and I have our issues like anyone else. And we didn't have the smoothest of starts either, if you recall."

"It's hard to remember a time when you weren't the perfect couple."

Dani laughed. "Please. When she and I met, you two had just gotten past the awkwardness of your breakup and become friends again. She didn't want to get involved with another woman she worked with and repeat the cycle."

Ally nodded. Kathi had confessed her attraction to Dani, and once they worked through both feeling a little weird, Ally had tried to be a good sounding board for her.

"And I"—Dani grimaced—"I was convinced that she still had feelings for you and that's why she held back."

"I didn't know that."

Dani shrugged. "I didn't talk about it. I'd been on job sites where working with women brought all kinds of drama. I was the new girl and didn't want to cause trouble. Plus, you were Kathi's friend. So, tell me, what is it about Maggie that has you so wound up?"

Ally wanted to talk *to* Maggie. Getting permission to talk *about* her would have to do. "I'm such an idiot. There are plenty of women out there I could be dating."

"Where are you meeting all these women? You work and then you go home." Dani lifted her brows. "Did you secretly join an online dating site?"

"You know what I mean."

"Let's set aside who she is, and just tell me who she is to you."

"She's smart and beautiful. And strong. Imagine what she's dealing with, and she's down there at court making sure that the guy who—" She surged to her feet. "Damn it. I can't get around who she is. Yet I'm thinking about her all the time. Wishing she was someone else—or I was—or Carey was. Wanting her to call me because she can't stop thinking about me either."

But she'd phoned. And Maggie hadn't answered or returned her call. Now, she needed to move on, take Dani's advice and look after her own emotional health.

"We're here for you, kiddo." Dani rested her hand on Ally's arm, then brushed some sawdust off.

"Did you just go into full-on mom mode on me?"

Dani stood and ruffled Ally's hair, then said, "Yes." She took off her jacket and laid it on her chair. "Now, teach me how to make a table. I don't want to go home to an empty house."

"You're a weirdo. You have a wife and two young kids. You should relish some alone time."

"It's too quiet."

Ally grabbed another pair of safety glasses off the workbench along the wall. "Wear these."

For the next hour and half, they worked together, talking only about the project in front of them. But Dani's words kept rolling through Ally's head. Even after everything she'd been through with Carey, she couldn't imagine what Dani's childhood had been like. She had happy memories of her and Carey's younger selves to lean on when she was angry or disappointed with him. She didn't know if Dani had anything good to reminisce about. But she'd clearly found a way to forgiveness. Ally had been around Dani's mom several times and hadn't picked up on any tension between them.

Chapter Eight

"Yes, sir, we do have your records request. We haven't finished fulfilling it yet. But we'll certainly contact you as soon as it's ready." Maggie shoved her hand into her hair at her temple and raked it back over her ear. The ache she'd been nursing all day throbbed under her fingers. She'd already been talking to this guy for longer than she should have to. He, like more than half the people she dealt with, thought the records he'd requested should be the most important project on her desk.

She glanced up as Inga leaned against the edge of her cubicle. "You have a great day, sir." She disconnected the call and caught Inga rolling her eyes.

"You're so nice to these people."

"It's called customer service. I know you've been a manager for so long the concept must be foreign to you."

"We pay you to deal with the public so I don't have to."

"Right now, I need a break." She locked her computer and stood.

Inga gave her a curious look but didn't say anything. She didn't have to. This was the third time in the two hours Maggie had been at work that she'd stepped away from her desk. Usually, Inga had to drag her away from it at lunch and then again in the evening. But Maggie had been distracted and restless, unable to focus for very long.

When she went to the employee break room, Inga followed. They shared the lounge area with the two other departments on their floor. On one side of the room, a secondhand couch faced a seldom-used television mounted on the wall. Several small tables provided space to sit and eat in the center of the room. On the far wall, two microwaves and a coffeemaker filled most of the small counter space.

Maggie passed up the fruit and yogurt she'd put in the full-sized fridge earlier and went directly to the vending machine. In the two months since the robbery, she'd graduated from mild insomnia to stress eating and irrational anxiety. She bent to fish the Butterfinger bar and bag of chips from the machine, then turned to find Inga blocking her path back to the office.

"Maggie, what can I do?"

"About what?"

"I know you've been paying every day to park in the open lot across the street to avoid going to the garage."

Maggie's face flamed with embarrassment. She'd thought Inga had caught her crossing the street a couple of days ago. Confronted with that observation now, she couldn't force out the excuse she'd come up with that day—that she had to rush off to an appointment after work and wanted to be close.

"You're eating junk all the time, and you look like you're not sleeping. I know this isn't work stress because I've purposely been assigning more new projects to Greg instead of giving them to you."

"I don't need you to do that."

"But I do. I know how good you are at your job. Lately, you're jumpy and irritable, and you don't stay in your chair for more than forty-five minutes at a time. I can't, in good conscience, pile onto what you're dealing with."

Her cheeks heated even more. In the two months since the robbery, she'd been struggling personally. But she'd always taken pride in her work, and hearing that Inga noticed she'd been failing there too hurt.

"So, what do you need? Would you like to take some time off?"

Maggie shook her head, grateful no one else was in the room to witness this exchange. Sitting at home wouldn't solve her problems. In fact, she worried that being there more would exacerbate the issue. She could envision herself becoming a shut-in more easily than she would like. With Amazon Prime delivering anything a person could need, she'd rarely have to leave the house.

"I want to help, but—"

"There's nothing you can do." She hadn't talked to Inga about the nightmares. Or sleeping with the television on so she wouldn't have to decide if the noises she heard were real or not. Or about parking closer because she couldn't bring herself to walk alone to the garage, let alone go inside the darkened space.

Inga would offer for Maggie to stay with her so she wouldn't be alone at night. She would wait around and walk with her to her car. But Maggie needed to find the strength to handle things on her own.

"I'm sorry I've been distracted at work. I'll try to keep my butt in the chair more often." She spoke to Inga-her-boss because she didn't want to tell Inga-her-friend that she couldn't allow herself to need her right now.

She squeezed past Inga and headed back toward the office. Inga said, "Take your time."

Maggie passed through the doorway without turning around. Back at her desk, she glanced at the clock and resolved to stay seated and working diligently until one o'clock. The chips and candy would hold her over until her late lunch.

❖

Despite her resolution to spend more time at her desk, Maggie didn't think she'd been much more productive. By the time she pulled into her parking space at the apartment complex, she'd reconsidered the merit of her hermit idea. She'd hang a bin on the outside of her door and pay her neighbor's teenager to retrieve her mail and put it in there. She'd already decided Amazon would deliver the essentials. Now, she just needed a job where she could work from home. Since she wouldn't need a car, she could sell hers. Without the additional expense she could accept a smaller salary for the convenience of working there.

Attempting to offset her junk-food binge, she limited herself to a grilled chicken breast on top of a large salad for dinner. She added crumbled blue cheese, sliced red onion, and dried apple slices, then drizzled a vinaigrette over it, because she hated a boring salad. A glass and a half of wine and most of her salad later, she'd scoured two job-search websites for at-home employment.

She finished her second glass of wine and poured a third. Settled on the sofa, she toyed with her phone, feeling just enough of a buzz to scroll through her contacts and find Ally's name. Despite her mixed feelings, she wanted to talk to Ally. After she'd calmed down, she understood Ally's confusion about how to broach the topic of Carey's identity. When would Ally have told her had she not overheard that conversation? But she'd fought the urge to call, hoping as the weeks slid by that she'd forget how easy Ally had been to talk to.

The wine had made her head fuzzy, and she wasn't in any condition to have a rational talk about Ally's relationship to Carey Rowe now. But the desire to hear Ally's voice had her staring at Ally's name on her phone. The blur in her brain gave her an excuse to push Call. She activated the speakerphone function and laid her phone on the arm of the sofa next to her.

Ally answered, sounding a bit out of breath and distracted. Had she taken time to look at the display to see who it was?

"Hi, it's Maggie. From the courthouse."

"I remember you, Maggie."

"Yeah. I figured."

"How are you?" Ally didn't sound like she was asking

casually, as one would an acquaintance. She seemed to really want to know.

"Having a bit of a rough time," she answered honestly. "And a little tipsy at the moment." Maybe too much honesty there.

"Hm. I've just opened a beer, but it sounds like I'm pretty far behind you."

"I'll slow down so you can catch up."

Ally chuckled softly. "If your aim is to get drunk, you might be on your own. I need to work on an important project tomorrow."

"What kind?"

"I mentioned that I do carpentry, right?"

"Yes. Are you framing a house? Because that does sound like the kind of thing you should be clearheaded for." Her words came out slightly slurred and jumbled together.

"No. I have a side gig that's really more my passion. I build furniture. I'm supposed to be building a crib. My client wants to surprise his wife with it. And at this rate, the baby will be born and up and walking before I finish it."

"Should I let you go, then?"

"No." Ally paused, and Maggie heard the slight pop of her mouth against the beer bottle. "I've been thinking about you."

"I didn't return your call."

"That's okay."

"It's kind of rude."

"You're calling me now. What's wrong?"

How did she say she felt like everything was wrong without sounding dramatic? Well, not everything. Her wine was good. And talking to Ally felt nice. She didn't want to ruin that by bringing up Carey and her apparent inability to move past what had happened to her.

"Maggie? Is that short for Margaret?"

"Yes. I'm named for Margaret Chase Smith."

"I'm not familiar with her."

"She was the first woman to hold a seat in both the House and the Senate. My mother heard her speak while in college in 1974." Maggie readjusted her position on the sofa, bending her legs and pulling her feet close to her butt.

"She must have been quite impressive."

"I'm not sure I'm living up to the namesake."

"How so?"

"I live an ordinary life."

"Don't we all."

"At least you have a passion. Any piece of your furniture could potentially be a family heirloom, passed down through generations. That baby's great-grandchildren could sleep in that crib."

"It is kind of neat when you put it like that. What are you passionate about?"

Maggie shook her head, then stopped when the motion made her dizzy. "Nothing."

"Maybe we don't shoot so high. What do you enjoy? Hobbies? Interests?"

"When I lived with my ex, I liked gardening. We had a raised bed in our tiny condo yard, but now that I'm in an apartment, that's not an option. I suppose I could put a planter on the balcony and grow some herbs. Or maybe a couple of tomato plants in five-gallon buckets."

"If all you're lacking is a plot of land, I have a decent-sized backyard. I'd happily loan you a corner of it in exchange for some of the fruits of your labor—or vegetables."

"I don't think I could do that." Drunk-dialing was a far stretch from purposefully spending time at Ally's house. But was she even drunk? Since they'd started talking, she'd slowed her wine consumption. She hadn't even finished the glass she'd poured before calling.

"The offer stands. But if you think it's inappropriate or you'd be uncomfortable, I won't be offended if you decline."

"Can I think about it and let you know?"

"Absolutely."

They chatted for a while longer, shifting to more casual topics. Maggie didn't refill her glass again, and she soon sobered up enough to be nervous about the fact that she didn't want to get off the phone with Ally. Eventually, she could hear Ally stifling her yawns, so they said their good-byes. She plugged her cell in to charge, then washed down some ibuprofen with a whole glass of water. Trying to mitigate some of the hangover she would take to work tomorrow, she forced herself into bed for a few hours' sleep.

❖

Ally awoke to the obnoxious sound of her alarm going off. She could just hit snooze or, better yet, turn it off and wake up whenever she wanted to. But part of her plan to step away from home-building for the summer included treating her furniture hobby like a business—as sort of a trial run. In addition to testing out the financial feasibility, she needed to prove that she could be self-motivated enough when she didn't have to report to a job site.

She lurched out of bed, pausing to stretch her neck and shoulder muscles. She'd spent too many hours on the lathe yesterday working on spindles for the crib. She'd finished most of the pieces, and today she would build the side rails. Grabbing her phone off the bureau, she sent an email to her client firming up a delivery date next week. Having a concrete schedule would keep her moving on the project.

She dressed in an old pair of jeans and a comfortable T-shirt. In the kitchen, she filled a travel mug with coffee and added creamer. Her stomach wouldn't tolerate food this early, but she'd grab a frozen breakfast burrito on her first break in a couple of hours. In the garage, she leaned against her workbench and let the first few sips of coffee work their magic.

Was Maggie dragging like she was this morning? Probably

worse. She'd heard the effects of the wine in her voice while they spoke last night and, she thought, the pouring sounds of at least one refill. Maggie was probably thankful today was Friday.

She'd made the offer to let Maggie garden at her place without much thought. The situation between them had so much potential for tension or, at the very least, awkwardness. But the kick of her heartbeat in her chest when she'd seen Maggie's name on her cell-phone screen had nothing to do with discomfort. She'd abandoned her work on the crib for the chance to talk to Maggie.

Dani had suggested she start taking care of herself. She hoped Maggie took her up on the offer, because spending time with Maggie made her feel good. And she didn't want to avoid that pleasure because of Carey.

For now, she'd direct her attention to this crib. She set her coffee mug on the bench and focused on the pieces she'd laid out the night before. As she assembled them, she thought about Maggie's idea that future generations would fall asleep there. Parents would stand at the rail and gaze down at their peaceful child. Or they would get up in the middle of the night and lift their crying baby from the crib to rock it back to sleep. According to Shirley, Ally had been a fussy infant, and Carey had slept through the night almost immediately.

When she checked her phone on her breakfast break, she had a text from Maggie indicating she'd like to accept the gardening offer. Ally was so excited she forgot to let the burrito she'd just taken out of the microwave cool. Rereading Maggie's message, she took a bite, then yelped as she burnt her mouth. She gulped down some orange juice, then texted back an invitation to come over the next day, followed by her address.

❖

Maggie followed the directions to Ally's house on her phone. As she pulled into the driveway behind Ally's SUV, the front door opened, and Ally stepped out. Maggie stayed in the driver's seat, distracted by watching Ally saunter, which was really the only word for the sexy swing in her hips, down the walk toward her. The slash in the leg of her jeans just above the knee provided an enticing hint of thigh. Her sage-green T-shirt had a faded spot in the shape of some kind of chemical spilled just over her abdomen. *And now I'm noticing how flat her stomach is.* Ally's strong body, a little thick in all the right places, probably came from daily labor rather than sculpting workouts.

To keep her leering from turning creepy, she averted her eyes and got out of the car. Ally waved as she crossed the lawn.

"Cute house. I love the color." The one-story ranch home stretched across the lot. The brick had been painted dark gray, and the white trim stood out against it in bright contrast. Cedar shutters and front-porch pillars added a touch of rustic charm.

"I'm not usually a fan of painting brick. But this wasn't pretty brick. It was mustard yellow, so something had to be done."

She knew the style. Homes in established neighborhoods built in the seventies sometimes had the tan or yellowish brick with brown roofs. The black shingles on Ally's house looked fairly new as well.

"Do you want to see the inside first? Or go right to the backyard?"

"I'm dying to know if it's as spacious as the front."

"It's about the same size. I have a little over an acre. That's why people are renovating these older places. New construction is fresh and clean, but it's all jammed together on postage-stamp lots. Come on around." Ally took her hand and led her up the driveway and into the backyard.

They followed a crushed-stone path through a gate in the privacy fence. Around the corner of the house, several large trees shaded an expanse of lush, green grass. When Ally dropped her hand, Maggie wished the walk had been longer. Ally's fingers laced against hers felt warm and comfortable.

"What do you think?" Ally swept her arm as if indicating a grand vista in front of them.

Maggie planted her hands on her hips and pretended to consider the view. "Are you sure you want to give up your yard?"

"Take as much as you need. I'm rarely back here, anyway, except to mow. I spend most of my free time in the garage."

"Okay. If this were my yard, I would probably build raised beds over there." She pointed to the spot she'd scoped out. "That area seems to get plenty of sun, but it's close enough to run the hose for water."

"Go for it."

Getting permission energized her creativity. They wandered closer to the area, and Maggie could already envision two rectangular beds. She described them to Ally, pacing off the dimensions of the space.

"Do you know what you want to grow?"

She wanted something easy to care for. She wasn't sure how often she would be here, and she didn't want to impose on Ally to care for her hobby. "What do you think about tomatoes, cucumbers, and carrots?"

"Whatever you want. And feel free to come by as often as you need to. But if you'll show me how much to water and when, I can take care of that when you aren't able to get by."

"Are you sure this isn't too much of an imposition?" She offered them both one more out. Ally had made a generous offer, but maybe she hadn't been smart to accept.

"Stop asking. I wouldn't have offered otherwise. And I still had time to make an excuse when you texted yesterday."

"Okay. If anything changes—"

"I'll let you know." Ally's expression softened, and she touched Maggie's arm. "And you'll tell me if things get weird for you, too?"

"Deal." She stuck her hand out, but what started as an exaggerated handshake just turned into them holding hands again. And she didn't want it to end. Leaving her hand in Ally's warm, firm grasp, she turned to study the yard again.

"When do you want to start?"

She squeezed Ally's hand. "Would it be too enthusiastic of me to say today? I could grab some supplies and still have most of the afternoon to work."

Ally smiled. "Sounds like a plan." Ally released her hand slowly, and Maggie imagined that she did so reluctantly.

When they circled the garage, Ally eyed Maggie's Prius. "How many trips do you think you'll have to make in your tiny car?"

"Hey. My little car has some space when I lay down the seats."

"Do you want a ride?" Ally nodded toward her SUV, which was larger than the Prius.

"I don't want to take you away from your work."

Ally shrugged. "I can spare some time to run to the garden center with you."

"As long as you don't mind. I'm thinking Lowe's. I can get lumber to build the beds and some basic planting stuff all in one place."

"I'll grab my keys."

Ten minutes later, Maggie wished she'd insisted on driving. Ally tapped her fingers against the steering wheel and tightened her jaw.

The driver of the blue car in front of them left two car lengths between her and the pickup truck in front of him. The traffic in the left lane passed them, and several cars slipped into the space in front of the blue car. Ally huffed.

"Everything okay?"

"Yeah."

The driver of the blue car slowed down so much Maggie thought she might be looking for a street to turn on. Two more cars merged in front of her.

"What is this lady doing?" Ally waved her hand at the windshield. "What the hell are you doing?" She leaned forward and spoke more sternly, directly to the driver, though she couldn't hear her.

"We're all going the same place. And no one is getting there very quickly." She suspected there might be a wreck somewhere up ahead, given the unusually heavy traffic.

"Everyone that this idiot is letting in front of her is getting there faster than us. Why can't she just close that space?" As traffic slowed again, Ally rolled up closer to the woman's bumper than Maggie was comfortable with.

"You can't push her into it."

Ally squeezed her hands around the wheel, then sighed and forcibly relaxed them. The line of cars crawled forward, and when they got close enough to the Lowe's parking-lot entrance, Ally swerved around the blue car's bumper.

"Impressive." Maggie hadn't thought Ally's car would fit through the space without curbing a tire.

"Sorry. I get impatient when I drive." Ally swung her SUV into a spot close to the front of the store.

"No kidding."

"It's something I need to work on."

"It's good to know you have faults."

"I have tons. Hey, I'm going to grab some sandpaper while I'm here. I'll meet you over by the lumber."

Maggie found the rack of pressure-treated lumber. She consulted her phone, where she'd made notes on the dimensions she wanted for the beds, and tried to calculate in her head how much wood she'd need. She didn't want to make another trip back for more, but she had no place to put the extra if she over-bought.

"Do you want some help with that?" Ally asked.

Maggie hesitated.

"Construction is kind of what I do, you know. This will probably go more smoothly if you let me give you a hand."

"Okay."

Ally nodded and pulled a small notebook and pencil out of the pocket of her light jacket. Within seconds she had a rough sketch of the beds Maggie had described to her earlier. "Is this what you want to do?"

Maggie glanced at the drawing and nodded, and Ally grabbed a large rolling cart from farther down the aisle and transferred lumber from the display rack onto it. Maggie helped stack the boards. She followed Ally down another aisle, where she added a box of nails.

"When we get back to my place, I can cut the boards to size for you."

"I don't want to inconvenience you."

"Honestly, Maggie, this whole thing will take me less than an hour to build. How long do you think you'd have to spend on it?"

"Do you mean how many days?"

"Then it's settled. Let's go get the rest of the stuff. Then we can hit the Starbucks drive-through on our way home."

Chapter Nine

Ally had been right. The work went a lot more quickly with her help. Within an hour of arriving back at Ally's house, they had built the frame on the first bed. And it was nicer than what Maggie's rudimentary carpentry skills would have managed. The box was perfectly square, and when Maggie thought they were finished, Ally described her idea to secure another board to the top in order to provide a ledge for Maggie to lean on while working in the soil.

Maggie had never been the manual-labor type. She wasn't opposed to a little work, but, living in an apartment now, she didn't have the space or the need for big projects. Her ex would hire someone to do work around their house rather than get her hands dirty.

"Isn't it funny how you can spend years with someone, yet when it's over, they cease having a name. They just become 'the ex' in your mind."

Ally paused in the middle of measuring one side of the garden bed and gave her a curious look. "Where did that come from?"

"I was thinking about house projects and—never mind. My thoughts are usually a long and winding road."

"That end with you randomly speaking them aloud?" Ally's grin softened any judgment Maggie might have inferred from her words.

"Maybe."

"I like that."

"Even if you don't know how I got there."

"Especially then."

Ally's ringing phone interrupted a nice moment of eye contact between them. When Ally pulled it from her pocket to check the screen, Maggie wished she'd been able to resist in favor of whatever was happening between them just then.

"I'm sorry. I have to take this." Ally stepped away as she answered her phone. She went to the other side of the yard.

Maggie debated trying to cut the next board by herself. Ally had run an extension cord for the saw to their corner of the yard. Even though Ally had moved far enough away that Maggie couldn't hear her conversation, the saw might still be too loud. Instead, she measured out the area for the second bed. Then she grabbed the hand tiller Ally had found in the garage, apparently courtesy of the previous owner, and loosened the soil. Ally paced while she spoke, pausing every so often to pinch the bridge of her nose or rub a hand down her face. She was as animated on the phone as she'd been in traffic. After Ally scowled at her phone, touched the screen, and shoved it back into her pocket, Maggie spun around to avoid being caught watching her.

Ally strode back across the lawn, picked up the next board, and marked the spot for her cut. Her expression didn't invite conversation, so Maggie didn't pry. They finished the first bed in a mildly uncomfortable silence.

The second frame got done even more quickly, whether due to their experience building the first or the lack of distracting conversation. Ally spoke only to convey a measurement or an instruction about their work. Maggie started to inquire about her mood several times—in her head. But the words never materialized.

By the time they'd finished, she was eager to escape the awkwardness. She gathered up the wood scraps and placed them in the bin Ally indicated, while Ally packed up and stowed her tools. She returned from her last trip to the garage with scraps and found Ally sitting at a table and chairs on the patio at the back of the house.

"Thank you for your help." Maggie glanced over at the finished beds, still empty of plants.

Why had she accepted Ally's offer? She'd wanted a distraction from the limbo created by months of waiting for the trial to start, and work wasn't doing it. Exercise had proved to be good stress relief in the past, but she'd canceled her gym membership last year in favor of the walking trails around her apartment complex. Now, just the thought of traveling those paths alone could send her into a full-blown panic attack.

So she'd convinced herself Ally's idea of gardening was just what she needed. She'd sent the text accepting Ally's offer with that thought in her head, completely ignoring the voice that said she really wanted to see Ally again. But even that hadn't gone the way she'd planned. After the tense silence following Ally's phone call, Maggie couldn't leave fast enough from the disappointment drowning her.

"Would you like a drink? I have hard cider, or I can open a bottle of wine?" Ally's offer seemed to be sincere rather than just polite, so Maggie replied honestly as well.

"That depends. Are we going to talk or sit and drink in silence?"

"What do you mean?"

Maggie stepped from the grass to the concrete patio but didn't take the opposite chair just yet. "We don't know each other that well. But I can tell you have something on your mind."

"It's nothing." Ally's brush-off of the subject lacked any trace of conviction. She sighed and rolled her eyes. "Carey's getting sprung from rehab tomorrow. Ma wants me to take her to pick him up."

"Oh. Maybe I will have a cider."

Ally leapt up and went inside. She returned with two bottles, their caps already popped, and handed one over. "I'm sorry. You don't want to talk about him."

"I don't."

Ally nodded and looked away, her expression a mix of hurt and understanding. They were becoming friends, weren't they? And friends shared family stuff. But surely she had other people she could discuss this with. Maggie *had* dragged it out of her. Was it fair to turn her back now?

"Listen, I can't summon up any sympathy for him or his situation. But maybe we could discuss this in terms of how it's affecting you. You don't want to go with her?"

Ally sat back down, gesturing for Maggie to take the other chair. "Not really. He's been sober for just over sixty days. I know that's an accomplishment, given his history. But she's going to fawn over him like he's graduating from college instead of from a mandated stay at a halfway house."

"Youngest child?"

"Typical, right?" Ally took a sip of her drink. "But it's not just that. He's more like her than I am, so she relates to him better."

"Are you like your father?" Maggie remembered a snippet of conversation in the courthouse café. "I'm sorry, but you said he wasn't around now."

"Yeah. I don't really know. I was four when he left. But Ma says I'm like him, only more reliable. Yet she only says that because I run her errands and stuff. As soon as she doesn't think I'm pulling my weight, that's when I'm just like him."

"Did you agree to go?"

Ally nodded reluctantly. "It feels selfish to say, but a part of me has been relieved that he's been away. I hate how what he's done—his choices—always bleed into my life."

"How do you mean?"

Ally set her bottle on the small patio table beside her. She scooted to the edge of her seat, and their knees nearly touched. Her hands twitched as if she wanted to cover Maggie's. Maggie shifted her hands from her lap to her sides, uncomfortable with how much she wanted that contact.

"For starters, you. If I hadn't been at the courthouse, I wouldn't have met you. And I like you, Maggie. I like talking to you and spending time with you. But what hope do I have—I mean, I've never felt so ripped in two directions in my life." Ally made a sound of disgusted frustration. "I'm sorry for dumping this on you."

Maggie could see Ally shutting down. She'd folded her arms over her chest and angled away from Maggie, as if protecting herself from Maggie's reaction to what they talked about.

She should walk away—they should both walk away from this whole situation. Even if she could get around the perceived conflict of interest involved, how could they ever have a meaningful friendship when there was a whole part of Ally's life Maggie couldn't care about? Truthfully, her feelings about Carey were stronger than just apathy. But Ally had just spent her afternoon helping Maggie build garden beds. She'd done that—not to get something back from Maggie, but because Maggie had talked about needing to find a positive outlet in her life.

Since she couldn't address what was really between them at that moment, she offered the only thing she knew for sure—she wasn't ready to disappear from Ally's life. "Do you mind if I come back Monday to start planting?"

Ally's soft smile touched Maggie's heart. "I'll be here."

"It'll be after work."

"No problem. I'll spend the day planning and starting a new project."

"What's next?"

"I don't have another commission yet. So, I'm debating a dining-room buffet piece."

"If you aren't crafting something specific for someone, do you sell your stuff online?"

"Mostly. This summer, I'm going to try taking some pieces to one of the larger flea markets to see if they sell there."

"That's a good idea. So Monday's all work, then?"

Ally nodded.

"Do you think you'll be ready for a break when I get here? I could bring some Chinese food for dinner."

"I have a better idea. Why don't you come straight here and get started on your planting, and I'll take my break and go pick us up some dinner? That way when you're finished, we can eat together."

❖

Ally pulled into an empty parking spot at the far end of Shirley's apartment building. She pushed the button on the dash that opened the rear hatch, leaving Carey to grab his bag. As she circled the back of her vehicle, he tapped a hand against the open hatch as he walked away, leaving it up.

"Door, Al." He'd done stuff like that since they were kids—ever since his growth spurt left him taller than her.

She smirked at him and hit the button on the remote to close the door, depriving him of the satisfaction of seeing her reach up and pull it shut. "Watch your head."

She cut him off and strode up the sidewalk toward Shirley's place. On the way to the recovery house, Shirley had insisted she come inside when they got back for lunch. She'd made Carey's favorite—chicken and dumplings.

Ally hadn't spoken to Carey since he got in the car, except to coldly return his greeting. He'd apparently decided to act as if she hadn't walked out on him last time they spoke. Once more, he expected to ignore the conflict, and she was supposed to let it go.

As Ally stepped inside, Shirley lifted the lid on the crockpot. The aroma of savory chicken filled the apartment, a welcome change from the usual stale cigarette odor.

"Biscuits done?"

"Dumplings. Not biscuits," Carey said as he shoved her

farther inside so he could close the door. "Guest room ready, Ma?"

"I put fresh sheets on the bed for you this morning."

"Thanks. This is just until I get on my feet and put this court business behind me."

"Stay as long as you want to, honey."

Carey disappeared down the hall, and Ally forcibly unclenched her jaw. She didn't want to start an argument about how he foolishly believed this situation would end with his freedom.

"You need to be nicer to him. He's going through a tough time right now." Shirley had told her repeatedly that she shouldn't cling to her anger. She'd even said she didn't get why Ally would be upset over some rusty old gun.

"A tough time? That's what you call this?"

"You never have enough compassion for him. He doesn't have things as easy as you do."

Ally turned her back to help contain an uncensored reply and pretended to be busy pulling a pitcher of iced tea from the fridge. She'd worked one job or another since the day she turned fourteen, beginning with babysitting for the single mother in the apartment next door.

She understood that Carey's addiction wasn't all his own making. His doctor had prescribed strong painkillers when he hurt his back, and he'd never successfully gotten off them. But she couldn't give him a pass on robbery because of addiction. He'd coldly told her that he saw her father's gun as a means to make more money. She hadn't raised him to be so uncaring about another human being. And that's what it came down to. She felt as responsible for the person he was now as Shirley, if not more so. She'd failed as much as their mother had.

Suddenly, she didn't think she could fake her way through a family dinner. She could see the conversation exploding with her disdain for Carey's actions and Shirley's denial about the severity of his issues. While she thought he deserved to deal with that turmoil, maybe his first night out of rehab wasn't the time to test his recovery.

"Hey, Ma. I just remembered I promised Kathi I'd watch the kids tonight." Shirley didn't like Kathi and Dani and would never check her story. She'd convinced herself that Ally's sexuality was a phase, brought on by Kathi's influence, which was just another layer of her denial since she knew Kathi wasn't even the first woman Ally had dated.

"Surely that can wait until after dinner."

"Nah. They want to have a date night. So I have to give the kids dinner."

Shirley screwed up her face in annoyance, and Ally decided to ignore the trace of disgust in it as well.

"It's my first night back," Carey said.

"Sorry, man. I'll stop by later this week." She left, feeling a bit like a coward for fabricating a reason to leave. Maybe she would drop in on Kathi and Dani on her way home, so her story wouldn't be a total lie.

❖

Monday, Ally finalized plans for her next project. She'd scrapped the buffet-server idea. Such a large piece might be harder to sell. She'd been thinking about booking a booth at a big flea market coming up, but several smaller items would be easier to transport, as well as not being so cumbersome for potential buyers to take home.

She had some reclaimed barn wood left that she'd been hoarding in the garage that would make a great top for a coffee table. She'd sketched out an idea for two slabs made up of barn wood separated by four thick, turned pedestals, one at each corner. A soft-gray wash would showcase the grain, and grays were so in fashion right now.

After spending the morning on the plans and prepping the barn wood, she took a break for lunch. She sat at her kitchen table with a can of Diet Coke and her chicken salad on toast and scrolled through Twitter. Part of the reason she'd wanted to take a break from construction was to have some flexibility in her schedule. But if she was serious about making a business of furniture making, she'd have to build some structure into the days she worked. So she granted herself a proper lunch break, without feeling guilty about the work waiting in the garage. But she did post a couple of pictures of the coffee table in progress on her own Twitter. She had a number of followers who'd purchased from her before, and she never knew when a piece would find a home before she'd finished it.

Working had distracted her from thinking about anything else. She'd lost herself in imagining a rustic-chic living room where her coffee table could be both a complement and a conversation piece. She would give it enough weight to pair with either a larger couch and love seat, or a slimmer, modern sofa and patterned chair.

She'd planned to start by assembling the top, but after lunch, she changed gears. The shape of the pedestals had crystallized, and she wanted to get at least one completed while the image was clear. She hefted a large blank into the lathe, then donned safety glasses and a dust mask. With a pencil, she scratched a few landmarks. The dimensions on the first piece didn't need to be precise. But it would be the blueprint for the remaining three pedestals, so she'd have to duplicate them exactly on each piece.

For the next several hours, she carved the basic shape with a roughing gouge. Then, switching between several tools, she refined the large swell that would pull the weight toward the lower half of the spindle. She squared off a couple of inches on either end, creating angles that would bracket all the smooth, rounded shapes.

By the time Maggie pulled her Prius into the driveway, Ally's arm and shoulder muscles had tightened to the verge of cramping. Shaking out her arms, wrists, and fingers, she walked to the front of the garage, near the open overhead door.

Maggie climbed out of the car and retrieved a backpack from the back seat. She still wore her work clothes, classy and professional, much like that first day they'd met at the courthouse. Today, she had on a beige jacket, periwinkle skirt, and nude flats. Her legs were bare, no hose, and so smooth Ally had to force herself to look away.

"I came straight from work. I hope you don't mind if I change here."

"Of course not. You didn't even get the tour of the inside last time. Come on through here." Ally led her in the door connecting the garage to the house.

They entered through the kitchen, which opened only to the eat-in area. She'd painted the cabinets white to brighten up the smallish space. She'd also updated the countertops but hadn't done any more work in the kitchen. Eventually, she'd make it back in there to do a backsplash and update the light fixtures. She'd done enough work to clean it up, but the kitchen didn't inspire her in the least.

"This is nice," Maggie said.

As they passed into the living room, Ally saw Maggie eyeing the wall on the other side of the kitchen.

"I know. Most people would knock out that wall, open it up. That's the trend in these older houses."

"So why didn't you?"

Ally shrugged. "When I cook, I prefer simple meals. I don't spend a lot of time in the kitchen. I plan to live here for quite a while, so I made choices based on what works for me, not what sells houses. I can always change my mind and lose the wall later."

"That makes sense."

"I restored all the hardwoods, but the living room only got paint."

Down the hallway, she indicated the guest bathroom. Maggie set her backpack on the floor inside the door. But instead of going in, she turned to Ally.

"You said you started in the master."

Ally nodded.

"Can I see it?"

Ally smiled. "A beautiful woman just asked me to take her to my bedroom. Why would I refuse that request?"

Maggie's blush paired with a sexy wink made an interesting combination. Ally enjoyed a glimpse of Maggie's confidence. She tilted her head to indicate Maggie should follow her.

"Oh, Ally, this is gorgeous," Maggie said as they entered the bedroom.

When Maggie continued through to the bathroom, Ally stayed in the bedroom, giving her space to explore.

Maggie poked her head back out the bathroom doorway. "You weren't kidding. This is definitely a sanctuary."

She'd eliminated the third bedroom, previously next to the master, then split the space. Half the area made up the new master bathroom, and the rest of it, she'd framed into a walk-in closet, both of which had been lacking in the original 1960s floor plan. She knew the risk of making the home a two-bedroom. But she needed only one guest room. And she had space in the backyard for an addition if she decided to add another bedroom.

"I don't know much about renovation, but it seems very well done." Maggie wandered back into the bedroom, tracing her hand over the woodwork on the door casing.

"Thank you." Ally had cleaned up and painted the original moldings. But her attention now was on Maggie's fingertips tripping over the ridges of the wood. Ally, unable to resist her desire to be closer to Maggie, moved farther into the room. "These rooms are finished, but the rest of the house is kind of in limbo while I focus on the furniture business." She rubbed her hand over the same stretch of woodwork, inches below Maggie's.

"That seems fair. You have only so many hours in your day."

Ally flicked her gaze down to Maggie's mouth, where she'd sucked her lower lip in slightly. Was that a nervous gesture? Was she also wondering what their kiss might taste like? Why were they talking about inane things like furniture and home improvement when there was a bed just a few feet away? She searched Maggie's eyes for an answer to at least one of those questions. Maggie's brown eyes were lighter than Ally's. Up close, they reminded her of a warm pecan wood stain.

"I should change my clothes so I can get to work."

"Okay." Ally blinked and held Maggie's gaze a moment longer. Then, reluctantly, she stepped aside.

Chapter Ten

Maggie closed the guest bathroom door behind her and leaned against it, the back of her head thudding lightly against the wood. What the hell was she doing here? She'd just stood in Ally's bedroom ready to forget who she was—and who she was related to—and just kiss her. Luckily, she'd escaped that moment, but somehow she knew it wouldn't be their last.

Thus far, Ally had offered her friendship and an escape from the ever-present fear that had taken up residence in the back of her mind. She didn't want to give that up if she didn't have to. But she wasn't in the habit of fooling herself about reality. This friendship had to be temporary. In a few months, when her court case and Ally's family obligations complicated things, they could go their separate ways with some good memories.

She pressed her hand against the ache in her chest at the thought of cutting Ally loose. But she couldn't see how they would navigate anything more permanent. She didn't even know if Ally was interested in friendship under those terms. Maybe she'd keep this plan to herself. She'd be the best friend she could be to Ally until the criminal trial began. Ally would likely be distracted by her and her mother's concern for her brother while Maggie eased away from her.

She changed into appropriate clothes for getting dirty, then folded her work clothes and stowed them in her backpack. She returned to the living room, but it was empty. She followed the sounds she heard from the kitchen.

Ally had just opcned the refrigerator and looked over her shoulder. "I'd offer you some wine, but I'm not sure I'm up for another marathon phone call after you leave here."

"Very funny."

Ally smiled and held out a bottle of white wine in invitation.

"One small glass. I'm driving later."

Ally grabbed two stemless glasses and poured them each a conservative amount. She handed one to Maggie, then rested her butt against the counter. Her faded jeans looked soft from many washings, and a few small holes had frayed threads around the edges. She tucked in her navy-blue flannel shirt. Did she do that to contain the loose hem while working around power tools? Or did she simply prefer to wear it that way? And why did seeing Ally in work clothes entice Maggie so much? She wanted to pull the shirt free, unbutton it, and find out if it looked as good hanging open to reveal her chest and stomach.

Maggie grappled for something interesting to say that didn't include an inquiry about Ally's fashion choices. But what came out was, "The weather's warming up."

"No kidding. Too much warmer and the garage will get stuffy. I'll have to break out the industrial fan soon."

"I love summer."

"Said the woman who works in an air-conditioned office."

Maggie smiled. "You have a point. I have to be in the heat only when I want to. Summer afternoons in the sun by my friend Inga's pool are heavenly. So, then, what is your favorite season?"

"Fall. I'm a big fan of cool, crisp days and those nights when you need a hoodie or a sweater to ward off the chill."

"Honestly, there's something to love about every season, isn't there?"

"No."

"What about spring? Everything smells new and fresh. Then the flowers start to bloom."

"My allergies act up from the pollen I'm breathing in all day out there." Ally exaggerated a scowl. "And summer in Tennessee is like being in a sauna every day."

"We covered summer already."

"I agree that autumn is glorious. But I challenge you to find something nice to say about winter."

"Christmas."

"That's only December. And winter's not even really here yet then. I'm talking about January and February, when it's just cold and dreary and incredibly unpredictable for construction."

"Snow." Maggie grinned as if she'd just provided the key to enjoying winter.

"We get snow maybe one weekend a year, unless you're counting the random ice and freezing rain. Which I don't, by the way."

"Wow. You really don't enjoy the weather here."

Ally laughed. "I mostly just endure it."

"If you could move anywhere else, where would you go?"

"If I didn't have to work outside, I'd like to try a desert climate."

"Put an air-conditioned shop on the list when you open your own furniture business." Maggie moved to the sink and rinsed out her wineglass. "Is it your family that keeps you here?"

Ally shrugged. "I grew up here. It's what I know."

Maggie glanced at the dining room and archway to the living room beyond. She could easily settle on the sofa and chat with Ally for the rest of the night. But she'd come here to accomplish something, and so far she'd made zero progress. "I should get to work outside."

"Right." Ally started as if she, too, had forgotten everything but their conversation. "And I promised you dinner. I haven't shopped for groceries in a while, so I'll order some takeout. Any preferences?"

"You really don't have to do that. I can get something on my way home later."

"I want to." Ally stepped closer, and Maggie backed up, retreating into the corner by the fridge.

Ally leaned in and Maggie froze, having no further escape. Ally's gaze flickered to Maggie's mouth before coming back up to meet her eyes. The curl of arousal she'd felt in the bathroom earlier echoed within her. She'd been the one to break the spell earlier. But she didn't think she could do it again. What would happen if she didn't? She glanced down. Scant inches separated their bodies. She wanted to move into Ally, feel their chests pressed together, Ally's arms around her.

Ally reached an arm out, and Maggie anticipated the embrace and, hopefully, a kiss. She wanted it, no matter the consequences. At the crinkle of paper, she turned her head to identify the sound. Ally had pulled a flyer from under a magnet on the side of the fridge.

"I was just getting this menu." Ally thrust the folded paper into the space between them.

Maggie's face flamed with embarrassment. "I thought you were about to—"

"I mean, I would—but I wasn't sure if you wanted—"

Maggie grasped Ally's face and pulled her close, burying the rest of her words against her lips. Ally's hesitation lasted only a second before she responded, though seemingly content to let Maggie lead. Maggie caressed Ally's lower lip fleetingly with her tongue, not deepening their kiss. She tasted the crisp, tart flavor of their wine. When she eased back, her head swam, and if Ally's hazy look was an indication, hers did as well.

Ally recovered before Maggie did. She held up the crumpled brochure. "The Chinese place that delivers here has great egg rolls."

"I'm sorry I crushed your menu."

"It was totally worth it."

"In that case…" She drew Ally back to her, seeking another kiss. This time, Ally took over, controlling the pressure and intensity. She slipped her fingers into Maggie's hair, and the gentle rake of her blunt fingernails made Maggie shiver with anticipation. Seduced, she lost herself in the taste and texture of Ally's mouth. The fever of the kiss tapered off as they drew apart again. Ally ended the kiss with a tender touch of her lips.

"Wow."

"Yeah." Ally grinned. "I knew you'd be good at that. But I had no idea."

"You did?"

"Sure. You have a vibe like you know what you're doing around women."

Maggie chuckled. "Well, once upon a time anyway." Before her confidence about everything had been shaken.

Concern shaded Ally's expression. "Are you okay?"

Maggie nodded. She wasn't, in some ways. But with the high from their kiss still humming through her, she was so much more than okay in others.

"Do we need to talk about the kissing?"

"Can we not?"

"That depends. Are you going to leave?" Ally bracketed Maggie's hips loosely with her hands, not restraining her, but letting her know what she wanted Maggie's answer to be.

Maggie glanced out the window at the backyard. "No. But I'd like to go do some work in the dirt. Clear my mind."

Ally nodded agreeably, but a trace of disappointment colored her expression. "Sure. I'll call in the dinner order."

"Thank you." Maggie stroked Ally's jaw, then eased out of Ally's arms before she could change her mind.

❖

Ally tried not to be offended that Maggie needed to clear her mind of their first kiss. She felt just the opposite. She wanted to hold on to it, examine it, and figure out why it felt different than any other one.

She placed the dinner order, then decided to spend the forty-five minutes until the food arrived working on her latest project.

In the garage, she raised the overhead door and propped the door leading to the yard open in order to create a cross breeze. But she had to force herself to stay away from that back door. She didn't want Maggie to catch her staring like some creepy stalker.

While Maggie apparently was out there wiping her memory, Ally couldn't think of anything but that kiss. She'd been aware of the change in the air between them, but she'd still been caught off guard when Maggie kissed her. Blissfully—amazingly—taken by surprise, she'd kept her head enough to let Maggie stay in control.

Not trusting herself to use the lathe in her distracted state, she began choosing the boards she would use for the top of the coffee table. She laid them out on a large worktable in the center of the garage, checking them for warping. She swapped a couple, arranging them for the most interesting wood-grain pattern. She hadn't completely decided if she would paint or stain this piece, so she proceeded as if the grain would be visible.

Their food arrived, and she met the delivery guy in the driveway. She called out the back door for Maggie, then began setting out the various cartons, two plates, and some silverware on the kitchen counter. By the time she'd finished, Maggie had come inside and washed her hands.

"I wasn't sure if you enjoyed the chopsticks, but I don't have the patience for them, so we have forks, too. Would you like to eat out on the patio?"

"Sure."

Ally grabbed two bottles of water and took them out to the small, cracked concrete patio. She'd outfitted it with a basic table and four chairs from Target when she moved in. Someday, she planned to bust up the current patio, then pour a larger stamped-concrete pad with a wooden pergola. She wanted to build chaise lounges, a table and chairs, and some benches around a stone fire pit.

She returned to the kitchen for a lighter and citronella candle to ward off any mosquitos. Then they carried their plates outside to the table and settled in. Ally worried the conversation would be awkward after their kiss, but they talked easily, avoiding any serious topics. Maggie shared stories from her childhood, so different from Ally's. And Ally described her ideas for the outdoor furniture she wanted to build.

"I'm amazed you can have all of that in your head. I don't have any creative inspiration in me." When Maggie deftly picked up a piece of chicken, Ally tried not to watch her fingers manipulate the chopsticks. And she certainly didn't notice the way Maggie's tongue darted out to curl and grab rice off the implements.

"Like I said, I don't get out here much, especially when I was working full-time and building furniture. But I have visions of someday having enough free time to host outdoor gatherings with my friends and their two kids."

Maggie rested her elbow on the table and propped her chin on her hand. "Tell me about them."

Ally grinned and launched into an explanation about how she'd briefly dated Kathi years ago.

"This was before the ex who kept your house?"

"Yes. I'm so glad we stayed friends after we split. It's a much better dynamic for us. And Dani is amazing for her."

"You said they have children?"

"Yeah. Two awesome little ones. Grayson is five and June is four. Grayson comes across as soft-spoken sometimes, but once he's comfortable in a situation, the kid is nonstop talk. And he gets so excited about things that interest him. I can't wait to see what he develops a passion for as he gets older. And June is a little girlie-girl. She's all about pretty things. And she has the biggest heart." She talked for several more minutes about the kids before she realized Maggie was giving her a look of amusement. "Sorry. I forget people don't love to hear about other people's kids."

Maggie covered Ally's hand where it rested on the table. "It's great how much you love them. Kids can never have too many strong role models and people who care about them."

"They're great. But they can also be exhausting. I'm perfectly happy being a fun godmother, then sending them home to the moms." Ally chuckled. "What about you? Did you ever think about having kids?"

"Maybe. When I was younger. But now that I'm in my forties…"

"Barely."

"Nonetheless. I start doing math and deciding between retiring while I can enjoy it or helping my kid through college."

Ally shrugged. "Your kid could put him or herself through college."

"True. Who knows if my kid would even pursue higher education?"

"Right. Maybe he would be a star athlete or one of our homegrown Nashville singer/songwriters and buy you a house to retire in."

"Maybe. But I think my decision's been made."

"I'm sure you'll meet Grayson and June eventually. I suppose I could share their attention."

A shadow crossed Maggie's expression, but she stood, picked up her plate, and turned away before Ally could analyze it. "That's very generous of you. Can I get you anything else from the kitchen?"

"Maggie." Ally stood, but Maggie had already fled inside.

Ally stared at the door. Should she go in and push Maggie to talk? She didn't want to end their night with things unsaid and their status in limbo. But she didn't want to hear that Maggie didn't want to be with her either. And that could happen. Maybe she'd kissed her only because she was caught up in the moment.

When she entered the kitchen, Maggie stood at the sink with a glass of water in her hand. But she stared out the window to the backyard where Ally had just been. Ally leaned against the counter on the other side of the kitchen and shoved her hands into her pockets, because she really wanted to take Maggie in her arms.

"What are we doing?" Maggie asked.

"Maggie, I—"

"I mean, really? I admit, I'm wildly attracted to you. And you've been so amazing, letting me come over here and garden—it's really taken my mind off everything. And kissing you was—simply fireworks. But what's the end game here? Do we pretend that I'm going to meet your friends and their kids and be a part of your life? And what about your family?" She stuttered slightly over the word *family.*

"You're attracted to me?"

Maggie stared at her. "That's what you took from that?"

"That and all the fireworks." Ally grinned.

"I'm being serious."

"So am I." She pushed off the counter and crossed to Maggie, then took both of her hands in hers. "I don't know what this is either. Or how it could ever work. But man, that kiss was the stuff of legends—for me, at least."

"We aren't teenagers anymore, Ally. Mad chemistry is not enough to justify—"

"You're right. We aren't kids. Which means we should be mature enough to figure this out." Ally looked down at their joined hands between them. "Just holding your hand makes my heart rate go crazy."

Maggie eased her hands free, but Ally imagined she did so reluctantly. "There's nothing to figure out. The most we can hope for here is a fling that has to run its course before the trial begins."

Ally tried to imagine a scenario where they were still involved when that date came. She wanted to be there in the courtroom, holding Maggie's hand—it was the first image that came to her mind. But that thought brought a flood of guilt. Shirley expected Ally to support Carey. How would she do that and still be by Maggie's side?

"Is that what you want?" Maggie asked, meeting Ally's eyes.

It wasn't. Not at all. She'd already known she cared about Maggie before kissing her. And now, recalling the feel of Maggie's body against her had only deepened her feelings. It was too early—way too soon to say she was falling for her. And the fear in Maggie's expression cued her in that she might not be ready to hear that yet either.

"Hey, what's wrong with a little distraction as long as we both know the rules?" Ally forced a casual tone that sounded stiff even to herself.

Maggie looked like she might challenge her about the truth of her statement. The fleeting bravado in her expression gave way to the same uncertainty that churned in Ally's gut.

"Distraction?"

"Yeah. If you want a label, that seems the simplest, doesn't it? I mean, we can be friends and spend some time together."

"I hate to pull the age card again, but I'm in my forties—a little old for flings."

"And I'm thirty-nine, so normally I'd agree. I want another long-term relationship someday. But we have a unique set of circumstances here. Spending time with you—I've been the most relaxed and happy that I've been in quite some time. I don't know how you're okay hanging out with me after my own brother robbed you. But I hope you know that if I can ease some of that stress for you in any way, I will."

Maggie's eyes filled with tears, and a quiet, strangled sob escaped.

"Maggie, what's wrong?" Ally grabbed for one of her hands, devastated that whatever she'd said had caused Maggie to cry.

Maggie rolled her eyes up and pulled in a breath, clearly trying to maintain control. The motion pushed several tears over her lower lid, to trail down her cheeks. Ally cupped her face and wiped them away with her thumbs.

"You believe me—about the robbery?"

"Oh, honey, yes, I do." Was that the first time she'd said it aloud? Certainly it was the first time she'd acknowledged it to Maggie. But to be fair, she often avoided talking about it so she wouldn't stress Maggie more.

Maggie stepped close and wrapped her arms around Ally's waist. As they embraced, her lips brushed Ally's ear, and she whispered against it, "Thank you."

Ally held her, soaking in the closeness, breathing in Maggie's light floral perfume, ironically mixed with the earthy scent of the dirt she'd been digging in outside. She rubbed her hands over Maggie's back, hoping to soothe her.

As Maggie regained control, she snuggled closer to Ally, aligning their hips more fully. Her arms tightened, and the touch of her lips against Ally's neck felt deliberate and very intimate. Ally's skin tingled, and her nipples had hardened where they pressed against Maggie's breasts. She slid her hand up Maggie's back to cup her neck. Maggie rolled her head slightly in response to Ally's fingertips caressing her.

Desire swamped Ally, and she wanted so much to give in to it. She would, easily, surrender to the need to touch Maggie, but first she needed to know that Maggie was feeling the same.

"Maggie?"

"Yes." Had Ally's voice sounded as breathless as Maggie's?

"Unless you're intending to start that fling right now, I'm going to need some space."

Maggie cleared her throat and loosened her embrace. "I'm sorry."

"No. Don't be." Ally would probably pay for her chivalry later when she lay in bed imagining Maggie there with her.

"I should pick up my tools from outside before I go." Maggie dropped her arms to her side.

"Will you be coming back?"

Maggie's small smile and nod unfurled the knot of tension in Ally's chest.

"Okay. Let me know if you need help with the tools."

While Maggie cleaned up outside, Ally stayed in the kitchen gathering her composure. Maggie had admitted to the physical attraction between them. And Ally agreed, but she hadn't added how the gentle timbre of Maggie's voice when they talked on the phone made her ache to be near her. She also didn't mention how she warmed inside when she watched Maggie working in her yard. All of that she'd have to keep buried while they enjoyed whatever they could have.

Chapter Eleven

Maggie logged her records request as completed and sat back in her chair, rolling her shoulders to lessen the tension from staring at her computer screen for the past two hours. Sometimes her posture seemed to worsen in direct correlation to how involved the project she worked on was.

According to the clock on her computer, she had an hour left in her shift. Not quite enough time to complete another request. In the past, she'd have started the next one, then stayed late to finish it.

If she left work now, she could get to Ally's a little early tonight. She hadn't seen her in the two days since their first kiss. They'd texted each day, but Maggie kept things light and brief from her end, citing a heavy load at work. Ally had reached out that morning to ask if she should water the garden beds, since it hadn't rained lately. She'd added that she wasn't busy if Maggie wanted to come over to tend them and stay for dinner.

Maggie didn't have to think about whether she wanted to accept the invitation. She'd been thinking about Ally since leaving her house two nights before. She hadn't met anyone in years who got to her like Ally. Yet any sane person examining their situation would probably say she should avoid Ally. So she'd left Ally's with the agreement that they would—what? Get to know each other, pretend they didn't grow to care about one another, then never see each other again? What could go wrong?

She locked her computer and headed down the hallway. After wasting a few minutes using the restroom, she filled her travel tumbler from the water cooler. Then, only forty-five minutes before quitting time, she angled into the doorway of Inga's office.

"Hey, Boss." She knocked on the inside of the open door.

"What's up?" Inga glanced up, then turned back to her computer screen.

"I'm at a stopping point. Would it be okay if I take off a little early today?"

Now she had Inga's full attention. "Of course it's okay. Is something wrong?"

She shook her head. "Just want to get ahead of traffic for a change."

"Are you sure? Because I wasn't going to say anything, but you've been different lately."

"Different how?"

Inga picked up a pen and fiddled with it, something she did when she was collecting her thoughts before she spoke. "You've seemed more relaxed. Not back to your old self, but—close."

My old self. She knew Inga came from a good place, but she didn't know how anyone could think she'd ever find that version of herself again. In fairness, she'd pulled back from her friendship with Inga after the robbery. She couldn't judge Inga's assumptions about her when, rather than confide what she was going through, she'd turned to Ally, a stranger, for comfort.

"And now here you are, asking to leave early. I was beginning to think no one else knew how to turn off the lights around here." Inga smiled. "Yes. Get out of here. Have a good night."

Inga's understanding made her want to confide in her. She considered pulling the door closed and dropping into the chair on the other side of Inga's desk. But she'd have to go back to square one, fill in all the details she'd omitted when dealing with Inga. The very idea exhausted her.

So, to assuage some of her guilt about cutting Inga out, she cleared her throat to regain Inga's attention. "I have been doing better, thank you. I know I haven't leaned on you, but knowing you're a good friend, available if I need you, really does help."

Inga nodded, then went back to her work. Her tense posture indicated she might want to say more, but she kept whatever it was contained.

Maggie gathered her things from her desk, catching several surprised looks as she shrugged on her coat and headed for the door. She passed through the building lobby with a wave to the security guard.

As she walked across the street to the lot she'd been parking in since the robbery, she recalled Inga's words about her seeming to be doing better. Was she? Certainly, when she was with Ally she felt better, stronger even. And some of the changes in herself she imagined would be permanent. What was the harm in double-checking her locks every night? But this parking situation should change. Her office had a contract for reduced rates with the garage where she was robbed. She could reclaim some power by parking there again. She'd always known, working downtown, that she should be cautious. But crime had been such an abstract idea until it had hit her directly. Tomorrow, she would park in that garage again.

❖

"You feel amazing." Maggie's words vibrated against Ally's neck as she dropped a path of kisses down to the base of her throat. "Have I mentioned how much I like you in these V-neck shirts and how sexy your collarbones are?"

"You haven't. But feel free to say it as often as you want." Maggie's lips against said collarbone pulled a thread of pleasure through Ally.

Ally stroked her hands into Maggie's hair and tilted her head to meet her mouth. Maggie's lips were soft and responsive, opening to her as she swept her tongue against them. Kissing Maggie was her new favorite pastime. Just when she was thinking she could do this all day, she felt Maggie toying with the band at the top of her athletic shorts.

"If I knew seeing me in my lounge-around-the-house clothes would get you this worked up, I'd have done it weeks ago." She'd been enjoying a lazy day catching up on television when Maggie texted to say she was off work and wanted to stop by. As soon as she answered the door, Maggie stepped into her with a searing kiss that left her knees wobbly. Aggressive-Maggie was incredibly hot. They hadn't made it past the sofa.

"I like you casual, although I'm certain I'd like you all dressed up, too. Maybe even wearing nothing at all. In fact, I think we should explore that idea." Maggie balled the hem of Ally's T-shirt in her fist and shoved it up.

Maggie's hand moving across her stomach threatened to make her embarrass herself. She wanted to slow down, to map Maggie's body under her hands, and to explore each other together, but maybe next time. Right now, she just needed Maggie's skin against her. When Maggie slipped her fingers inside the waistband of Ally's shorts, Ally's hips bucked in response. Damn, she could completely lose it, and Maggie had touched only her stomach.

She grabbed Maggie's wrist, pulling it away so she could regain some self-control.

"Stop." Maggie's softly spoken plea registered enough that Ally eased her grip but didn't release her. "Please, stop." This time panic edged Maggie's voice, and she panted for breath.

"Did I hurt you?" Ally let go of her wrist and searched her face for some explanation for Maggie's distress.

When she reached for her, intent on comforting her, Maggie shrank back against the sofa, casting her eyes around the room as if searching for an escape. Ally slowly unfolded herself from the sofa, careful not to startle Maggie further. Maggie's stress level visibly deescalated as Ally put some distance between them.

Her heart ached with the realization that her nearness made whatever was going on worse for Maggie. A part of her needed to get away from the vulnerability, both Maggie's and her own. She wasn't sure if escaping to the backyard would be far enough, or if she needed to grab her car keys on the way out. Opting for the yard, she strode away, holding her breath to dam her tears until she'd yanked open the door and passed through it. When she finally did exhale, her breath trembled past her lips.

She stopped in the middle of the yard, her back to the house, and pressed the heels of her hands against her closed eyes. Everything in her screamed for her to go back inside and take Maggie in her arms, yet that was the last thing Maggie wanted.

❖

Maggie stared out the kitchen window at Ally's slumped shoulders, and her chest ached. She was out there beating herself up, and Maggie wasn't sure if she even knew why. Why did this situation between them just keep getting more complicated? And why couldn't she walk away when she was certain that would be the simplest thing for both of them?

She went into the yard, seeing the change in Ally's posture as her shoes sounded on the concrete patio. Her heart wanted her to embrace Ally, to touch and comfort her, but her fear kept her several feet away.

"I'm sorry," she said quietly into the tense space between them.

Ally turned around, unable to adequately hide her devastation. "Do you want to talk about it?"

Maggie shook her head.

"Why not?"

Maggie sucked in a deep breath. How did you tell the woman you were making out with that her moves made you think about her brother? Harsh.

Ally surged forward a couple of steps, clearly frustrated. When Maggie flinched at the sudden motion, Ally backed farther into the yard. "I gave you space when you asked for it after our kiss the other day. But this feels different. You were afraid of me just now." Ally's concerned expression broke Maggie's heart.

"I'm not—afraid of you. But when you grabbed my wrist—I panicked."

Comprehension spilled across Ally's face so viscerally that Maggie could feel Ally's nausea. Ally eased close to the patio, sank into a chair, and covered her face. She breathed a huge sigh. "Oh, my God, Maggie. I'm so sorry."

Maggie knelt in front of her and pulled her hands away from her face. She held them, resting both of their hands on Ally's knees.

"It wasn't you I was reacting to." She caressed the back of Ally's hands with her thumbs, trying to underscore the physical connection between them. "I've barely been touched by anyone since that day, and clearly I still have some things to deal with surrounding that trauma."

"I didn't even think about how you would feel—"

"And you shouldn't have to."

"But I do. If you're having trouble separating me and my touch from—oh, my God, he didn't try to—"

"No. No. It's not like that." Maggie rushed to calm the terror racing across Ally's expression. She drew a breath, needing to find a way to explain so Ally could understand how she'd felt. She owed Ally that. "You're a physical person. You have been since we met, now that I think about it. And I like that about you." She ran her finger along Ally's jaw and down her neck. Ally sat completely still, as if terrified to move. "And I like touching you. But I think, for now, I need to feel a little more in control."

Ally nodded slowly, holding her gaze. "I understand. You need for me to be careful about touches that feel restraining to you."

"That sums it up." She laced her fingers into Ally's, letting her know that hand-holding was okay.

"I can do that. You just let me know if anything makes you uncomfortable." Ally winked. "And I don't mind you telling me what feels good, too."

"Thank you. How about for tonight, we go back inside and find a movie to snuggle in front of?"

"That sounds perfect." Ally took Maggie's outstretched hand and followed her inside.

❖

Ally released the trigger on her circular saw as the end of the two-by-four clattered to the floor. She set aside the piece she'd cut to size and reached for another one just as a car horn sounded. She glanced at the clock over her workbench—still a little too early for Maggie. She set the saw down and brushed sawdust off the front of her pants.

"Al, you in there?" Carey's voice carried as he came down the driveway.

She went to the open overhead door just as he reached it. He'd parked Shirley's car at the curb. He'd cleaned up his appearance since she last saw him. His hair had been cut, and he'd shaped his facial hair into a goatee. His jeans and black T-shirt were clean and in good condition.

"Carey, what are you doing here?"

"I can't visit my big sister? That's what family does. They visit each other. Not that we've seen you around lately."

"Yeah, sorry. I've been busy."

"Doing what? I heard you weren't working anymore. That must be nice."

She didn't have to ask where he'd heard that—his words had Shirley written all over them. If Ally didn't have an employer, then she didn't have a job. She didn't understand Ally's ambition for something more than a paycheck, or that she'd tired of furthering someone else's dream.

"I'm building a business here."

"So you're setting your own hours. Yet you can't take time to come by Ma's? I've been home two weeks."

"I figured you had your own stuff going on. Ma said you're going to meetings."

"Every day."

"That's good." She glanced back at the clock in the garage. Maggie would be getting off work soon. She couldn't let her come here if Carey was still here. As if thinking about Maggie had cued him in some way, he angled to look out the open back door into the yard.

"What's going on out there? Are you building something?"

"That's—a garden."

"Gardening?" He laughed. "Since when do you have a green thumb?"

He headed for the backyard, and she followed slowly, using the time to text Maggie that something had come up and she shouldn't come over tonight. She added that she would water the plants. Maggie texted back three question marks, and she responded that she'd explain later.

Carey bent and feathered his hand through the leaves of the tomato plants. "Ma didn't say anything about your garden."

"She—uh, she doesn't really know."

"So it's a secret garden?" He grinned, and she saw a flash of the funny, sweet kid he once was.

She actually laughed with him. "Yeah, something like that."

She shook her head. She didn't believe Carey was elementally a bad guy, but he'd fallen into this spiral that led him to a horrible act. Maybe she hadn't done enough when she first noticed his dependence on pain pills. By the time she truly believed he had a problem, he'd already started stealing from her. In fact, right now, she was glad he was in the yard and not inside her house, where she'd have to keep a close eye on him. That was a terrible way to think about your own brother. But that's where they'd gotten to. And she wasn't sure their relationship could ever recover.

He crossed to the patio and sat in one of the chairs, then glanced at the opposite chair as if he expected her to sit with him. She stayed standing in the yard, just to spite him. She knew she was acting childish and stupid, but she didn't care.

"So, tell me about the new girlfriend." Something in her expression must have given away her surprise. He laughed. "Thanks for confirming my guess. You haven't been by the house, so I had to come see who you were spending your time with."

"I told you what I've been doing."

"Too late, big sis. You already gave it away."

"Okay. I have kind of been seeing someone."

He grinned. "I figured. I was hoping by surprising you, I might catch her here."

"Funny." He'd come way too close for her comfort. She couldn't even wrap her mind around what a disaster that would have been. Was this what her life would be like now? A coordinated dance to keep her girlfriend apart from her family. Wait—girlfriend?

"I get why you haven't brought her around Ma. But why haven't I met her yet? Are you that ashamed of me now?" He looked genuinely hurt that his addiction might have kept her from introducing him to Maggie.

"No. It's complicated."

"How so? Is it a friends-with-benefits thing?"

"No. Come on, Carey. You know I don't do that." Not exactly. Though she didn't know how she could call what she had with Maggie much more. They weren't all going to gather around a Thanksgiving table any time soon.

"How the hell do I know what you do anymore? You've kept her a secret for some reason. In fact, you don't talk to me about anything."

"You've had your own shit going on."

"That's a cop-out."

"Okay. Yeah, it is." They'd been close once. And she'd been so busy being mad at him she hadn't realized how much she missed that bond. "We've had some tension lately. And I just haven't wanted to talk."

He nodded. "I gotta own my part in that. I've been talking to my shrink about my relationships—with you and with Ma. I'm trying to do better, Al. That's why I'm here. I don't want to let us grow apart like we have with the rest of our family."

His father lived forty minutes away, but, though Carey had called him when he got out of jail, he hadn't visited. She didn't know where her own father was. And Shirley had never let them spend time with either of their fathers' families.

"I'm having a tough time, and I'm trying like hell to stay sober. I could use a little family support."

This was the conversation she'd been avoiding since he came home. Over the past two years she'd tried to help him, foolishly believing she could still be the hero her younger brother needed. But her own willpower wasn't enough to keep him clean. She'd been covering for him at work, but she got busted when their boss visited a job site and had nearly lost her job.

Remembering the stress of trying to keep his life together when he didn't seem to care enough to do it himself snapped something inside her. She let loose with everything she'd been wanting to say.

"Where's the line, Carey? Where does unconditional love stretch too far? When you're strung out and can't meet your obligations, I'm supposed to blindly support you? You steal money from Ma and me, and get coddled and forgiven. Now you've done something that will likely land you in prison, and you want fucking support?"

"Yes. You're my sister. I'm an addict and I'm getting help."

"This wasn't stealing money out of Ma's sock drawer. You put a gun in a woman's face, and she feared for her life. She still has nightmares. And you're still making excuses for your behavior. You are my brother. And a part of me will always love you. But you don't get my support until you can admit what you've done and accept the consequences." Tension pulled her body tight, but her voice grew softer. She wasn't a yeller when she was mad. In fact, the quieter she got, the angrier she was.

"So you need me to plead guilty, go to prison, and ruin my life in order for you to forgive me?" He surged to his feet, his hands balled into fists at his side.

She shook her head. He didn't get it. "You lost your job. Until recently, you couldn't go a day without the pills you were buying on the street. You've lost the trust of those closest to you." She gave him a hard look and steeled herself to walk away from him. "You ruined your life a long time ago. I just need you to want to fix it."

With the perfect parting shot, she strode away, ready to leave him standing alone in her yard.

"What do you think I'm trying to do? I'm working on it. I've been talking to Reuben about getting my job back."

She stopped. "He's not seriously considering it."

"He's not thrilled, but he's short-handed since you left, so I think I can convince him to give me a shot, on a trial basis."

"I hope that works out for you." As exit lines go, it wasn't very strong. But she left him there just the same.

Once inside, she continued to her bedroom, so she wouldn't be tempted to see how long he stayed out there. She flopped down onto her bed, replaying their conversation. God, she'd talked about Maggie—referenced her nightmares. Carey hadn't caught on that she spoke about his victim more personally than she should. How would she have explained that? Thinking about Maggie made her want to talk to her. She pulled out her phone, then just held it limply in her hand. She needed to reach out to Maggie to explain why she blew her off. But not yet. She'd have to find some distance from her confrontation with Carey before she could engage with Maggie.

Chapter Twelve

I'll be right with you, ma'am," one of the two employees yelled across the crowded gun store in Maggie's direction.

Between checking in the several people waiting in line for the range and assisting the other customers in the store, they appeared to have their hands full. She'd hoped to take a private lesson. But unless another employee was in the back of the store, she might have to come back later. Perhaps she should have scheduled something ahead of time so they could have staffed accordingly.

She'd just turned toward the door when she almost ran into someone. She pulled up short, just as arms came up on either side of her. She jerked away from them at the same time that she mumbled an apology.

"Maggie? Hey, I thought that was you." Charlie Bell stood in front of her, dressed casually in a T-shirt and jeans.

"Detective Bell, hello."

"Please, call me Charlie." Charlie glanced over her shoulder at the range check-in counter. "I'm going to the range for a bit. You?"

"Oh, I figured you all would have someplace to go—just for police or something."

"The academy does have a range, but it's on the other side of town. This place is closer to my house. If I just want a little practice, I run down here."

"I see."

"Are you headed down?"

"Um, no—I was just—leaving, I think." She glanced again at the people checking in with the man behind the counter. Both of the employees still looked very busy.

"Are you thinking about buying a gun?"

Maggie nodded. "I'm considering it."

"Ever handled one before?"

She shook her head. "Not really. I was here once before, and a woman showed me a couple of things, but I've never fired one."

"Okay. Well, I don't recommend having a gun in the house if you're not comfortable with it."

"They give private lessons here. But they seem quite busy today."

"Do you want to go down with me? I can show you a few things."

"I don't want to keep you from your practice."

Charlie waved a hand dismissively. "I was bored. And shooting is good stress relief."

"Still—"

"Come on. I can shoot by myself any time." She held her arms out at her sides and swept her hands toward her body. "Who better to give you some pointers?"

"If you're sure you don't mind."

"Great. Let's go. I assume you didn't bring any safety equipment."

"That's right."

Maggie stood nearby while Charlie checked them in at the range counter. She returned with two paper targets and a pair of safety glasses and ear protection for Maggie.

Maggie followed Charlie down a set of stairs. Though they descended to a basement level, the space was brightly lit, clean, and painted a pleasant light gray. To the right, an open archway led to a lounge area with two sofas, a coffee table, and a television mounted on the wall. Charlie moved through to an even smaller space, with a counter-height table flush against one wall. Charlie set her backpack on the table.

"Let's cover a couple of things before we go in. It's harder to talk once we have ear protection on." Charlie took a nylon pouch out of her backpack. "I don't have anything smaller than a 9mm with me, because that's what we carry on duty. We'll use this one. It's my personal backup weapon, not paid for by the city, so you can shoot it."

"I spoke with one of the employees on a previous visit. And it seems like I should decide if I just want something in the house, or if I want to carry it." She didn't even feel comfortable saying the word *gun* yet. Maybe she wasn't ready for this.

"Sure. Those are things to consider when purchasing. Otherwise, you may buy something too large to comfortably carry on a daily basis." Charlie unzipped the nylon pouch and removed a gun. "But before you decide all that, you could just try firing one to see how you feel about that."

"Okay." Right now, she felt scared. What would it be like to pull the trigger? And this was just target practice. The idea of using a gun, even for self-defense, frightened her.

"We'll start with three really important rules. Always assume a gun is loaded until you've checked it for yourself, no matter who hands it to you. And, second, when handling one, always point it in a safe direction."

Charlie demonstrated how to maneuver the gun while being mindful of the direction the barrel was pointing. And if the gun was to be fired at any given time, she should be aware of what the path of the bullet could potentially be.

"Third, keep your finger off the trigger until you're ready to shoot. You put it here, along the trigger guard. Keep it close enough to move to the trigger quickly when you need to, but not on it, so you can't accidentally pull it."

"Back to the first one. How do I check to see if it's loaded?"

Charlie showed her how to push the button to drop out the magazine, the part that held the bullets. Then she locked back the slide and told her to check in the chamber for a round. For the next ten minutes, Charlie talked about the mechanics of the gun while letting Maggie handle the pistol. This one—Charlie called it a Sig—was smaller than some she'd seen, but it still was heavier than she'd have thought.

Once Maggie felt somewhat comfortable, they donned safety glasses and ear protection, which just looked like very large headphones to Maggie. Charlie handed her the paper targets, then grabbed her backpack. She led Maggie through one door into a tiny room between two doors—for sound dampening and ventilation reasons, Charlie explained. After the first door closed behind them, Charlie pushed through the second one.

They passed several occupied lanes, and Maggie started as, even with the earmuffs, she found the sound of gunshots louder than she expected. A large man stood with his back to them, arms extending, firing what had to be the biggest handgun she'd ever seen. At the end of his lane, a paper with a person-shaped silhouette fluttered with every round that impacted it.

Panic crept in, making her heart race and her stomach twist painfully. Maybe she couldn't do this. She numbly followed Charlie to an empty lane, searching for an opening should she want to back out.

Charlie picked up one of the paper targets and began securing it to a frame on a pulley down the middle of the lane, so it could be positioned as close or far as the shooter liked. Maggie stared at the image on the target, the shape of a man standing partially behind a woman. One of his arms was wrapped around the woman, restraining her, and in the other hand he held a gun. Targeting circles painted the bodies and head areas of both figures, so they bore only a faint resemblance to actual people. But for just a moment, Maggie saw herself in the woman's place and Carey Rowe as the perpetrator. Her breathing quickened, and her chest tightened. The air in the room felt heavy, and the gunshots around her made it hard to focus on calming down.

Charlie glanced over her shoulder and froze, then glanced back at the target. She ripped the paper down and folded it in half. "Maggie, I'm sorry."

Maggie shook her head, trying to chase away the edges of the parking garage and the snarl of Carey Rowe's voice.

"Hey, we can go back outside, if you want to."

"No." She needed to defeat this fear. She was safe here, and she shouldn't run from the memories just because they were difficult. "Give me a second."

Charlie held up another target. "How about zombies?"

Maggie laughed at the cartoon zombie that filled the page. "Sure."

Charlie secured the target, then pushed a switch on the wall that sent it zinging away from them until she stopped it halfway down the lane. She set out the Sig and a box of bullets and showed Maggie how to load the gun, reminding her to always keep it pointed down range.

"Okay?" Charlie paused with the weapon in her hand, sighted on the target, seeking Maggie's permission before firing.

Maggie moved behind Charlie, then nodded, and Charlie gave an answering bob of her head. She returned her attention to the target, talking while she did about how to use the sights on top of the gun to aim. Though she didn't move, something in her posture changed, an alertness, just seconds before she fired two quick shots. Maggie jumped, even though she'd said she was ready. The spent shells that ejected had landed near Maggie's feet, and two holes ripped through the center zombie's chest. Charlie laid the gun on the counter in front of her.

"You good?"

"I am. You're a good shot."

"I've had a lot of practice. Do you want to try it?"

She did. She'd expected fear and felt a trace of that, but she experienced a jolt of anticipation as well.

Charlie moved to the side, letting Maggie occupy the center of the small space. "Pick it up. Finger off the trigger."

Maggie did, carefully. Was the gun that much heavier loaded than it had felt empty? Or did she imagine the added weight, knowing the bullets were there? She grasped the pistol with both hands, like Charlie had shown her, and aimed at the target.

"Firm grip, but don't choke it." Charlie was beside her, with one hand on the center of her back and the other on her left arm. She guided Maggie's down a little, which reminded her to look at the sights on the top of the gun instead of haphazardly aiming at the target. "Squeeze the trigger evenly. Don't jerk it."

Her heart pounded so loudly, Charlie could probably hear it. Her arms trembled, partly from nerves and partly from adrenaline. She stared at the pistol she held for what felt like a very long time. *Come on. Squeeze, don't jerk.* The gun bucked in her hand with a flash of fire and a wisp of smoke at the end of the barrel. She set it down and fought the urge to jerk off her glasses and earmuffs. Charlie had already warned her that the noise and pressure from shots in a neighboring lane would hurt her ears without protection.

"You okay?" Charlie asked.

She nodded. "Did I at least hit the target?"

Charlie held down the switch until the target swept up to them. She fingered a hole that touched the edge of the zombie's left shoulder. "You grazed him. Not enough to stop a zombie, I'm afraid. Do you want to try some more?"

"I think I have to. I can't leave here knowing I'm useless in an apocalypse."

Maggie exited the range door and pulled off her earmuffs and glasses. She followed Charlie upstairs to the counter, where she handed over her safety equipment. At Charlie's direction, she went into the ladies' restroom and washed her hands. When Charlie had showed her how to reload, gunpowder had transferred from the magazine to the pads of her fingers. Shooting was dirty business.

In the parking lot, Charlie stowed her backpack in the trunk of her car, then nodded toward the Mexican restaurant across the street. "Want to grab some dinner?"

Maggie glanced at her phone, and seeing no missed calls or texts, she accepted. She hadn't heard from Ally since her text the previous night telling her not to come over. She'd spent her Saturday morning cleaning her apartment and pretending she wasn't waiting for at least a text from Ally. Then, seeing the card from the woman at the gun shop on her fridge, she'd decided to see about getting a lesson. She'd been lucky to run into Charlie and now expected to enjoy a nice dinner with her.

Leaving their cars in the parking lot of the gun shop, they crossed the street. The restaurant wasn't busy, so they were seated quickly and soon had a basket of chips and a bowl of salsa on the table between them.

"Thank you for the tutoring session," Maggie said.

"Not a problem. I enjoyed it. How did you feel about shooting?"

"Um—I have mixed feelings. It was intimidating and quite scary. But empowering, too."

"I can understand that."

The waiter placed two glasses of water in front of them and took their orders. After he'd left, Charlie rested her forearms on the table and leaned in.

"Gun ownership isn't for everyone, Maggie. I know officers who recommend it to all victims they come in contact with. I don't make a blanket statement. You need to consider a lot of things."

"Such as?"

"Your safety and that of any family members in the home. You don't have kids, so that simplifies that point. You should think about your comfort level handling a gun. You could definitely find other ways to make yourself safer and increase your awareness of your surroundings. It's a very personal choice. And while I agree with the laws that make it so, just because someone *can* own a gun doesn't mean they should."

"I have some thinking to do first, I guess," Maggie said. "Once the trial's over, I should have a better handle on how to move forward. Will you have to testify?"

"Probably not. If you remember, I was at the scene, but only because I caught the call-out. I had a full case load, so after your initial interview, I handed the investigative part off. Detective Graves will be in court. And the officers that arrested the defendant."

Their food arrived, and for a few minutes they ate silently. Maggie put a tiny dent in the huge taco salad. Instead of a bowl shape, the salad had come in a large fried shell shaped more like a canoe and nearly the size of a small boat.

Charlie set her fork down and swiped her napkin across her mouth. "Hey, I'm sorry again about that target. I like to practice with that hostage one because it gives me the added challenge of where not to shoot. I didn't even think about it triggering—"

"It's fine, really. I was already struggling a little before seeing the target. I need to work through this stuff."

"Are you talking to anyone?"

"Like a professional?"

Charlie nodded.

"No. I'm not against it as a concept. But I've tried therapy for other things before, and I didn't find it super helpful. I don't think it's the answer for everyone." Maggie used the expression Charlie had about guns, and Charlie grinned in response. "I'm not stuffing my feelings. In time, I'll work through everything. I'm still figuring out what makes me feel safe."

"Are you talking to any of your friends?"

"Um, my closest friend, Inga, not so much." She thought about Ally and wondered how to explain that relationship. "But I have been sharing with someone."

"That's good."

"You might not think so when you find out who it is."

Charlie raised her brows and waited.

"Do you remember the woman from the courthouse lobby?"

Charlie nodded.

"She's Carey Rowe's sister." When Charlie's expectant look didn't change, Maggie went on to explain how they'd met before knowing who each other was. She didn't go into detail about their current situation, simply saying that they'd been talking and hanging out.

"And you trust her enough to discuss the case with her? You know that legally, nothing stops her from telling her brother or his lawyer anything you say."

"I do trust her. But spending time with her isn't about the case. If we talk about it, it's more about feelings. Besides, she has as much to lose as I do—at least her brother does. I could tell the DA anything she tells me."

"True." Charlie's expression was still cautious. "I'm not sure it's a good idea for you to socialize with her. Ultimately, she's going to side with her brother, don't you think? He's family."

Maggie had gotten the impression that Ally disapproved of Carey's decisions. She'd purposely not let Ally say much about him. But it seemed he'd been burning bridges in the family before the robbery.

"Do you have any siblings? You've got that protective-older-sister thing down pat," she asked.

Charlie smiled. "Hazard of the job probably. I'm actually the youngest of three. Two older brothers."

"How nice. I always wanted a brother."

"Only child?"

Maggie nodded.

"Are you close to your parents?"

Maggie shrugged. She'd always had a healthy parent/child relationship with her folks, but not so close that she told them everything. After her father passed away, her mother had moved to a senior-citizen community outside Indianapolis, where her sister, Maggie's aunt, lived. The first couple of years had been rough, and only in the last two had she started to make friends there and get involved in activities. Maggie hadn't even told her about the robbery, not wanting to add to her stress.

"When I was younger, I'd have gladly given you one of my brothers. But we're very close now. One is a police officer and one a firefighter."

"So being a hero just runs in the family."

"I guess so."

Charlie paid the check, waving off Maggie's argument, but she did let Maggie leave the tip. Then they walked back to their cars together. As night fell, the air grew only slightly cooler, but much more humid.

"I had a good time today," Charlie said as she opened Maggie's car door for her. "If you want to do it again some time—well, you have my card, right?"

"I do. Thank you." She hesitated with her hand on the door, half in and half out of the car. "Is it okay? Are you allowed to be friends with people you meet while working? I mean, is it a conflict of interest?"

"Now you're worried about your inappropriate friendships?"

"Okay, smartass." Maggie laughed and slid into the driver's seat. She rolled down the window. "Maybe I'll lose your number."

Chapter Thirteen

Monday afternoon, Ally hurried around her house, picking up discarded clothes and the glass she'd used to finish a bottle of wine the night before. Maggie would be here in ten minutes. She'd had all day to prepare, but she'd gotten distracted that afternoon working in the garage.

She stuck a stack of mail, mostly bills that she'd get to later, in a drawer. She opened a new bottle of her favorite sweet, red wine. Her tastes weren't sophisticated, but she drank what she liked. After pouring two glasses, she left them on the counter to retrieve later.

Her doorbell rang as she was folding the throw for the back of the sofa. She let Maggie in, moving back to give her space to enter. Maggie paused and gave her a peck on the cheek. When she made a move to continue into the living room, Ally slid an arm around her waist and gently steered her back for a hug.

She smothered the urge to apologize for blowing her off Friday. She'd already done that via text Sunday morning, while also admitting that she'd missed her. She'd helped a friend move on Saturday, then spent Sunday taking a much-needed lazy day. She'd wanted to see Maggie Sunday, but the shadows of Carey's visit still lingered. He'd asked her for support, and she didn't know how to give it to him while still following her heart. And she had no doubt that her heart was involved, whether she could admit it to Maggie or not.

So she'd stretched out on her sofa and binge-watched a zombie-apocalypse series Kathi had been raving about. It'd been good enough to keep her attention, but not a new favorite show.

"How was your day?" She took Maggie's coat and hung it on of a row of hooks by the door.

"Long. Incredibly long. And it's only Monday."

"Is it too early for a glass of wine?"

"Is it ever too early?"

Ally grabbed the two glasses from the kitchen and handed one over.

"I'm so glad you texted yesterday." Maggie rested on the arm of the accent chair and sipped her wine.

"Yeah?"

"Sure. I couldn't have known it then, but getting my hands in the dirt will be cathartic today."

"Right. Well, that's what I'm here for." Ally hoped she managed to hide her disappointment. In the next breath, she chastised herself for being so needy. This was not her norm, and she didn't like it one bit. She turned, intent on heading for the garage to distract herself.

Maggie grabbed her hand as she went by. She bent and set her wine on the coffee table, then tugged Ally closer. She cradled Ally's face in her hands and kissed her softly. "I missed you terribly this weekend. And it's a little scary to admit that."

Ally didn't ask why it was scary. She knew. They'd promised to keep this light, and Maggie's words hinted at something delightfully heavy—something that made Ally's chest ache with the desire for it to be true.

"I really should get in the backyard, before I change my mind and decide to drag you into your bedroom." Maggie placed her hands flat on Ally's chest, her fingers curling against her collarbones.

"I wouldn't complain one bit." Imagining Maggie shoving her down on her bed, Ally tightened her thighs to dampen the heat building between them. Too late, she realized that Maggie felt her muscles tense where their legs pressed together.

"You okay, there?"

"All good. Though I can think of a few ways I could be better. Maybe we could explore them in that bedroom you mentioned." Ally slid her arms around Maggie's hips and buried her face against her neck.

"God, I want you." Maggie's voice shimmered with desire.

"Me too." Ally drew in a steadying breath. She felt like Maggie was on the edge, and with only a nudge from her, they'd give in and tear each other's clothes off. But she wouldn't push. She'd promised Maggie control, and though she might be walking funny for the rest of the night, she'd keep her word. "Maggie?"

"Yeah. I'm—um—I have to go outside." Maggie eased free, catching her hand as they backed up and releasing it slowly, their fingers sliding against each other until she was out of range.

"Maggie, no."

Maggie smiled then, a flirty, teasing pull of her lips that said she knew exactly the effect she had on Ally and she loved it. "The garden is calling, love. I'll come find you when I'm finished."

Ally stood in the archway between her living room and dining room and watched Maggie go out the back door. Good God, she was already so close to finished. Ally had reacted immediately when Maggie voiced her desire to take her to bed, and every teasing word that followed had only pulled at the thread until Ally thought she'd certainly unravel. They were going to be combustible together, and Ally had no doubt it would be worth the wait.

But for now, she needed to find some other way to burn off some of this energy. Her body hummed, and if she held out her hands, she was certain they'd be trembling. She dismissed the idea of heading to the garage. Power tools were not a good idea when she was this distracted. The treadmill in her spare room, the one that doubled as a guest room and office, would tire her out, but the idea of running and going nowhere was too symbolic right now.

A series of knocks on the door simultaneously saved her from deciding and made her heart race, too. She knew those knocks. They were made by tiny fists. On her way to the front door, she calculated her odds of not answering and acting like she wasn't home. Her SUV and Maggie's Prius in the driveway spoiled that idea for her. Instead, she'd open the door to two little cuties and whichever mom accompanied them today.

With her hand on the knob, she paused, looked up at the ceiling, and whispered, "Please be Kathi."

❖

Her tiny prayer was answered as June and Grayson spilled into her house, followed by Kathi.

"Hey, kiddos. What a nice surprise." She scooped June up into a hug. Grayson, having recently decided he was a big boy and didn't do hugs anymore, gave her a high five as he walked by.

She squeezed June once more, catching the tropical scent of the fancy shampoo Dani used on the kids. Cruelty-free, GMO free, dye-free, and all-natural fragrances. Grayson had experienced milk sensitivity as a baby, and since then, Dani was very careful about what they were exposed to and what they ate. Ally didn't think either kid had even had a glass of Kool-Aid.

"What are you up to, girl?" Laughter lilted in Kathi's voice.

"Well—Maggie's here. But then I guess you knew that, which is why you came by." They passed Ally's house every day on their way from picking the kids up at school. But, needing to get the kids home for dinner, they stopped to visit only occasionally, so sometimes she just heard a car horn honk as they drove past.

"Oh, was that her car in the driveway?" Kathi's exaggeratedly innocent face lacked only batting eyelashes.

"Mama said we had to 'vestigate whose car it was." Grayson's serious face combined with the adorable pronunciation almost broke the stern look Ally directed at Kathi. She pressed her lips tight to contain her smile.

"Thanks, Grayson. Let's go outside and you can meet her." Ally ruffled his hair and steered him and June in the direction of the back door. Over her shoulder, she said to Kathi, "Congrats on raising an honest boy."

Both kids ran into the backyard, then stopped suddenly. The two raised garden beds were new since they'd last visited, but they both seemed more fascinated by Maggie and what she was doing. June strode forward a few steps, then paused. She looked back at Kathi, where Grayson stood hugging one of her legs. June blinked and gave a small nod, as if having decided how to proceed, and then she turned and crossed the remaining lawn.

Maggie knelt on a foam gardening pad next to one of the raised beds. She braced one elbow on the ledge of the box and reached inside with the other.

As June leaned to peer into the bed, she rested her hand on Maggie's shoulder for balance.

"Hi there. You must be June," Maggie said.

June nodded and flicked a thumb over her shoulder. "That's my brother, Grayson."

"I see. Ally has told me about both of you. It's nice to meet you." Maggie included Grayson in her welcoming smile, but he only inched farther behind Kathi.

"What are you doing?" June asked.

"Pulling out the weeds."

"What weeds?"

"See these plants here?" Maggie touched the leaves of one of the taller stalks. "These are carrots. I take out anything that's not the same so the carrots have room to grow."

June shook her head. "Carrots are orange."

Kathi laughed. "She's only ever seen those baby carrots we buy in the snack packs." She squatted down next to them. "The orange part grows in the ground, Junie. Those are the leaves."

"If you come back over when they're a little bigger, you can help me take them out of the ground and you'll see the carrot. Would you like to do that?"

June's eyes got big, and she glanced at Kathi for confirmation. Kathi nodded, and June turned back to Maggie. "Your gloves are dirty."

"Yes, they are." She tugged one off. "But they keep my hands clean. See? No dirt under my fingernails."

"Could I wear gloves when I help you?" June held out her hands, fingers spread so Maggie could admire her light-pink nail polish.

Ally made a mental note to look for kids' gardening sets next time she shopped at Lowe's.

"Yes, you can. We wouldn't want to mess up this pretty manicure." Maggie glanced across the yard. "Grayson, will you come back with June to help us pick the vegetables?"

He nodded, tentatively shuffling into view.

"Grayson, come see the weeds."

June's endorsement convinced him everything was okay, and he ran to her side. They looked into the garden bed together. June pointed out the stalk of one of the carrots, seeking confirmation from Maggie that she'd identified the right sprig of green. Maggie nodded and shared a smile with June.

"The rest of them's weeds and don't belong in there," June said.

Kathi angled close to Ally and said, "Aren't they just adorable."

"They are." Ally couldn't take her eyes off Maggie's face. Her broad smile, as she watched June and Grayson together, made Ally's chest ache. She seemed genuinely charmed by the two kids. Her throat grew tight and her eyes stung. She shouldn't be entertaining domestic thoughts about Maggie. They'd already established that whatever this was couldn't go anywhere.

"I meant the kids. But your girl is pretty cute, too," Kathi whispered.

"Hush. She's not—"

"Don't even lie to me. She's your *something* all right."

"Quiet." She glanced at Maggie again, but she didn't appear to have heard them.

"Ally?" Grayson ran across the yard, with no regard to speed or terrain. She knew from experience he had about a thirty percent chance of stumbling and falling down. He probably knew it, too, somewhere inside, yet he hurled himself over the grass just the same. When was the last time she'd acted without care for consequences? She caught Maggie's gaze drifting from Grayson to her. Well, right now, actually—this thing with Maggie.

"Yes, Grayson?"

"Mama said you're coming to our house."

"I am. Next weekend. Your moms want to go out to dinner. So you and June and I are having a date night." When she'd told Dani about her lie to get out of dinner with Shirley and Carey, Dani insisted she follow through on the idea.

Grayson gave a cheer and threw his arms in the air as he ran away to tell June.

"A date night. I love the idea of you wrangling those two," Maggie said as she approached them. Her smile was radiant, and for the brief seconds it was directed only at Ally, warmth spread through her. Then Maggie turned to Kathi, still smiling and friendly, but more reserved.

"Hi. I'm Maggie." She shook Kathi's hand.

"Kathi."

"As in one half of Kathi and Dani. Ally has told me about how the two of you try to keep her in line."

"Dani's the taskmaster of the bunch. Even I wouldn't try to put one over on her." Ally reengaged in the conversation, wrapping her arm around Maggie's waist because she needed to touch her.

"I suppose every family has to have a leader." Maggie grasped Ally's hand where it rested on her hip. She eased it away from her body and took a step to put distance between them.

But she threaded her fingers through Ally's and kept ahold of her hand. Ally gave her a curious look, but Maggie had turned her attention to Kathi. "Your kids are adorable."

"They can be a handful." Kathi tilted her head in Ally's direction. "But she's really good with them. In fact, she's very good at taking care of the people in her life."

Ally glanced at Kathi, wondering at the warning tone in her voice. Kathi's expression remained welcoming.

"I definitely get that impression," Maggie said.

"Hey." Ally's exclamation sounded loud, even in the open air of the backyard, and very awkward. Maggie and Kathi looked at her expectantly, so she soldiered on. "I think I have some juice boxes inside. Grayson, Junie, do you want one?"

Both kids yelled out "yes" from where they still bent over the garden beds, playing their fingers in the dirt.

"Guys, don't pull out any plants unless Maggie tells you which ones. We don't want to ruin her nice garden," Kathi said.

"Great. Drinks here, ladies?" Ally waved her hand among the three of them. "I have water, beer, cider, and diet soda."

"I'm fine," Maggie said.

"I'll have water."

"Good." Ally grabbed Kathi's hand. "Come help me get the drinks. Maggie, can you keep an eye on them?" At Maggie's apprehensive look, Ally rushed to reassure her. "They'll be fine. We'll just be a second." She jerked Kathi after her, toward the house.

"Are you and Ally girlfriends?" Grayson asked as he sidled up to Maggie.

Great. The kid finally gets brave enough to talk, and this is what he asks? "I—um—we're friends and we're both girls."

He didn't seem satisfied with the answer, but he didn't

pursue the subject. Maggie moved over to the patio and sat down. Grayson stayed standing nearby, shuffling his weight from one foot to the other as he spoke.

"Why did you make your garden here at Ally's house?"

"I live in an apartment, and I don't have a yard."

He nodded. "My grandma lives in an apartment. And she has a button in the bathroom that I'm not allowed to push. It makes the ambulance come."

A panic button in the bathroom. Grayson's grandmother apparently lived in an assisted-living complex, and now he thought she did, too.

"Do you live close to here?"

"About twenty minutes away."

June, having lost interest in the plants, joined them on the patio. She patted Grayson on the shoulder as she walked by, absently, like it was an impulse rather than a conscious thought. She grabbed the edge of the table to steady herself, then climbed up into Maggie's lap.

"We live close. Mama picked us up from school. I'm in kindergarten and June is pre-K."

"Do you like school?"

He nodded. "All except for nap time."

"I used to hate naps too when I was your age."

They chatted about his school and the activities he liked, while June sat contentedly and listened, only interjecting occasionally. Maggie smiled at the shift in dynamic between them. Grayson had opened up, and June's outgoing personality gave way to his. She suspected after he was finished talking, June's energy would take over again.

❖

"You really need help carrying two juice boxes and a bottle of water?" Kathi chuckled as Ally yanked her inside and closed the door. She looked back outside through the window to ensure that Maggie's attention was diverted.

"Let's have it." She folded her arms over her chest.

"What?" Kathi opened the refrigerator and bent to find the drinks.

"Bottom shelf." Ally provided the location of the juice, though Kathi certainly would have found it. She hadn't been shopping in almost two weeks, and the fridge looked pretty empty. "You have something to say."

Kathi grabbed the drinks and set them on the counter. "Since you asked. We're just concerned about you."

"We? So Dani's on board."

"Dani's always on board, whether she knows it or not." Kathi grinned. She liked to joke that she really pulled the strings behind the scenes and Dani only *thought* she was in charge. "What's going on between you and Maggie?"

"We're friends." She definitely did not want Kathi's opinion on their kiss.

"That's not what it looks like."

"I don't really care what it looks like." As she said it, she realized it was true. For once. She didn't care about the outcome or anyone else's opinion. She wanted Maggie close, and she was prepared to deal with any consequences to make that happen.

"Oh, honey, no." Kathi's sympathetic expression brought a flush of embarrassment to Ally's cheeks. From anyone else, she'd call that look pity, but she knew Kathi came from a place of genuine concern, though she didn't like it any more.

"What?"

"Please tell me you are not in over your head with this woman."

Over her head? Yeah, she probably was.

"How does this all play out? Are you going to take her home to meet your family? Oh, wait, she already knows your brother."

"Kathi." Ally intended her voice to be stern, like a warning, but it wound up more pleading than she'd like.

"Shirley is going to lose her mind when she finds out who Maggie is."

"I know."

"What's your plan there then?"

"I don't have one." Ally rubbed her hand against the front of her neck, feeling hot and itchy. She met Kathi's eyes, still finding sympathy with a bit of tough love. "I don't know. But I like her. And I like the way I feel when I'm with her. It's been a long time since I could truly say that about anyone. Why do I have to give that up for my family?"

"Have you met your family?" Kathi's short quip hurt a little because of its accuracy. She touched Ally's arm. "We want you to be happy, Al. And honestly, Shirley demands a lot from you. If that's the kind of relationship you want with her, that's great. But if it's not," her voice softened, "it's okay for you to make a change in your life."

Ally blinked against a sting in her eyes. She needed to end this conversation—now. She made a show of glancing out the kitchen window. "We've left Maggie out there defenseless with the kids. This is no time for a heart-to-heart."

"I agree. But you're the one who dragged me in here to 'help' you with juice." She made exaggerated air quotes around the word *help*.

"Let's go." Ally led the way to the yard but stopped only three steps out of the door.

Maggie sat at the patio table gently rocking side to side, and June had curled up against her chest, nearly asleep. Grayson had climbed into the other chair, quietly playing on the table surface with a small toy pickup truck that he habitually carried around in his coat pocket.

Ally couldn't ignore the soft sigh of her heart at the sight, but she didn't address it verbally. Instead, she turned to Kathi and said, "She's almost out. Do you want me to carry her to the car for you?"

"No. She needs to stay awake now anyway, or she'll be up

all night. Lately, she doesn't want to go to bed. And Grayson has started wanting to sleep with us. Even when we make him start in his room, he sneaks in during the night."

"Mood killer," Ally mumbled just loud enough for Kathi to hear.

"Exactly."

"Okay, kiddos. Say good-bye to Maggie and Ally. We need to go home and get dinner ready."

June reached up and wrapped her arms around Maggie's neck and said good-bye in a sweet, slightly sleepy voice, then slid off her lap. Grayson offered a high five. Ally walked them out, saying her good-byes at the door. She accepted a hug from Kathi, along with a reminder to call them if she needed anything.

Chapter Fourteen

Maggie walked into the parking garage while gauging her level of panic. Today—not so bad. She felt a tiny quickening of her heart, nothing unmanageable. But as she tucked her keys between her fingers and looked around the dimly lit garage, she didn't see any danger. The shadows didn't come alive as they had when she'd tried this in the days and weeks following the robbery.

She'd been forcing herself to park back in the garage where the robbery happened. Maybe it shouldn't matter. Some people might not blame her for never going inside again. But to Maggie the garage was symbolic. She refused to give up her power. And this plan seemed to be working for her.

After she left the garage in her car, she turned right toward Ally's house. But for a second, she debated heading the other way—toward her apartment. She'd had a busy week at work and wasn't sure she'd be good company. In the past, she'd often enjoyed a Friday-night glass of wine, probably in a hot bath, and then gone to bed early. But today, seeing Ally held more appeal than her usual game plan.

Since the first night they'd tried to move beyond a kiss, three weeks ago, Ally had been maddeningly patient. They'd fallen into something of a routine. A couple of times a week, Maggie arrived after work and went directly out to the plant beds. After she'd finished, she would find Ally working in the garage.

Ally had finished the coffee table and sold it, and had moved on to an entertainment console a client had commissioned. They would eat together, then linger in the living room, talking, lightly touching, and kissing. But, though she had left plenty turned on most nights for the past two weeks, she didn't advance their physical relationship, and Ally didn't push her to do so either. Maggie hadn't experienced any further episodes of panic.

She enjoyed what they had—when she didn't let herself think too hard about it ending someday. As the days flew by, she found new things about Ally to like—her laugh, as well as the way she made Maggie laugh, her sensitive side, and even the impatience she displayed if she as much as talked about driving in traffic.

Even as Maggie let herself fall for Ally, the pending criminal trial loomed over them both. And today, she'd received a voice mail from the victim/witness coordinator at the district attorney's office that a court date had been set and they would be contacting her to schedule a pretrial conference. She'd requested a call back to confirm Maggie got the message and to talk about her availability for an interview in the coming month. Thinking about meeting with the prosecutor regarding the trial felt like a harbinger of the end of things with Ally. And she wasn't ready. So she would put off returning the message for a couple of days, pushing up against that deadline and holding on to Ally.

When she reached Ally's, the garage door was already up, and Ally stood at a workbench with her back to Maggie. The scrape of sandpaper against wood set a cadence that masked Maggie's footsteps. As she drew closer, she could see that Ally also had wireless earbuds in, so most likely it actually was her playlist that allowed Maggie to sneak up on her.

Maggie wrapped her arms around Ally's waist and pressed against her back. She nuzzled against Ally's neck behind her ear, smelling sawdust and the fresh-shampoo scent of her sweat-dampened hair. Ally pulled one earbud out and dropped it onto the bench in front of her.

"Hey, you."

"Can I help?" She slipped her hands under the hem of Ally's T-shirt and stroked her stomach. "Or maybe we could go inside and make out on the couch like teenagers."

Ally moaned and pressed her hands over Maggie's, holding them to her skin. "That sounds amazing. But I need to finish up out here so I can paint this piece tomorrow."

Ally gently took Maggie's hand and pulled her around to stand beside her. "I'll accept your offer of help, though." She secured a new strip of sandpaper onto a sanding block. As she held it out, Maggie gave her a skeptical look.

"You don't have one of those power sanders."

"I do. But it's more satisfying to do it this way." She demonstrated the stroke Maggie should use on the top of the console, sanding with the grain.

"Are you trying to Mr. Miyagi me?" Maggie moved to the other side. She braced one hand on the surface, and with the other, she mirrored Ally's motion with her own sandpaper.

"Maybe. Let me know if it works." Ally chuckled.

"What's so funny?"

"It's just nice to talk to someone who gets that reference."

"You've been dating that young?"

Ally lowered her head and looked away, obviously pretending to focus on a stubborn rough spot in the wood. "The last woman I went out with was twenty-five."

"I'm not sure if I'm impressed or repulsed."

"She was mature for mid-twenties."

"Oh, yeah. I'm sure you were dating her for her maturity."

Ally laughed.

"The ex you lived with, she wasn't younger, right? You said she had a teenager?"

"That's right."

"You're okay dating an older woman, then?" She'd meant to tease. But as she said it, she realized her comment brought up more questions. Were they dating? She didn't need to have another conversation where they couldn't define what they were. So, she amped up the flirtation to distract from any seriousness. "Just slightly older, that is."

Ally raised her brows, a smile twitching at the corner of her lips. Maggie eased back to Ally's side of the console, intent on kissing that little grin right off her mouth. "Do you mean a mature woman who could teach me a thing or two? You know, in the bedroom."

"I'll assume you're talking about me and not your ex, or some other mature woman. Also, I'll pretend *mature* is a compliment and not just you calling me old." She trailed her hand across Ally's shoulder and up the side of her neck. Ally tilted her head, and Maggie walked her fingers into the edge of Ally's hairline, just behind her ear.

"That feels amazing." Ally made a sound of contentment as Maggie sifted her fingers through the back of her hair. "I like your hands on me."

Maggie's kiss lingered just shy of letting it turn passionate. Ally didn't deepen it. Maggie didn't know where she found the self-control, but Ally had consistently let her lead. "Someday soon, I'm going to reward you for all of this patience you've been showing me."

"Anything worth having is worth waiting for," Ally murmured with her lips pressed to Maggie's jaw.

"So, no pressure to make sure it's worth it, though?"

"None. I already know I'll wait for you as long as I need to." Ally's eyes locked on her and held. Her voice still carried a teasing note, but her gaze said she was serious.

Did Ally want to change their self-imposed rules as much as she did?

"Ally—"

"Would you like to stay here tonight?"

Maggie hesitated. Given her last thought, she should say no. She couldn't let this thing between them get any more emotional. Maybe the invitation to spend the night was strictly physical.

Maggie wanted Ally, but getting intimate still made her nervous. What if she freaked out again? She hoped she'd only had an issue with Ally's hand tightening around her wrist, but what if there was more to it than that? She didn't want Ally to think she was leading her on, then pulling back after winding her up.

"Nothing has to happen that you're not ready for. I realize I sort of sprung this on you. But I had an idea about something that might make you more comfortable—physically, and I figured we could test it out."

"You had an idea?"

Ally nodded. "But if you aren't ready, we could try another night. When you've had time to bring a few overnight things with you."

Ally's willingness to let Maggie set the pace gave her a shot of confidence. Surely she could believe in their relationship as much as Ally did.

"Do you have an extra toothbrush?"

Ally grinned. "I do."

❖

"Are you going to tell me about your plan?" Maggie asked during one of the many slightly awkward silences during dinner.

Ally had grilled turkey burgers and an assortment of vegetables. She poured them each a glass of wine and put on some soft music. She stopped short of lighting candles, not wanting dinner to feel too much like a seduction scene.

She smiled and covered Maggie's hand. "If you really want the details, I'll tell you so you won't worry."

"I'm not worried." Maggie turned her hand over to lace her fingers together with Ally's, and as if on cue, her fingers trembled against Ally's. "Okay, maybe a little nervous. Should I do something to prepare? I didn't come here today expecting—um, intimacy. So—I haven't done any of those things we women do to prepare to have sex but don't talk about because it's not so sexy."

Ally raised her brows. "You haven't shaved your legs."

"Among other things. But yes, let's focus on that one."

Ally sat against the back of her chair, adopting a serious expression. She acted like she was giving Maggie's confession careful consideration. "Are we talking weeks or months?"

"Oh, God, no. A day—eh, maybe two."

Ally's lips twitched, and then she gave Maggie a full grin, enjoying the flush that crept up her neck. "I think I can work with that. Besides, for tonight, no sex."

"None?" Maggie shoved both of her hands under the edge of the table, and judging from her fidgety motion, Ally could practically picture her wringing them together.

"It's completely off the table."

"For real? Or are you just saying that to make me take it as a challenge to get you to give in?"

"Would that work?" Ally rolled her empty wineglass between her hands, trying to appear relaxed about this whole conversation. If she could put out calming energy, maybe Maggie would absorb some of it.

"Maybe. You know it's not that I don't want to sleep with you, right?"

"Good. Because it's very important to me that you do want to sleep with me." She saw Maggie's confusion at her choice of words and hoped it would all be clear to her in a little while. She set her glass down, then filled it with the nearly empty bottle on the table between them. "I'd really like for you to trust me. And to keep open communication and tell me if anything pushes you too far. And, most important, to relax."

Maggie drew an exaggerated breath, then let it out slowly. "I can try."

After dinner, they settled on the sofa and watched a cheesy '90s rom-com that Ally had seen at least a half dozen times. She didn't think she'd be able to focus with Maggie sitting on the cushion directly next to hers but soon found herself caught up in the love story on-screen. She registered the warmth of Maggie's thigh pressed against hers and forced herself to think of the warmth, soothing like a fireplace on a cold winter night, as opposed to the knowledge that it was Maggie's *thigh* just under those jeans.

She stretched her arm along the back of the sofa and rested her fingers against Maggie's opposite shoulder. Maggie cuddled against her, resting her hand on Ally's knee, and she wondered if maybe Maggie had decided to test her resolve. No sex. She'd made the rule, and she would stick by it in order to make sure that Maggie was totally comfortable with the progress between them physically. She pressed her own thighs together and repeated the words in her head. *No sex.*

❖

"If, at any point, you're uncomfortable, just say the word." Ally had turned off the television and now took Maggie's hand.

Maggie stared into Ally's eyes, seeing her concern and caring, and she nodded.

Ally led her to the bedroom and pulled back the covers. "You get comfortable. Help yourself to some comfy clothes if you want them. You'll find a new toothbrush in the cabinet under the sink. I'll be back." Ally grabbed some clothes out of a drawer, leaving it open slightly for Maggie, and left the room.

Maggie brushed her teeth and washed her face. She selected a T-shirt from the same drawer and replaced her own shirt and bra. She shoved her shorts down and stepped out of them. Wearing only her underwear and Ally's shirt, she crawled into bed and pulled the sheet and comforter over her. Ally's plush bed enveloped her, and the softest sheets Maggie had ever felt caressed her bare legs.

After she heard a light knock, the bedroom door clicked open.

"All good?" Ally eased into the room wearing a T-shirt similar to Maggie's, along with a pair of capri-length pajama pants.

"Yes." Maggie flipped the corner of the comforter back in invitation.

Ally crossed the room and got in next to Maggie. But instead of reaching for her, Ally turned away and scooted back against Maggie, so that Maggie was spooning her.

Confused, Maggie rested her hand on Ally's hip, over the comforter. This was Ally's big plan? To get in bed and ignore her? Except she hadn't. She'd pressed back, touching her as passively as she could, giving the power of their embrace to Maggie. Maggie doubted the position came naturally for Ally, certain she was usually the big spoon. But she'd sacrificed her comfort for Maggie's.

Maggie pushed her hand under the covers and slid it around Ally, snuggling closer. Ally covered Maggie's hand with hers, lightly, not holding her there—just touching. Maggie nuzzled her cheek against Ally's hair and pressed her chest against Ally's back.

"Next time we should do this without these T-shirts between us," she whispered.

Ally chuckled. "Just don't get used to being the big spoon. That isn't going to be an every-time thing."

"I figured." She splayed her fingers against Ally's stomach and enjoyed the twitch of muscles under the smooth skin. "Thank you. This is perfect." She kissed Ally's jaw and closed her eyes.

Chapter Fifteen

Ally woke up slower than usual. She typically snapped awake in the morning as if someone had flipped on a light switch on her brain—from sleeping to aware in mere seconds. But that morning, she drifted into consciousness like she was being pulled reluctantly from a beautiful dream. At some point during the night, she and Maggie had shifted, and now she lay on her back with Maggie's head on her chest and her arm across her stomach. She didn't even know people slept like that in real life. She never had. She'd always rolled away from her partner during the night.

But last night, she'd wanted to make sure Maggie knew she was close, while also giving her the control between them. Maybe a part of her had tried to continue that reassurance, even in sleep. She rolled her eyes. Now she was playing amateur psychologist with herself. She shouldn't be overthinking this. She should just enjoy the fact that Maggie was lying here, in her arms, at peace. Her arm tightened involuntarily against Maggie's back, and Maggie stirred.

"Good morning," Ally murmured, not wanting to disturb the peace of the morning. "Should I assume since you didn't sneak out in the night that you were okay with everything?"

Maggie placed her hand on Ally's chest, just under her collarbone, then rested her chin on the back of her hand. "I guess so. I don't seem to want to move from this spot."

Maggie brought her leg up to lie across Ally's, and Ally moved her hand under the covers to touch her knee. As she rolled to her side, facing Maggie, she ran her palm up Maggie's leg.

"Whoa. You don't have pajama bottoms on." She paused with her hand high on the outside of Maggie's thigh—almost her hip.

"I don't."

"If you tell me you haven't been wearing underwear all night, I might cry."

"Of course I'm wearing underwear. What kind of woman do you think I am?"

"See. Now I don't know if that's better. Because I can't think about anything but whether they're cotton or lace. Or maybe satin?"

Maggie winked. "Why don't you find out?"

"Lord, save me," Ally murmured as she pressed her face into Maggie's neck. She kissed Maggie just below her ear as she inched her fingers up until they encountered fabric—lace-edged cotton, to be specific.

Maggie snuck her hands under Ally's T-shirt. "You're very warm."

"And getting hotter by the second." Suddenly, her pajamas and the added weight of the covers were too much for her. She kicked off the comforter, then fumbled with the sheet when it twisted around her leg, eventually freeing herself.

"You're the one who said no sex."

"I said no sex *last night.* I made no such promises about this morning."

"Ah." Maggie's fingers danced up her stomach and caressed the underside of her breast. "I like your idea of a loophole."

Ally's nipples tightened and tugged a spot between her thighs. "Maggie," she rested her hand over Maggie's on the outside of her shirt, "we're nearing a point where I'm going to be very uncomfortable if we don't stop."

"I have some idea of how you feel." Maggie moved her hand

again, sliding it up between Ally's breasts. "However, I'd very much like to feel more of you."

"Maggie," Ally moaned.

"It's okay, Ally."

"I don't want to push you." Her stomach flipped with arousal, but something else, too. Worry that Maggie might feel pressure. And something darker, which she couldn't put into words aloud, that Maggie might flash on a memory of Carey at an inopportune moment. That thought had her withdrawing physically from Maggie. She started to release her and turn away, but Maggie held on.

"Hey, you're not pushing. If anything, I'm pulling." Maggie rolled onto her back, dragging Ally with her, until Ally hovered over her.

"What I said about stopping—"

"I know."

"I need to say it. I need to know you hear me." She waited for Maggie's nod. "If at any point you want to call a halt to this, that is entirely your prerogative."

Maggie cradled Ally's face in her hands and held her gaze. "Hey, I want this. And I'm right here. With you. If any part of that changes, I'll let you know."

Ally's apprehension melted under the heat of Maggie's kiss. Feeling Maggie's hands slide against her skin brushed away her fears.

"More. I need access to more of you." Maggie tugged at the hem of her shirt.

Ally eased away and pulled off her shirt. Then, at the intense look of desire in Maggie's eyes, she also stripped off her pants, leaving herself completely naked, before bringing their bodies flush again.

"Wait." Maggie planted a hand in the center of Ally's chest. "You were going commando under there all night?"

"Sure." Ally grinned. "I never wear underwear to bed. You gotta let stuff breathe."

Maggie trailed her hand down to Ally's hip and squeezed. "That is so good to know. I'm going to need a bunch more sleepovers."

"We're not done with this one yet."

"No. But I have a good idea how I hope it's going to end."

Ally kissed Maggie's neck. "We're going to get there. Let's not rush."

"Okay. But let's be clear. *You're* going to get *me* there first." The teasing in Maggie's voice didn't obscure her permissive tone.

"Oh, yes, ma'am." Ally pushed up Maggie's shirt, dropping kisses across her stomach as she went.

Maggie's hands in her hair encouraged her higher, until her lips brushed the underside of Maggie's breast. Maggie sat up and took off her shirt. As she lay back down, Ally cupped her hand around the swell of that one breast and brushed her thumb against her puckering nipple. She bent and lathed her tongue against it, feeling it tighten even further. Maggie sighed and arched her back.

"Beautiful," Ally whispered as she stroked her hands around Maggie's back, hugging her close.

Her head swam with the feel of Maggie's skin and the soft sounds of pleasure she made as Ally caressed and kissed her. She forced herself to be patient, though her body clamored for more—now. More of Maggie flush against her. More of Maggie's hands and mouth on her own skin.

She focused on Maggie and her reactions to each touch as she stroked down her stomach and over her hip, dragging her underwear over her thighs and off. Maggie encouraged her with whispered words and light touches against her shoulder and her neck.

"Touch me." Maggie's demanding tone erased Ally's desire to go slow.

Sliding up, she kissed Maggie deeply as she traced a path up the inside of Maggie's thigh to her center. Her small moan echoed Maggie's sound of satisfaction as her fingers slipped into Maggie's wet folds.

"Oh, God, yes," Maggie breathed.

Ally echoed the sentiment in her head. She found Maggie's clit and teased. She watched Maggie's face as she curled her finger and slid inside. Maggie grabbed the back of Ally's arm, pulling her deeper.

Emboldened by Maggie's hand on her arm, and the feel of Maggie squeezing around her, Ally withdrew, then pushed back in. Maggie tilted her head back and whispered pleas for "more." Ally added another finger, and Maggie's answering groan left her feeling empowered, yet more humbled than she ever had. Bracing herself with one hand, she buried her face in Maggie's neck and thrust, letting Maggie's hips moving against her set the pace.

When Maggie tensed, Ally's heart kicked with fear, but she resisted the urge to stop and check in. If everything was good, she didn't want to pull Maggie out of the buildup. So, trusting Maggie to tell her if something was wrong, she continued stroking in and out. Maggie grasped at her shoulder, then gripped the back of her neck. She cried out as her hips jerked against Ally's hand.

Need throbbed through Ally, and she wanted to reach between her own legs and topple over the edge with Maggie. But she kept her focus on drawing out Maggie's release, reveling in each tremor that vibrated between them. As Maggie's orgasm ebbed, Ally lay on her side and drew Maggie close, holding her but careful not to restrain her from moving away if she wanted to.

"That was—very nice." Maggie burrowed into her embrace.

"I strive for amazing, but I'll settle for nice."

"Good. It's important to always know there's room for improvement." Maggie's laughter echoed against Ally's chest.

"I'll show you improvement in the form of a second orgasm." Ally smoothed her hands toward Maggie's hips.

"No, you don't. It's my turn to be nice." Maggie batted Ally's hands away. She swung one leg over and straddled Ally's midsection.

"I'm so close after touching you that you don't have to be nice to get it done."

Maggie tilted her hips, rotating them against Ally's stomach. "Hm. Maybe I could manage that second orgasm myself."

"Lord, please do. You look so damn sexy right now." Maggie, on top of her, in control of her own pleasure was nearly enough. Ally squeezed her thighs, feeling how wet and swollen she was. She would need only a couple of strokes.

"You're so close, aren't you?" Maggie bent and whispered in her ear. "I could just slide my hips down—" She moved as she spoke, slipping a leg between Ally's and rolling her hips.

"Jesus, yes." Ally's hips jerked reflexively as Maggie ground against her.

She had a fleeting thought about slowing down, about waiting for Maggie's fingers, maybe even her mouth. But her body was way ahead of her mind, racing toward a peak she desperately needed.

"Let go now. And you can have my mouth for the next one." Maggie bit lightly on her neck.

Ally's control spiraled away, her legs clamped closed, and she rode Maggie's thigh into a quick, sharp release. She felt like she did when she was a kid and had gone into the ocean for the first time. She'd immediately waded out too deep, lay back, and closed her eyes, letting each wave rock her.

When she opened her eyes again, Maggie was staring at her, her expression serious but unreadable.

"What are you thinking?" Ally wasn't sure she wanted to know. If Maggie had regrets, Ally would rather have another moment to bask.

"You are absolutely gorgeous when you come."

That wasn't what she'd been expecting.

"I mean it." Maggie lay down beside her and stroked her

cheek. "You're so unguarded. And I love this little flush you get right here." She played her fingers against the heat on Ally's neck.

"What are you doing today?" Ally caught her hand and laced their fingers together.

Maggie shrugged. "I have a million errands, laundry piled up from the week, and I need to clean my place."

"That's a shame." Ally stretched, an exaggerated, full-body pull from her fingertips to her toes. "I was hoping you'd hang out here, maybe spend some more time in bed this morning. Then you could go on a field trip with me this afternoon."

"I suppose I can stick around for a while. I could take care of my cleaning later this evening."

"How long can that take anyway? What do you have, about eight hundred square feet?"

"Nine-fifty."

"You know, we've been—friends for over a month, and I haven't even been to your apartment."

"Well, the garden—"

"Right. I'm not complaining. I just—I'd like to see it so I can picture you there." She used the same phrase Maggie had used while on the phone together so many weeks ago.

She didn't want to sound clingy, or like she just sat around all the time imagining what Maggie was doing when they weren't together. She did—but only sometimes. "Unless you have some weird neighbors. Or maybe you love your neighbors. I'm imagining a hot widow lady who lives downstairs and you've always had a thing for her, so you don't want her to think you're off the market."

"Wow. That was—wow." Maggie chuckled. "No hot widow neighbors."

"Okay."

"How about tomorrow night, we do this again, only at my place?"

"Is my visit contingent on more sex? Not that I mind, but I need to do all those things women do to prepare for—how did you say it—intimacy." Ally grinned, warming with Maggie's answering smile.

"After I've had your hands on me, I don't know how I could say no to more sex." Maggie gave Ally a quick peck. "Now, down to serious business, where are we going on this field trip?"

"First things first," Ally said as she kissed Maggie and slid her hand against Maggie's stomach.

❖

"Where are we going? And how did you find this place again?"

Ally laughed. "Why do you sound so nervous?" They'd been driving for about thirty minutes, and now, instead of the suburbs, the interstate they cruised down was surrounded by fields and country homes.

"I'm not. Not really. I've already decided you aren't taking me out here to kill me and dump my body."

"And how did you reach that conclusion?"

She lifted one hiking-boot-outfitted foot off the car's floorboard. "Because you wouldn't have told me to wear sturdy boots that I could get dirty. That wouldn't matter if I wasn't walking out of whatever backwoods place you're taking me."

"Not backwoods. Just rural. But you're right. You'll be making the return trip with me." She glanced over at Maggie with a grin. "Unless something happens to both of us, of course."

Maggie gave her shoulder a gentle shove. "Stop."

Ten minutes later, Ally exited the interstate. A long stretch of country road later, she turned down a winding driveway.

"A farm? Are you thinking about relocating?"

"Maybe someday. But not now and not here." Ally pulled up in front of a large red barn. "Come on."

By the time she got out and circled the car, a white-haired gentleman in a plaid shirt and overalls exited the barn.

"Ally Becker. We spoke on the phone."

"Yes, ma'am. Miss Becker."

"Please, call me Ally. And this is my friend, Maggie."

"Good afternoon, Miss Maggie."

Ally waited while they exchanged pleasantries, but she was itching to see what she'd come here for.

"Are you ready to see the old barn?" He nodded toward the fields behind the white farmhouse nearby.

"Yes, sir."

"It's in the back forty. I'll carry you there on the Gator."

He led them around the back of the red barn to a four-door, green utility vehicle with a dump bed on the back. He pulled a handkerchief from his pocket and wiped down the passenger seat, then the one in the back as well.

"She's a little dirty."

"No worries. I'd expect that's because she does real farm work." Ally waved off his apologetic tone.

Maggie jumped into the back, so Ally climbed in beside him in the front. He tried to apologize for the ruts as they bounced through the fields, but Ally wouldn't have it.

"If you've got what you said out here, it's all worth the trip."

He nodded and smiled. "I think you'll be pleased. And I can already tell I'm selling to the right person."

Maggie touched Ally's shoulder as she leaned forward. "She's keeping our mission today under wraps."

"You won't be disappointed." He chuckled, a hearty laugh that brought more color to his ruddy cheeks.

As they rounded another bend past one of the biggest oak trees Ally had ever seen, the remains of an old hay barn also came into view. The basic shape remained standing, but most of the outside boards had been removed. The roof had partially caved in. Ally's heart rate picked up, and the anticipation had her jumping out of the Gator before it had fully stopped.

Maggie got out more slowly, and by the time she reached Ally's side, Ally was already taking inventory of the piles of barn wood closest to her.

"My boys started pulling the boards off the outside. But I made them stop when the roof started to collapse," their host called from the driver's seat of the Gator.

"I can see why. Doing any demo on the main structure is going to be delicate work." Ally walked as close as she dared to the skeleton. The wood was gorgeous—varying shades of weathered silver-gray, dark tones, and golden hues. "I'd love to buy the whole thing. But even if I had the manpower to take it down, I don't have the storage space."

"Be careful."

In her peripheral vision, Ally saw Maggie tense. Ally stepped back to a safer distance to examine the stacks in front of the barn again. As she passed Maggie, she briefly grabbed and squeezed her hand.

"Isn't it beautiful?"

"Yeah." Maggie met her eyes, then dipped her gaze to Ally's lips and back.

"Behave," Ally murmured so they couldn't be overheard.

Maggie glanced down at the barn wood. "Are you already sketching furniture in your head?"

"Maybe."

"I like how excited you are about this."

"Are you kidding? This stuff is the real deal. And it has provenance. When I sell a piece, I can tell the buyer that I handpicked the wood from a barn in Smith County." She turned toward the Gator and raised her voice. "I want as much of these front stacks as I can fit in my buddy's enclosed trailer. Okay if we come back one day next week?"

"Sure thing. If you let me know when, I'll get my boys out here to help you load it up."

"How old are they?"

"Fifteen and seventeen."

She nodded. "I'll pay them for the labor. Can I load some of these smaller pieces in the Gator to take today?"

He nodded, and she bent to select an armload of shorter boards that would easily fit in the back of her SUV.

"Can't leave without a taste, huh?" Maggie asked.

"You weren't complaining when I said the same thing this morning." Ally winked.

Maggie flushed, but her smile said she enjoyed the banter. "Shut up and load me up." She held out her arms.

"I'm not touching that one." Ally laughed as she carefully laid several boards across Maggie's outstretched arms.

Chapter Sixteen

Maggie put her lasagna into the oven and closed the door. Earlier, she'd made a tossed salad, and when the pasta dish was almost done, she would throw in a loaf of frozen garlic bread. When she was certain things were under control in the kitchen, she headed for her bedroom to shower and change.

She showered quickly, taking time to run a razor over her legs. And when she got out, she moisturized with her favorite lotion, thick and satiny, and smelling of blackberries and amber. She dressed with both comfort and style in mind, pairing drawstring linen pants with a bold-printed, sleeveless cotton shirt. Though Ally had tossed the idea of visiting Maggie's apartment out almost casually, for some reason, Maggie now thought of tonight as a real date. And she wanted Ally to think she looked pretty.

After spending most of the day with Ally yesterday, she'd returned home in the late afternoon with little desire to complete her tasks. She'd made a simple dinner, paid some bills that wouldn't wait much longer, and went to bed early. She'd unlocked her tablet and found an ebook she'd been putting off starting, only laying it down when her tired eyes wouldn't focus on the words.

So this morning, between loads of laundry, she'd cleaned her apartment thoroughly. She wasn't one of those weirdos who enjoyed cleaning. Rather, she saw it as a necessary task that she made bearable by streaming her favorite station on Amazon music.

She gave her bedroom onc final check before heading to the main living area to do the same there. She'd just finished lighting some candles when the doorbell rang. After counting to five, so as not to appear too eager, she opened the door. Ally waited on the landing outside her apartment holding a pie.

She'd spent more time with Ally in the last forty-eight hours than she had with anyone since her ex. Yet, looking at her now, she wanted to pull her inside and shove her up against her front door. The V-neck of Ally's T-shirt begged for her lips against the hollow between Ally's collarbones.

"It's not flowers. It's store-bought. And if you'd already planned for dessert, well, you can never have too many sweets." She held out the pie as she stepped inside.

"It's great. And I don't have anything for dessert." Maggie took the pie, kissed Ally's mouth, then went to the kitchen and deposited it on the counter.

Ally followed, and as soon as Maggie's hands were empty, she wrapped her arm around Maggie's waist and drew her in for a more thorough kiss. "It's apple," she said between kisses.

"My favorite kind."

"Dinner smells amazing."

"The lasagna still has about twenty minutes. I'd planned for us to open that wine on the counter and sit on the sofa like civilized women." She grasped the front of Ally's shirt and tugged her even closer. "But now, I'm getting some other ideas about how we could spend that time."

"I like spontaneity." Ally winked, bracketed her hands on Maggie's hips, then slid them around to her butt.

Maggie narrowed her eyes. "You want to think you do. But I suspect you prefer things to have order." As soon as she said it, she wished she hadn't. She didn't want to take their conversation into a serious place just now. Given the chaotic nature Ally had described in her family, Maggie understood her need for predictability.

"I'm making strides."

"You are. Taking time off to grow your business, for example. Have I told you how impressive that is?" Maggie clasped Ally's hand and led her toward the bedroom.

"I'm all for you being impressed by me." Ally pulled back with her own hand, giving token resistance, though her eyes said she was all in. "Where are you taking me?"

"Don't you want the tour? You've already seen the living room and kitchen. This is my bedroom." She stepped back and let Ally precede her into the room.

"It's nice. Light. Airy. It suits you."

Maggie tried to see what Ally was seeing. The walls were the same neutral shade as every other apartment in the complex. The only bit of color from the room came from the pale-yellow and gray comforter on her queen bed. She'd have preferred a king, but her apartment-sized bedroom wasn't large enough. No photos stood on her nightstand, only a simple lamp and a wireless charging dock for her phone. But Ally saw something in this room that fit her. She wasn't sure if that was insightful or sad—maybe both. Or maybe she should stop reading too much into polite comments when she had a beautiful woman in her bedroom.

Ally turned to face her and said, "You've got me in your room now. What do you plan to do with me?"

Responding to the challenge in Ally's eyes, Maggie moved next to the bed, beside her. "Turn around."

Ally smiled, and then, not challenging the direction, she turned away from Maggie.

Maggie placed her hand in the center of Ally's back and pushed Ally's upper body onto the bed, facedown. Ally's arm splayed out instinctively, and she didn't quite catch herself. Maggie reached around and unfastened Ally's khaki shorts, then tugged them down, leaving them pooled at Ally's feet.

Maggie bent, lying against her back to speak close to her ear. "Later we'll have a drink and polite conversation over dinner. But first, I need to put my hands on you."

"What are you waiting for?" Ally kicked one leg free from her shorts so she could spread her legs a little farther.

Ally's willingness bumped Maggie's arousal. Ally's head was down, her posture both relaxed and anticipatory at the same time. Her back sloped gracefully from between her shoulders to her ass. And her legs flexed as if waiting for Maggie to lean into her. When Maggie traced the line of Ally's spine, her fingers tingled against her warm, soft skin. Ally's legs twitched, and she lifted her hips, inviting the next touch—practically begging for it, really.

"Maggie."

"Are you ready for me?" She reached between Ally's legs and laid her palm against damp cotton. Her own knees nearly buckled. She couldn't wait much longer to touch her. "You are."

"So ready."

Maggie shoved her underwear aside and entered her smoothly but firmly. Ally arched and pushed back to meet Maggie's thrust. As Maggie hugged close to get a better angle, Ally's hip bumped her crotch. Maggie pressed into her, seeking just a little pressure—a fraction of relief for the pounding between her legs.

"I can—" Ally swept her arm along the bed, reaching for Maggie.

"No. This is for you." She captured Ally's hand, then directed it underneath Ally until she cupped her own breast. "If you want to touch something, start there." She squeezed her fingers around Ally's, pinching her nipple. She kept her hand resting over Ally's even when Ally took over toying with her own breast. She paced the thrusts of her other hand with Ally's.

Ally tensed beneath her, practically chanting for her not to stop. Maggie wouldn't—not yet. Even when Ally's moans crescendoed, then stopped and she sagged beneath her, Maggie continued to pump her fingers, slowing only slightly. When, with a gasp and a whispered curse, Ally began to thrust against her again, Maggie circled her arm around Ally's hip and rubbed two fingers against Ally's clit.

The speed of Ally's second orgasm surprised them both. She cried out and pushed back hard, seeking strong, steady pressure as she pulsed around Maggie's fingers. Maggie obliged, sinking into her and holding her through each trembling breath. As Ally's breathing slowed, her legs went limp, and she rested her weight more fully on the bed.

Maggie crawled up and flopped down on her back next to Ally. She tangled her fingers with Ally's, delighting in the pull of soreness already setting into her arm muscles.

"If I had anything other than Jell-O in my body right now, I'd climb up there with you. As it is, I'm going to stay right here." Ally's torso lay on the bed, and her legs stretched out behind her.

A singsongy chime came from the kitchen.

"Time's up," Maggie said, rolling toward Ally. She nuzzled into her neck.

"Oh, thank God. I was afraid you might go for three. And I'm not sure I'd have survived that."

"I wasn't. But that's an idea for after we get some carbs in you."

"Sure. Say, do you mind bringing my plate up and putting it here in front of me so I don't have to get up?"

Maggie laughed. She shoved off the bed and, still holding Ally's hand, pulled Ally with her. "Let's go. I've worked up an appetite."

❖

"Would you pour the wine? I have a white chilling in the fridge." Maggie bent to remove the lasagna from the oven.

"Sure."

Maggie straightened and pivoted to set the casserole dish on the trivet on the counter. Ally stood in front of the fridge with a wine bottle in one hand and a small card in the other, looking at Maggie quizzically.

"The opener is over there. It's one of those electric gadgets." Ally didn't move. "I got distracted and didn't put the bread in. But I'll do it now. We should let that pasta cool so we don't strip a layer off the roof of our mouths anyway."

"What is this?" Ally held out a business card. "Why do you have a card for a gun shop?"

"I stopped by there one day, and the saleswoman gave me that." She'd stuck it under a magnet on the fridge and, frankly, had forgotten about it, even after she went to the range with Charlie.

"And you forgot you had it?" Ally's condescending tone grated. She seemed to expect Maggie to deny the intent behind the visit.

"I put it there on the fridge so I'd know where it was when I was ready to make a decision."

"Are you thinking about purchasing a gun?"

"Maybe."

"Why would you want to do that?"

"For self-defense."

"No, no." Ally raised a finger in front of her. "One of those classes where you learn to beat up on the dude in the overly padded suit. That's self-defense. This," she waved her hand away from her body as if the card itself was as offensive as what it represented, "this is just stupid."

Ally's self-righteous tone riled Maggie, not to mention her use of the word stupid. "While I appreciate your *opinion*, sleeping with me doesn't give you the right to tell me what to do."

"Whoa. I'm not trying to tell you what to do. This is just—not what I expected. Why would you want a gun?" Ally tossed the card onto the counter. But Maggie imagined that she'd rather have thrown it in the trash can.

"I don't ever want to be just a victim again."

"The odds of that happening to you again—"

"It won't. Next time I'll fight back." Maggie smothered the urge to try to explain what she'd felt like that evening. Ally would probably never be able to understand what it was like to be powerless. And it didn't matter. This was her decision, not Ally's. "Can we table this discussion in favor of dinner? I really am starving."

"Sure." Ally turned away to open the wine, but given the stiff set of her shoulders, Maggie didn't think this conversation was over.

By the time Maggie had plated the lasagna, the bread was ready. Ally set a glass of wine on the counter beside Maggie and wandered over to the eat-in area on the other side of the L-shaped countertop. The small rectangular table with two chairs on one side and a narrow bench on the other had been one of Maggie's favorite furniture purchases when she first moved in. But she didn't use it when she ate alone, so the corner of it had ended up as a catch-all for mail and bills she needed to pay later.

She brought their plates over and returned for her wine. Ally sat on the bench side and folded her hands in her lap. Maggie considered taking the other end of the bench, to be close to her, but thought that might be awkward, so she pulled out one of the chairs.

"This is good. Thanks for making it," Ally said after a few bites.

"I'd cook more, but I abhor going to the grocery store. So I often just grab takeout on the way home. There's a little deli on my route that does great subs and salads."

"You should try one of those meal-delivery services."

"I've thought about that. If I do, I'll let you know what I think."

Ally made a small sound that could either be agreement or simply a lack of anything else to say.

They ate, in the midst of the longest lull in their conversations since they first met. Maggie's frustration built along with the tension between them. They'd been having this amazing weekend.

She had a myriad of physical and emotional stuff to dissect later, but she'd been feeling good about everything between them and had even started to hope they could figure out a way through the inevitable complication of the criminal trial. And *gun control* would be their insurmountable barrier?

She lifted her napkin off her lap and dabbed at her mouth, then dropped it on the table next to her plate. "Why is this such a problem for you?"

"It's fine."

"Then why are you pouting?"

"I'm not."

"You are. Since you seem intent on ruining our evening, we might as well talk about it."

"Okay." Ally set her fork down a bit too forcefully on her plate, wincing as it clanged.

Maggie made a go-ahead motion with her hand.

"For starters, I'm not a fan of private citizens arming themselves."

"I'm not asking you to buy a gun."

"Just to be okay with you having one?"

She started to remind Ally that since they didn't have a future, it shouldn't matter to her if Maggie bought one. But her chest ached just thinking about losing this amazing connection just when they'd taken it to the next level.

"You should respect my right to own one under the laws as they currently stand. Especially if it makes me feel safe. I got robbed."

"The gun wasn't even loaded."

"I didn't know that when he threatened me, did I?" In fact, she hadn't found out until later that Carey Rowe had claimed the gun wasn't loaded. Charlie had told her when she called to inform Maggie that he'd been arrested. She tried to remember if she'd told Ally. Or had Ally learned that from Carey?

"So, if you'd had a gun, would you have shot my brother?"

Ally looked like she immediately wanted to pull that question back, and Maggie almost wished she could, so she wouldn't have to consider it.

"I don't know."

"Should you really be carrying around a gun if you don't think you could use it?"

"That's not what I said."

"Well, then what are you saying?"

"I don't know what I would have done if I'd had a gun that day. But I'm not the same person now that I was then, either." She'd changed in so many ways. Whereas before she'd let things happen and accepted them as fate, now she wanted to take control of her life.

"And now you know what you'd do?"

"I don't want to shoot anyone. The thought that I could take a life—"

"That's just great. He's done some stupid shit. But he's still my brother, and I don't want him dead." Ally surged off the bench and strode to the living-room area, pacing in front of the coffee table.

"I don't want anyone dead, either. But if it's them or me…" Maggie followed, though more slowly. She stopped behind the couch, leaving it as a barrier between them. She wanted to understand Ally's family stress around Carey's actions, but how could that compare to what she'd gone through? Carey had made a decision to do what he did, and maybe his addiction had contributed to it. But not all addicts committed robbery. Maggie hadn't had a choice in her part of their interaction. She'd been in the wrong place, and for whatever reason, Carey had targeted her.

"Are those the only options?"

"I didn't think so. Before." She picked at her left thumbnail, worrying a piece of dry skin. "Now, in the aftermath of what happened to me, I feel the need to examine what will make me feel secure again."

"And you think a gun will do that? How many times do you really hear about someone justifiably defending themselves with a firearm versus the people who commit crimes with guns?"

"So we're back to a gun-control debate?" Maybe they would be on more solid ground if they returned to a purely political conversation, because letting Ally's emotions get inside her was nearly as bad as examining her own feelings on the subject.

"How do you think the bad guys get them? They aren't out there buying them legally."

How many questions was Ally going to fire at her? And why did she have to be the one with all the answers? "I don't know. How did your brother get a gun?"

Ally made a sound like a growl in her throat as she turned away. Whatever she mumbled, Maggie couldn't make it out.

"Ally?"

"I can't."

She couldn't what? She couldn't believe that her brother had committed a crime? She couldn't believe Maggie? "I thought we were past the point of pretending this didn't happen. I get that he's your brother, but even if you don't want to believe he's capable of robbery, he had a gun on him when he was arrested. So where did he get it?" Her voice rose as she spoke.

"From me." Ally spun around and jerked to a stop, her expression a mask of agony. "It was my gun. Er, rather, my father's. But he stole it from my mother's house, where I'd left it."

Maggie stared at her. Even when she played the words back in her head, they still didn't make sense. The pistol that Carey Rowe had used to rob her had belonged to Ally. She said he'd stolen it, right? Ally didn't put the gun in his hands. Not really. So then why did she feel like that's exactly what happened?

"Maggie, I—oh, hell, what am I doing?" Ally rubbed two fingers and a thumb across her brow. "I should go."

"Yes. I think you should." Her voice sounded distant, like she heard herself from underwater.

Ally bit her lip, then gave an awkward nod before she went to the door.

The soft click of the latch as Ally carefully closed the door annoyed Maggie more than if she'd just slammed it behind her. Maggie circled the couch and sank down onto the center cushion. Why had she ever thought she could separate her feelings for Ally from what her brother had done?

❖

Yes, I think you should. Maggie had seemed so composed when she said the words. But given her shocked expression, more emotions might have been brewing below the surface.

As Ally got in her car and backed out of the parking spot, she was experiencing a cauldron of feelings herself—none of them good. She'd gone from having the best sex of her life, to arguing, to not knowing if she'd ever see Maggie again in a little over an hour. If she hadn't been in the middle of it all, she wouldn't have believed her evening could turn to such shit so quickly.

She left Maggie's apartment complex still picking apart their conversation. In the beginning, she hadn't known why things were getting so out of hand. The idea of Maggie buying a gun had stirred a visceral reaction in her that she had trouble sorting out. Yes, she was generally anti-gun. But that felt a bit hypocritical since technically she'd had a gun herself.

She'd held on to it because it belonged to her father. She had thought once about getting rid of it, but how did one dispose of a gun they no longer wanted? She remembered feeling funny at the time about selling it, not knowing who might eventually own it or what they would do with it. Which was ironic, now, given what Carey had done.

And Maggie was right. She really had no authority to tell Maggie she couldn't own one. She'd never been one of those people who had to force their opinions on other people. So why was this different?

"Are you fucking kidding me?" Ally grumbled as a white pickup truck pulled out and into her lane. She slammed her hand against the steering wheel and cursed again, both because of the idiot in front of her and because, damn, that hurt.

At the next stop light, the idiot put on his signal light for the same right turn that Ally needed to make. She considered going straight instead and taking a longer route home. But maybe extending her drive in her current mood wasn't the best idea. She turned and fell in behind him. When their side of the road split into two lanes, she whipped her car into the left lane and floored the accelerator to fly by him, sparing him only one glance in the rearview mirror. Once she was clear of his truck, that stress disappeared, and she could focus again on the other issue burning an ulcer into her stomach.

Why did she hate the idea of Maggie owning a gun so damn much? Maggie was afraid, and a gun might make her feel safe. The answer was clear, even if she didn't want to acknowledge it. Because her brother had germinated that fear. And he wouldn't have had access to that firearm if she hadn't been careless with it. She'd treated it like any piece of memorabilia instead of with the respect it deserved.

Chapter Seventeen

And you haven't heard from her since?" Kathi asked when Ally finished filling her in on most of their disagreement. She'd glossed over her part in Carey obtaining the gun and focused on their difference of opinion on gun control.

"No." She'd been avoiding her friends, pretending she had a deadline on a project. But after a week of Ally dodging their calls and texts, Kathi had cornered her in the garage.

"Have you reached out?"

"I texted her. She didn't respond." After moping around the house for two days, binge-watching romantic comedies, and eating too much chocolate, she'd made herself get up and move. She'd forced herself to go for a long walk in her neighborhood every morning in order to define a start to her day.

She'd borrowed her friend's trailer and gone back for that load of barn wood. Then she'd spent hours in the garage, churning out small projects that didn't need a lot of focus. She'd already sold two of the reclaimed-wood serving trays online. And she'd worked out a cool design for a side table using scrap wood.

"One text?"

Ally didn't have to say anything to confirm the answer.

"Come on, Al. This woman isn't worth more than one text?"

"It's complicated." The guilt about that damn gun was going to destroy her. She couldn't even bring herself to admit to Kathi where Carey had gotten it.

"It's really not. You're afraid, and you're hiding behind this bullshit about your brother being the guy who mugged her."

"It's not bullshit."

"Except that it is. If you didn't believe you could get past all that, you wouldn't have let yourself get in this deep."

"It's not serious. We—aren't—weren't serious." Ally picked up a small triangle of scrap wood and toyed with it.

"Bullshit."

"Stop saying that." Kathi had her on that one. She could try to lie to herself, but the truth was, she wanted to be serious about Maggie.

If they'd met under different circumstances, Maggie was exactly the kind of woman she was looking for. Maggie was an amazing mix of sweet and sexy. She made Ally laugh. On the way home after their trip to the barn in Smith County, Ally had let herself daydream about more weekends together.

"Why are you arguing *for* Maggie now? You were against me being involved with her."

"Sure. But that was before I met her. I've never seen you happier than you've been since you two started spending time together. And she won over my kids, which says something. Those two are surprisingly good judges of character."

"They really are." For a second Ally's heart felt lighter, until reality settled back in. "But none of that changes our circumstances. Can you see me introducing her to Ma? And how could she ever feel safe around Carey?"

"You think he's dangerous?" Kathi had been around Carey when he worked on the same crew as Ally.

"No. I mean, I never thought so before. But when I separate him from the situation and think about someone—anyone—pointing a gun at Maggie—"

"Like you'd do anything, including physical violence, to keep that from happening. Like a lifetime behind bars wouldn't be punishment enough."

"Yeah." Ally nodded. She started to straighten the tools on her worktable, putting them back in their rightful place.

Kathi put one hand on her shoulder and the other on her arm, halting her busywork. "I know how you feel. When I think about anything happening to Dani, or the kids, I feel the same way. Because I love them."

"I sure hope you do. They are your family, after all. If you didn't—" Her brain was a little slow putting together what Kathi was saying. As soon as she did, her language skills seized up, and she could only shake her head.

"I think you care about her a lot more than you want to admit."

"No. I—what—"

Her phone rang before she could gather her thoughts. She glanced at the screen, and her mother's name reminded her of the many reasons Kathi had to be wrong. She didn't love Maggie. She couldn't. She held up the phone so Kathi could see before she pressed the button to answer the call.

She couldn't make out Shirley's words through her crying, but she thought she heard her brother's name. "Ma? What's going on? You have to slow down and breathe so I can understand you."

This time she definitely heard Carey's name and—was that a hospital? "Ma? Where is Carey?"

"Ms. Rowe?" Another feminine voice came on the phone. Ally could still hear Shirley crying in the background.

"It's Becker. Ally."

"Right. I'm sorry. I'm a nurse at Skyline Hospital. Your brother was brought in to our emergency department by ambulance. We have him stabilized, and the doctor is in with him now. Your mother is asking that you come down here. Do you think that's possible?"

"Of course. What happened?"

"The doctor can advise you further when you get here. But I can tell you it appears to be an accidental overdose."

"Okay. Would you tell Ma I'm on my way."

She hung up and turned to Kathi, suddenly at a loss as to what to do next.

"I heard. Do you want me to drive you?"

"Thanks. But I'm okay to drive. And I'll probably have to take Ma home at some point. I'm sure she rode in the ambulance." She stood in the living room glancing around. Where were her keys?

"Do you have your wallet?"

She patted her pockets. "No."

"Go get it. I'll find your keys."

She ran down the hallway to her bedroom and grabbed her wallet off the nightstand and shoved it into her pocket. Back in the living room, Kathi held out her keys and a light jacket.

"Call us if you need anything at all." Kathi squeezed her in a quick embrace, then guided her toward the door.

❖

During the entire drive to the hospital, she tried to imagine what she would encounter when she arrived. Carey had overdosed, the woman had said. Accidental. What did that mean? How did one accidentally overdose? She supposed it meant he hadn't been trying to kill himself. That was good news. But he had to have been trying to get high, right? The panic in her mother's voice reverberated in her head, but, she reminded herself, the nurse had said he was stable. Certainly the odds for him taking a bad turn now were slim, weren't they?

At the hospital, she followed the signs to the emergency department. She gave Carey's name at a desk near the waiting room and was directed through a set of double doors to a treatment room. She'd just passed through the doors when she saw Shirley, nearly collapsed against the wall in the hallway. A tall man in a white coat held her arm and bent to speak to her.

"Ma," Ally called as she approached.

Shirley turned and practically sobbed. "Ally, thank God." She looked at the benevolent man, still hovering beside her. "This is my daughter, Ally."

"I'm Dr. Wilson. I've been treating your brother." He offered his hand, and Ally grasped it. His handshake was firm and warm, and his eyes held the perfect amount of sympathy and intelligence. She immediately trusted his medical opinion, then wondered if he'd learned that skill in medical school or came by it naturally.

"What happened?" Ally directed her question to Dr. Wilson, but Shirley began speaking instead.

"I thought he was napping. I went to tell him dinner was ready, and he wouldn't wake up. I called 9-1-1."

Ally shoved her reaction to Shirley's words into a box to examine later. She turned, shielding herself slightly from Shirley, and addressed the doctor. "The nurse on the phone said he was okay."

"Okay is a relative term. He ingested opioids that were probably cut with fentanyl. He's lucky your mother found him when she did, or this could have been much worse. He's stable. He's awake and mostly lucid. But this incident should be taken very seriously."

"I understand."

"An addiction counselor will come by in a little while."

"He doesn't need that," Shirley said.

"Ma'am, the counselor can talk to you as well. Families of addicts—"

"I said, we're fine. Just get my son well so we can take him home."

He was right. About Carey. And about their family. But Ally didn't give him any indication that she held a different opinion than Shirley. For some reason, she didn't want this man—this doctor—to think of them as the kind of family for whom overdosing on illicit drugs was commonplace. But they were, now, weren't they? Carey was an addict, and if the statistics she'd been reading were correct, he was likely to lose the struggle to maintain his sobriety several times during his recovery process. She didn't know how to handle this realization.

"Can we see him?"

He nodded and glanced at his watch. "Certainly. I'll be back to check on him in a little bit. We're going to admit him. If we can get him a room upstairs, you'll be allowed to go up there with him as well."

"I don't think she's leaving his side." Ally tilted her head in Shirley's direction.

"Let the nurse know if you need a cot for her to sleep on."

"Thank you, Doctor."

He nodded and gave her a sympathetic smile that seemed genuine—or maybe he'd practiced it with a lot of patients' families before her. He gestured to the security guard to open the doors leading to the emergency department. "Go through those doors. He's in the second room on the right."

Shirley hurried into Carey's room, and Ally followed more slowly. He lay on a hospital gurney, a light sheet over his body. Several machines seemed to be standing by in case he took a turn for the worse, but nothing appeared hooked up to him. Maybe they just stocked all the rooms with that equipment. She took inventory of the medical devices for several more seconds to avoid looking at Carey.

When she finally did, she had trouble meeting his gaze. He looked exhausted. Dark smudges colored the sunken half-moons under his eyes. He'd gained a little weight since she'd seen him last, but his skin was pale. His hair curled at his temples and around his ears like it did when he'd been sweating.

Shirley grasped his hand and half draped herself over his bed.

"Hey, Ma."

"Okay. Let's let him breathe." Ally pushed a chair closer to his bedside. "Sit here with him." Ally paced to the window and leaned against the sill. Now that the initial shock had faded, and she could see he was awake and presumably all right, her anger at him was building at a furious pace. Her face felt hot, and she was certain that spot on her left cheek that got red when she was mad would be glowing by now.

"How're you feeling?" Shirley asked.

"The doc says I can expect to feel like crap for a couple of days. Some of that's from the Narcan the paramedics gave me, and some from going through withdrawal again. Though it shouldn't be as bad as last time."

"How long are they keeping you here?"

"Probably just overnight. But that's not the worst of it."

"What do you mean?" Shirley raised her head.

"When Ma called 9-1-1 they sent the police, too. One of them was in here with me while you were talking to the doctor."

"Makes sense. They probably don't want you getting violent with the paramedics." Ally didn't blame the paramedics. With the rise in opioid abuse, they likely had a protocol that triggered a police response on any drug-related calls.

"I wasn't violent."

"I mean in general—as a policy. They would send police, too—I get it."

He looked like he still wanted to argue about his own personal situation. "Anyway, the cop said once the judge finds out about this, he'll probably revoke my bond. I'll have to go back to jail until the trial."

Two months. And that's if the court date stood. Jorge had told her there was always the chance their trial could get bumped from the courtroom for a higher-priority case. If that happened, they would get a new date, but it could be several months more or longer.

"I told you we should have hired him a better attorney." Shirley straightened and leveled an accusatory glare at Ally.

"Me? This is my fault?" She waved her hand at the room

around them. Ally whipped her eyes to Carey, but he didn't look like he was ready to jump in. "I can't—do this right now." She made it as far as the door before Carey spoke up.

"Ma? Can you go find a vending machine and get me a soda?"

"Just ring the thing and ask the nurse for one."

"Please, Ma."

Shirley sighed and dug through her purse. "I don't have any cash."

Ally pulled several bills out of her pocket, two ones and a five, and shoved them into Shirley's hand. She waited until Shirley had gone before turning on Carey. She'd make him regret that he kept her from leaving just now.

"What the fuck happened?" She strode across the room and grasped the rail at the side of his bed until her knuckles glowed white against the back of her hand.

He shook his head and looked away.

"If you wanted to ignore me, you could have let me leave." She moved to stand in his sight line. "What did you take?"

"That isn't your business."

"The hell it isn't. When I get called to the hospital because you've overdosed, it becomes my business."

"I didn't ask you to come down here."

She scoffed. "Yeah, 'cause she wouldn't have made my life hell if I didn't come running when she called."

"That's your deal with Ma. Not mine. I got my own shit to deal with."

"You can't separate the two of you. She expects me to take care of you and her both."

"I don't need you to take care of me."

She tilted her head and pointedly looked him up and down, lying in his hospital bed. "All evidence to the contrary."

"I was doing just fine. Reuben was giving me some work, under the table, until the trial. Them someone narced to his boss. He said he couldn't have me on a job site for liability reasons."

"So that's it? You lose a job, and that justifies throwing your sobriety away?"

"You don't know how hard this is." He raised his voice to match hers, but his was hoarser.

"You've stolen from your family, lost your job, been arrested for armed robbery, and now you're in the hospital from an overdose. Do you actually have to die before you'll wake up?"

"Allison Marie Becker." Shirley stood in the doorway, holding a can of soda and looking shocked to find her practically screaming.

"Ma—"

"Carey is sick. You shouldn't be shouting at him."

Ally looked from her mother back to Carey. He at least looked embarrassed. "He overdosed on God-knows-what drugs, no doubt laced with something equally dangerous. And you're not doing him any favors by pretending he has the flu."

She strode out of his room, ignoring Shirley when she called her name again. Shirley could find her own ride home. Ally was tired of babysitting the two of them.

Chapter Eighteen

How come your friend isn't here to show me how to do the carrots?"

"She's very busy. But I'm sure she wishes she was." Dani smoothed a hand over June's hair and met Ally's eyes over the top of June's head.

Ally nodded but didn't say anything. She hadn't heard from Maggie in a month, and she'd been miserable. At one point, the heartbroken part of her had decided to let the garden boxes go to weeds, as if proving that abandoning Maggie's project meant she could also let Maggie go. But she didn't want to tarnish the memory of Maggie's enthusiasm about the garden and her gratitude for using the space. So she faithfully watered the plants and pulled the weeds, and found she enjoyed watching the tomatoes grow and ripen. And that tiny, petty part enjoyed her tomato-and-mayonnaise sandwiches a little more thinking, *Maggie is missing out on this.*

Grayson yanked a carrot free from the ground, flinging soil as he waved it victoriously over his head. "Mommy, I pulled the carrot all by myself."

"Let me see it." June moved quickly to his side. She rubbed her hands together, brushing the dirt off the purple gardening gloves Ally had bought for her. Grayson's were lime-green. They bent their matching honey-blond heads together and studied the vegetable. "Mama, they do look like the kind we buy in the store. Only dirtier."

"Put it in the basket, sweetie."

He dropped it alongside the bounty that Kathi, Dani, and Ally had already helped them pick.

"You guys should take some of this stuff home. I'll never eat this many cucumbers, and I don't even like carrots."

"I don't like carrots either," Grayson said in solidarity.

"Yes, you do, sweetie." Kathi touched his shoulder. "And these will be extra tasty because you picked them yourself." She gave Ally a stern look.

"You know, you're right. They probably will taste better than store-bought ones. Maybe I'll keep some, and you can take the rest."

Dani picked another cucumber and added it to the pile. "I'm already looking forward to a fresh cucumber-and-tomato salad."

"Salad? Ew." June wrinkled her nose as she grasped a carrot stalk and tugged.

"Why do I get the feeling that you and I are going to be eating all these delicious veggies by ourselves?" Kathi asked Dani.

They finished harvesting, then went inside to divide up their haul. Dani stood at the sink, carefully washing each vegetable. Ally dug a medium-sized bowl out of the cabinet for her share and put the rest in a reusable grocery bag for Kathi and Dani to take home.

"Can we talk?" Ally asked Dani as she moved next to her and leaned against the counter.

Dani and Kathi exchanged a look that was so communicative Ally had to turn away. Would she ever share a bond like that with another person?

"Hey, Grayson, do you still have that dinosaur card game in your backpack?" Kathi asked.

"Uh-huh."

"Let's go in the living room and play. Junie, do you want to come with us?"

She nodded and followed them out of the room. Ally was so grateful to have them in her life. She'd never had the urge for kids, but she really did adore those two. And Dani and Kathi were the best friends she'd ever had.

"Those are some great kids you have there," she said.

"We like to think so." Dani dried her hands on a towel, then set it on the counter and gave Ally her full attention. "What's going on?"

Ally didn't know how to wade into the conversation, so she cannonballed into the middle. "How did you forgive your mom?"

Dani grimaced. "Partly time. And recognizing that I had to stop trying to make her who I wanted her to be and accept who she was. I didn't have a mom who baked cookies and went to my school functions. As an adult I was very aware of what I had missed out on. But she got sober. And she was trying to make her life better. And if she and I were going to salvage a healthy relationship, I had to let go of the things I wished I'd had in childhood, because I sure as hell couldn't change it."

"Why did you have to do all the letting go and changing? It was her mess."

"She did her share, too. We reached a point where I realized that she was doing her part and I was holding us back. Mom and I had a long talk once about where everything went wrong for her. She had a rough start in life, too—worse than mine. But that's her story to tell. Nobody taught her how moms are supposed to love their kids. Once I figured out she started drinking because she hated herself, and not because she hated me, it was easier to forgive her. And to realize that I wanted to do better for my own kids, and that wasn't going to happen if I carried all the dark stuff everywhere I went."

"You're an amazing mother."

"Well, I owe that partly to my psychiatrist, but mostly to Kathi. She was the first person in my life to show me selfless love."

Ally chuckled. "Yeah. Me, too."

"Are you thinking about forgiving Shirley?"

"It's not like she's asking for forgiveness. What do you think you would have done if your mother hadn't gotten sober?"

Dani shrugged. "That's a tough one. Our adult relationships with our parents are tricky. On the one hand, they're our moms. Aren't we supposed to love them unconditionally? But when there's drama and conflict, you might not keep around a friend you had that kind of relationship with. So where do you draw the line?"

"That's a good question. I don't think she sees anything wrong with our relationship, as long as I'm doing things her way. So, it's on me to change it." Shirley wasn't helpless, but the less she did for herself, the less she wanted to do.

"I don't think it's wrong for you to ask for respect for who you are and what you need."

"I don't have any real memories of her with my dad. But with Carey's—he never hit her, or us. Yet he was a very controlling dude. She didn't do anything without his say-so. And I'm just realizing that I blamed her for being a doormat. But he had her so convinced that she was nothing without him. When he left her, she was depressed for over a year. She never really recovered. Now she depends on me and Carey for everything—mostly me."

"And you've resented her for it." Dani didn't ask. Because she didn't have to.

"I've lived my entire life just trying not to turn into her." The admission wasn't as difficult as Ally might have thought. "But right now, I'm struggling more with my relationship with Carey."

"And Maggie complicated that."

Ally nodded. "Absolutely. But now that's a non-issue. Either way, I'm not ready to write my brother off forever."

"Understandable. But your relationship with him will never

be the same. It can't be if it's going to work. He's an addict—for the rest of his life. His first priority now has to be staying sober."

"And mine should be to support that attempt, at least where he and I are concerned."

Dani's smile carried a trace of the sadness Ally had been drowning in. "It feels a little like he gets a pass for infinity, doesn't it?"

"It does."

"It took me a while to figure out it's just the opposite. You still need to hold him accountable, maybe even more so than ever." Dani squeezed Ally's shoulder. "And even if you don't always see it. Everything he does is more difficult for him now. If he truly wants to stay sober and be healthy, he's going to work harder than he ever has at anything."

"What do you think his chances are of being successful if they send him back to jail until the trial? Not to mention the fact that he's probably going to do time in prison."

"I don't know, hon. But I do think you need to let both him and your mother be responsible for what their own lives have become. I hate to see you keep sacrificing your own happiness to be the peacemaker for people who don't appreciate how wonderful you are."

They were treading dangerously close to Maggie again, and Ally didn't think she could go there.

"All of this letting go and acceptance you're preaching." She waved a hand in Dani's direction. "Do you know how hard that is?"

Dani nodded solemnly. "I do."

"Okay." Ally shook her hands out, as if she could fling free the heaviness of the conversation. "That's enough serious talk. Thanks for the therapy."

"Any time." Dani wrapped an arm around her shoulders and pulled her close.

Ally sank into the comfort of that hug, letting the warmth envelop her. When she heard a throat clear behind her, she looked over her shoulder. Kathi stood at the entrance to the kitchen, both kids flanking her.

"Nobody told me it was family hug time." Kathi crossed the room and threw her arms around them both before Ally could move.

"Hugs," Grayson yelled as he and June flung their little bodies against their legs. Laughing, Ally reached back and placed her hand against his back, holding him to her.

Ally stood there in her kitchen surrounded by her family of choice, and only one thing was missing. She'd felt Maggie's absence all day and didn't think any amount of acceptance could make that void go away.

❖

"Can I get you ladies anything else?" The waiter set plates down in front of Maggie and Inga.

"We're good for now." Maggie picked up the small cup of dressing and poured it over her salad. Then she sifted through the lettuce with her fork, making sure some dressing got distributed throughout it. She hated reaching the bottom of a salad and finding plain lettuce.

"Salad again, huh? What is this healthy kick you've been on?" Inga picked up half of her meatloaf sandwich and took a big bite.

Vowing to be a better friend to Inga, Maggie had initiated a Tuesday lunch date. Their deal was that they had to leave the office, and their destination had to be within walking distance. Today, Inga had chosen a new place that boasted about their Southern specialties, like the side of fried okra on Inga's plate.

"It's a fried-chicken salad with a huge honey-and-butter biscuit on the side. What about that screams healthy to you?"

Inga shrugged. "Is Charlie coming?"

"She said she'd stop by if she didn't get called for a case."

Since the day they'd run into each other at the gun range, Charlie had been texting occasionally to check up on her. Without Ally, Maggie was lonely, but she hadn't confessed any of that to Charlie or to Inga. She simply kept her conversations with both focused on them, asking Inga questions about the baby, and getting Charlie to talk about her job and her own family.

The previous week, she'd included Charlie in their lunch hour, at Inga's insistence, and the two had hit it off right away. The plan had worked even better than Maggie expected, because while the two of them spent time getting to know each other, Maggie didn't have to talk.

She'd gotten Ally's *one* text and wanted to respond, but she didn't know what to say. Their difference of opinion about guns aside, the whole situation had only reminded Maggie that they hadn't had a future to begin with. She'd let herself become attached to Ally in a way that could only end in heartache, so she might as well deal with that pain right now rather than later.

"Tell me again why you aren't hooking up with Charlie?" Inga asked.

"I don't want to hook up with anyone."

Inga gave her a look that said she knew that wasn't true and that she knew exactly who Maggie wanted to be with. Before Maggie could respond, Charlie rounded the corner of their row of booths and strode toward them.

"Speak of the devil," Inga muttered.

"Sorry I'm late. I got hung up in an interview."

"Did you make him talk, or did he lawyer up?" Inga slid over to let Charlie into her side of the booth.

"You've been watching *Law and Order* reruns again, haven't you?" Ally said.

"I like to multitask during two a.m. feedings."

The waiter approached, and Charlie put in an order for a club sandwich with a side of pasta salad. As he walked away she said, "Maybe it'll be quick since no actual cooking's involved.

I can't stay long. We have another witness to meet with this afternoon." She snagged a piece of okra off Inga's plate. "Sorry if I interrupted. What were y'all talking about?"

"How Maggie needs to get back out there and start dating."

"No. *We* weren't."

"Why not?" Charlie grabbed a roll from the basket in the center of the table and tore off a chunk. "If we hadn't met on a case, I totally would have asked you out."

"And she'd have said yes, because you're hot." Inga sang the word hot in a high-pitched voice as she leaned into Charlie's shoulder.

"I would say I'm flattered, but I'm not looking to date right now," Maggie said.

Charlie didn't look too broken up by her rejection.

"Because you're hung up on another kind of inappropriate relationship." When Maggie turned to Inga in surprise, Inga raised her brows. "Did you think I hadn't picked up on that?" To Charlie, she said, "She's been—dating, I guess—Ally Becker." She could always count on Inga to lay out the truth.

"Ally Becker, as in Carey Rowe's sister?" Charlie asked. Maggie didn't know if she'd put together when they talked about her before that something more was going on.

"We're friends." Maggie didn't think she could sell the lie. But they weren't even friends now, were they?

"Friends who sleep together," Inga said.

"How do you know we slept together?"

"You just told me."

"Okay. Dial back the smug, Inga. God, remind me why we're friends again."

"Because I don't coddle you. And I put up with you when you shut down and don't tell me what's going on in your life"—she held up a hand to stall Maggie's interruption—"and I'm okay with that. I'm the needy one in our friendship. But you've had some big stuff happening lately, and I hope you know that I'm here if you need to talk."

"I do. There's really not much to discuss."

"It seems like there's something," Charlie said. "Whenever I ask how you're doing, you just say fine. I kind of assumed you were still dealing with the robbery and everything, but there's more, isn't there?"

Maggie sighed and set down her fork. So much for her stress-free lunches while Inga and Charlie distracted each other. "Ally and I aren't—anything, anymore."

"Oh, sweetie, I'm sorry." Inga reached across the table and covered her hand. "What happened?"

"Basically, we had a disagreement that we maybe could get past. But it brings to light all the other obstacles to a relationship between us, and, long story short, I haven't talked to her in over a month."

"Maybe that's for the best."

"How so?"

"What are you imagining is going to happen? That she's going to sit next to you in court and hold your hand while you put her brother in prison?"

"I know it's complicated. But we got involved in spite of that situation."

"*You* did."

"What does that mean?"

"I believe you're trying to get past who she is to be close to her. But are you really sure you know what her motives were?"

Maggie narrowed her eyes and waited, needing to hear Inga say aloud what she'd just implied.

"You said yourself that she knew about the relationship to your case before you did. Maybe it was even sooner than she let on."

Maggie didn't want to consider that the theory might be true. "No. She didn't seek me out. She was already seated in the café when I walked in. There were no tables left. Our first meeting was entirely by chance."

"And then?"

"I called her."

"After she made sure you took her number." Inga turned toward Charlie. "What do you think?"

Charlie gave Maggie an apologetic look, then said, "I think you should be careful."

"And I'm wondering why I introduced the two of you."

"Hold on. I'm not done. I don't necessarily agree with Inga. I've only seen this woman around you one time, in the lobby that day."

"That was immediately after I found out who she was."

"But I'm pretty good at reading people, and I didn't get a conniving vibe off her. She seemed genuinely concerned for you."

Maggie nodded. Not that she'd needed confirmation that Ally wasn't just out to con her. But it helped to have someone else say it.

"I don't know much about her. She was in court that day to support her brother, right? Are they close?"

"Yes."

"Parents still alive?"

"Their mom is very involved in their lives. But their dads aren't around."

"I can see that all being a sticky situation. So I say be careful. I'd hate to see you hurt if she decides being with you isn't worth the stress it puts on her relationship with her family."

"Well, it doesn't matter. Because I've already decided for her. I didn't respond when she reached out." Maggie picked up her fork again, but she'd lost her appetite, so she just pushed the remains of her salad around for the rest of their lunch.

Chapter Nineteen

Maggie stuck her head in Inga's office and knocked on the doorframe. Inga looked up from her paperwork and took off her reading glasses.

"Hey. I just wanted to remind you that I'm leaving early today."

"Oh, right. That thing with the DA."

Maggie nodded. A victim/witness coordinator with the district attorney's office had left a reminder message on her cell phone late last week. After the fight with Ally, she'd completely forgotten to call and schedule the pretrial conference. She'd returned the call when she got off work and set a late-afternoon appointment for this week.

She left the office and decided to walk the five blocks to the address she'd been given. She'd worn a light blouse and knee-length skirt that day, but even the shade from the towering buildings of downtown didn't abate the humid July air. When she arrived, she went straight to the lobby restroom, allowing the air-conditioning to cool her off. She blotted her face and neck with paper towel and fussed with her hair for a moment before leaving.

She took the elevator to the fourth floor and gave her name to the receptionist. Only a few minutes later, a tall African American woman came through a door behind the reception desk. Her quick stride, strong posture, and smart black pantsuit telegraphed confidence. Could this woman, please, be assigned to Maggie's case? She needed that energy.

"Ms. Davidson?" She slowed as she approached Maggie, leaving a respectful distance. Did she do that in deference to Maggie's status as a victim?

"Maggie."

"Maggie, I'm Sasha Westlake. I'm the prosecutor assigned to the state versus Carey Rowe."

Maggie grasped Sasha's outstretched hand. Did Sasha feel hers tremble when she said his name? She managed a firm handshake and didn't apologize for her slightly damp hand.

"Come on back." She led Maggie to a conference room just down the hall from reception.

"Make yourself comfortable."

Her offer to get comfortable felt futile. A large conference table dominated the room, the eight chairs around it basic black and chrome. The overall effect left the room feeling like an afterthought, although the blame probably fell to the same government underfunding she'd seen in her own office. She'd campaigned for two years to finally get a comfy desk chair.

She chose a spot at the side of the long conference table that allowed her to look out the window. When she swallowed, her throat felt sticky and dry. She should have accepted the receptionist's offer of a drink earlier.

"It's just going to be us today. The other attorney on the case had to go pick up his sick kid from school." Sasha sat across from her and opened a thick blue folder. "This is just a pretrial conference. We'll talk about your recollection of the events of that night. I'll review most of the questions I intend to ask you on the stand. Okay?" Sasha's eyes conveyed warmth and patience as she spoke to Maggie. But when she began leafing through the file in front of her, they looked sharp and alert.

Maggie nodded.

"Great. And as things evolve, if we have anything new to discuss, I'll have the victim/witness coordinator get in touch with you. You'll hear from her more than from me directly going forward. But I'm always available if you need to speak specifically to me."

For the next thirty minutes, Maggie recounted the details of the robbery, and Sasha occasionally stopped her with questions. When they took a break, Sasha pointed Maggie to a nearby restroom, and when she returned to the conference room, Sasha had brought them both back a bottle of water.

"This heat is killing me. And the air-conditioning in this building can't keep up."

"I hear you. They upgraded our system, and now it's supposed to be more efficient. But so far, it's just controlled remotely by some guy in another city building somewhere. The temperature swings seem even more dramatic."

"Great. They've been promising us an update as well. Thanks for dashing our hopes that things will be better then."

Maggie smiled. "Sorry."

Sasha smiled back, then closed her folder and set her pen down next to it. "I think that's it for my questions for now. You'll be fine on the stand, and I don't expect the defense to throw you any oddball questions."

"He won't try to make it look like I'm lying?"

"No. There isn't any question you were robbed. He won't want the jury to feel that he's attacking the victim. He'll look for a weak point in the evidence or something."

"Okay."

"The goal is a guilty verdict. I'm confident we can get that, in this case. Then the judge will set a sentencing date. Mr. Rowe likely will get time served for the time he's spent in jail, so that will be subtracted from his sentence."

"That was only a couple of days or a week, right?"

"Initially, yes. Plus, this last month."

"What do you mean?"

"I thought you'd been notified." Sasha flipped her file back open and consulted a page at the back. "He's been in jail again for nearly a month now."

"Why?" Had he committed another crime? How was Ally dealing with this?

"He violated the bond condition requiring him to stay clean. I'm so sorry. I thought someone from our office had called you. If nothing else, you can breathe easier until we go to trial. He's not getting out of jail before then."

"Oh, Ally," Maggie murmured.

"What's that?"

"Uh—nothing. No. No one called me."

"Apparently, he overdosed at home, and his mother had to call for paramedics."

Sasha walked Maggie back out to the lobby with a promise to get in touch if anything changed before the court date. Maggie rode down in the elevator, staring at the buttons while thinking about what Sasha had revealed.

Carey Rowe was back in jail. Sasha had said she could breathe easier. But Maggie didn't feel any more or less safe than she had before. Given what Ally had mentioned about his back injury on the job and eventual spiral into addiction to painkillers, she'd never felt that Carey was a continued threat to her. Her fear stemmed more from the awareness that danger existed—a fact she'd been able to ignore before the robbery.

Ally stepped into the visitation room at the detention center, searching for her mother and Carey. She didn't see them at any of the dozen tables spread throughout the space.

A uniformed guard approached her. "Ms. Becker?"

"Yes."

"The inmate is in a private room, because he requested a

conference with his attorney. This way." He led her to a door along the far wall. As they got closer, she could see into the room through a window, but nothing being said inside could be heard from the outside.

Ally had gotten stuck in traffic on the interstate, due to a vehicle accident. Just when she'd started to fear she would miss visiting hours altogether, traffic had started moving again.

"Sorry I'm late." She slipped into the chair next to Shirley, across from Carey and Jorge.

"Would you please talk some sense into your brother?"

Ally glanced at Carey. "What's going on?"

Shirley waved her hands in huge arcing circles. "Go ahead. Tell her what you're planning to do."

"Ma—"

Shirley exploded again. "He's going to plead guilty. Tell him how foolish that is." She turned to Carey. "Listen to your sister."

"I think it's a good idea," Ally said.

"What? Don't listen to her. What the hell are you saying?"

Ally met Carey's eyes for a long, serious moment. "Is the ADA still willing to reduce your sentence in exchange for the plea?" Carey deferred to Jorge, who nodded. "Then you're doing the right thing."

"No. We're going to fight this." Shirley's face grew red, and she jabbed a finger with every word. "Don't let that little bitch lie—"

"Whoa, Ma." Ally bristled, prepared to defend Maggie. In fact, she was ready to out her relationship with Maggie right here and now, if it meant she didn't have to listen to Shirley finish that sentence.

"I did it." Carey's words sent the room into silence. Jorge shifted in his chair, possibly uncomfortable with hearing such an admission from his client. But Carey made his statement calmly, as if the truth had settled something within him. He looked at Ally. "I think you need to hear me say it."

She nodded, understanding passing between them that she

desperately wanted to delve further into. But she didn't want Shirley involved in that conversation, so she'd wait until they were alone. Did he already know about Maggie? She'd never given him enough credit for being able to read her.

"Why are you doing this?" Shirley practically wailed.

Carey looked at Shirley, more focused than Ally had seen him in some time. "Because my life is out of control. I've been blaming everyone else for my problems. If I'm going to stay clean, I have to grow up."

Shirley tried for several minutes to change his mind. But he stood firm, gaining some respect from Ally in the process. If he could stand up to their mother about something as serious as this, then surely she could start doing the same. Their visitation time was almost up when Carey asked Jorge to walk Shirley out.

"Al?" he said when Ally stood to follow. He tilted his head toward Shirley, indicating Ally should wait until they'd left. When the door shut behind them, Ally turned to face him. "The woman who I—you've been in contact with her?"

"I have."

"Can you tell her I'm sorry?"

"Carey, I—"

"Please, Al." He drew his brows together. "Stealing money from Ma and from you. I don't know—that always felt like it was okay because it was family. I know that's messed up, but I needed the drugs so bad. I was in so much pain without them."

"And we let it slide for the same reason. Even though it made me so mad at you."

"But taking your dad's gun was wrong. And what I did to that lady—"

"Her name is Maggie Davidson." Something in her voice gave her away, because he narrowed his eyes as if she'd just told him how she felt about Maggie.

"What I did to Miss Davidson, she must have been so scared. I'm not that guy. At least I never will be again."

She wanted to believe him. And, she'd decided, she would give him the chance to prove himself. She wouldn't cut him off. But some things were going to change, with him and in her relationship with Shirley.

Chapter Twenty

Ally sat in her car in the parking lot of Maggie's apartment building and stared up at her living-room window. A soft glow shone behind the closed curtains. Maggie was home. There went Ally's one excuse for not being able to at least try to talk to her.

She'd been very brave after she left the detention center, practicing aloud in the car what she might say. She tried to imagine Maggie's response, but, in her mind, Maggie was quite unforgiving. Maybe she was just preparing for the worst.

The beauty of Maggie living in an apartment complex was that she could still leave. It wasn't as if she were sitting in Maggie's driveway. She thought about her conversation with Carey and the determination that had surged through her following that exchange. She wasn't here just to ask Maggie to forgive her for their fight about owning a gun. She was here to convince Maggie that they deserved a real chance to be together. Given who they each were and the complications of dealing with Ally's family, that was a big ask.

She opened the car door and set one foot on the ground. She wanted this. She wanted Maggie. If she let herself consider that Maggie might say yes, exhilaration sang through her body like the quiver of a releasing bow string.

She got out of the car, strode up, rapped on Maggie's door, and—waited. She was there. The light was on. Her car was in the lot. Oddly, Ally hadn't considered that Maggie just might not open the door. She scowled in frustration. Then, thinking Maggie could be looking through the peephole, she adopted a peaceful expression.

Maybe she hadn't knocked hard enough, so she tried one more time. She clasped her hands together in front of her, then behind her, then awkwardly hung them at her sides. Why didn't she know what to do with her hands? Her arms felt like they didn't belong on her body. Her pulse pounded in her neck. How long should she stand here?

She'd just decided to give up and had turned away when the door opened. Maggie stood in the doorway, and Ally nearly sighed. She wore a T-shirt and pajama pants with plump cartoon birds on them. Her bare feet peeked out from under the pants hems, toenails tipped in deep red. She looked beautiful.

"It's so good to see you." Ally couldn't help her breathy pronouncement.

Maggie's cool expression wavered just a bit before she fixed it again.

"Can I come in?"

"No." Maggie put her hand on the doorjamb as if she needed to physically block Ally from entering. Ally wasn't about to force her way in, but Maggie wanted to let her in. Ally could see it in the soft bend of her elbow and the angle of her body toward Ally.

"Why did you open the door, then?"

Maggie didn't answer, but she stepped back out of the way. Ally eased past her and moved into the living room, needing a little bit of distance to control her urge to touch Maggie. She wanted to brush her arm, to take her hand, to draw her into a hug.

"I've missed you."

"What are you doing here, Ally?" Maggie folded her arms across her chest.

"I wanted to talk."

"I don't want to argue about our impossible situation." Despite her posture, Maggie didn't totally pull off nonchalance.

She bit her lower lip and blinked quickly as if against the sting of tears.

"Neither do I."

"Then what are you doing here?"

"I'd like to fix it."

Maggie's reaction to Ally's words was immediate. Her shoulders rose with a sudden intake of breath, and she rolled her eyes upward as they filled with tears.

"See, that's the thing about an impossible situation, Ally. There is no fixing it."

Maggie's watery eyes broke Ally's heart. "Can't we try?"

"So we can end up here again? No. I can't get over you another time."

"You got over me? Then if you won't let me try to fix us, will you at least tell me how you managed that? Because I can't get you out of my head." *No. I can't get you out of my heart.*

"I'm not asking the DA to drop the charges, if that's what all this is about." Maggie straightened, drawing from a reserve of strength that Ally was certain she didn't possess herself.

"What? Why would you say that?"

"The ADA told me Carey went back to jail. I know how hard that must be for you. So if you're here hoping for—or worse, if that's what your plan was from the beginning—"

"No. God, no." Ally surged forward two steps, then stopped as Maggie backed up. "I wouldn't."

"That's kind of what it looks like." Maggie yanked open the door, inviting Ally to leave.

"Wait. Maggie." Now she did move closer, stopping directly in front of Maggie. She took the door from her and slowly closed it. "I'm not asking you to change anything about the trial. In fact, there's not going to be a trial."

"What?"

"I—can we sit down?" She gestured toward the couch.

Maggie nodded. Ally sighed and sat at one end, expecting Maggie to sit at the other. But Maggie took the adjacent chair, farthest away from Ally. Ally scooted across two cushions to the end of the couch closest to Maggie but didn't do anything to close the remaining space.

"I'm sorry we argued about you buying a gun. I should have handled that conversation better. I have my own beliefs about gun control, and they haven't changed. But I've never been in the situation you were in, and I shouldn't pass judgment on how you're handling things."

"I didn't buy a gun."

Ally hung her head briefly, then met Maggie's eyes. "I can't say I'm not relieved."

"I didn't decide not to do it because you disapproved."

"Okay. There were a lot of negatives in that sentence, but I think I got it."

"I went to a shooting range—with Charlie."

Ally grimaced, then quickly turned her expression into a not-very-genuine smile. "Go on."

"Ultimately, I don't want to be someone who has to carry a gun to feel safer. I'm coming to terms with the way the danger in the world has touched me. And I plan to live with the risk that it could happen again."

Ally nodded. She went through her day not worrying about her own safety. In reality, she could easily be in Maggie's situation. She worked alone in her noisy garage, not as aware of her surroundings as she should be. She often delivered furniture, by herself, in unfamiliar neighborhoods. History had proved that simply having breakfast at a Waffle House in Nashville put lives at risk. The world—and her city—would never be as safe as it had once been.

"Ever since the robbery, nothing has been simple. I work downtown. Do you know how many people I encounter walking from my car to my office, or to lunch? I used to like it. People-watching. The diversity, the energy—the bustle of people with a variety of goals for their day downtown. Now, I'm scanning for something shifty—something that hints at malicious intentions."

"I hate that Carey did that to you. It's still hard for me to think of the boy that I grew up with reaching a point where armed robbery was an option for him." She scooted forward on the cushion and caught Maggie's gaze before continuing. "And I felt guilty about how he got the gun. I was careless, and through a series of events, my actions put you in danger."

"You couldn't have known what he would do."

"No. But I can promise it won't happen again. I've already spoken with the police about what happens to that gun once it isn't needed for evidence. It will be destroyed, at my request."

"It was your dad's. If you want—"

"I don't have any good memories attached to it. I don't want it. And no one else should have it either." She rested her elbows on her knees and clasped her hands, rubbing the back of one thumb with the other. "I met with Carey, his attorney, and my mother today. He's taking the deal from the ADA. He's going to plead guilty. He admitted to me that he did it. I mean, I knew he did, but hearing him say the words..."

"I—I don't even know what to say." Fresh tears dampened Maggie's lashes.

"I figured you'd hear from the prosecutor or from Charlie or something. But I wanted to tell you myself. Did they discuss the plea with you before they offered it?"

Maggie nodded.

"He'll serve three years." Ally couldn't keep sadness from saturating her voice. Without having to endure a trial, this was the closest thing to justice Maggie could get. But how would three years in prison change Carey?

"I'm sorry."

"No." Maggie jumped at Ally's declaration, which came out more emphatic than she'd intended. "You don't have anything to apologize to me for."

"These past four months have been the most tumultuous of my life. Knowing that the end of it all is in sight—I'm not sure what to do now."

"I have some ideas about that." Ally inched forward a bit more, her knees almost touching Maggie's.

"You do?"

"For starters, you should come to my house tomorrow night for dinner."

"Dinner?"

Ally nodded. "But you should definitely bring these pants." She pinched a tiny bit of the fabric at Maggie's knee and tugged. "You know, just in case it gets late and you want to stay."

"Ally—"

"No, wait. I realized that I can spend the rest of my life looking after my mother and my brother. Or I can do what makes me happy. And I choose me—er, you. It's—because you're the person who makes me happy." She grunted in frustration. "I'm trying to tell you I love you, and somehow I'm managing to screw that up, too."

Maggie stared at her, then smiled. "You're doing just fine."

"Yeah?"

"Yes." She leaned forward and took Ally's face in her hands. "And I love you, too."

"You do?"

Maggie laughed as Ally pulled her out of the chair and into her lap. But given the way she was perched on the edge of the cushion, Maggie's momentum threw them both off balance, and they tumbled back onto the couch together. Ally gathered Maggie against her. She kissed Maggie softly, then more deeply.

"I don't know how everything is going to work out. But I promise to always put *us* first."

"And what would you say if I told you that I had some pajama pants with sheep on them that I think would fit you perfectly? In case you want to stick around tonight."

"Sheep?"

"Is that a deal breaker?"

"I suppose not."

"Great. I'll go get them." Maggie rolled off the couch and returned a minute later with the pajamas. "Oh, and I'm going to need you to be the little spoon again."

Ally laughed and snatched the pants out of Maggie's hand. She stood and shoved down her jeans, then pulled on the pajamas. "I know you're expecting me to balk at that one. But secretly, that was one of the best night's sleep I've ever had." She caught Maggie around the waist and buried her face in her neck, dropping kisses on every inch of skin she touched. "I'll be whatever spoon you need me to be."

❖

Maggie walked through the metal detector in the lobby of the courthouse, continuing when no alarm sounded, and retrieved her purse from the bin on the other side of the x-ray machine. She stopped in front of the coffee shop, which was nearly as busy as the first day she'd been in this lobby almost six months ago.

"Did you want to go in and get a cup for old time's sake?" Ally asked as she came to stand beside her.

Maggie shook her head. Her nervous stomach couldn't handle coffee right now. She walked straight to the bank of elevators and staked out a spot near one of the cars. She could feel Ally's presence behind her, even before Ally touched her lower back.

When the doors opened, Ally steered her inside and into the corner. Maggie didn't understand why Ally seemed so determined until she realized Ally had situated herself between Maggie and the other occupants of the elevator.

Ally turned her back to the rest of the crowded car and bent her head to speak in Maggie's ear. "Are you okay?"

"I'm good."

Ally squeezed her hand, and when she would have released it, Maggie held on. The doors opened on almost every floor, and people filtered out, until only two other people remained with them. On the sixth floor, Ally stepped aside and let Maggie leave first.

Maggie paused outside courtroom 6B and walked to the nearby window. Outside, a picturesque view of downtown spread out before her. The skyscrapers rose up to her right, bordered by the older two- and three-story commercial buildings along the edge of the river. Two bridges spanned the river, a long barge passing under one of them. She couldn't imagine a more peaceful view in a place that inspired such turmoil within her.

Ally stood beside her, their shoulders touching, but she didn't say anything. Maggie glanced at her and found her eyes scanning the scene outside as well.

"Are you sure us going in there together is a good idea?" Maggie said quietly enough to not be overheard by the other people filing into the two courtrooms at this end of the hall.

"Yes. I think you need to see this. And I don't want to be anywhere except at your side."

Maggie curled two of her fingers around Ally's index finger, pulling playfully. "I appreciate that, though—I'm not saying I'll ever be ready to be friendly with him. But Carey is your brother. Your history with him is vastly different than mine. So if you want to be in his corner—"

"Hey." Ally turned to face Maggie, took her hand fully, and waited until Maggie made eye contact. "I'm here with you. I talked to Carey about it, and he knows we'll be there together. He's going to continue working on his sobriety. I agreed to visit occasionally while he's incarcerated. When he gets out, we'll figure out where things stand."

"And your mom?"

"She's pissed." Ally smiled. When Maggie tried to pull her hand free, Ally kept hold. "We had a talk, too. I told her things are going to change. I'm not her caretaker. And I'm going to pursue my own life. She'll be mad at me whether I'm here with you or not. So don't worry about it."

Shirley had refused to come to court. She said she couldn't watch her baby boy taken away in handcuffs. Ally didn't know if they would put him in cuffs in the courtroom. But she suspected Shirley would only have made a scene anyway. Shirley had said her good-byes to him when they visited on Thursday. And she would be a regular visitor to wherever they transferred him after he was sentenced.

"And you're okay with the fact that your girlfriend and your mother will never have any kind of relationship?"

"Okay? Not really. But that's because I think you're amazing and can't imagine anyone missing out on knowing you." Ally turned them toward the double doors to the courtroom. "Let's get in there."

After they entered, Ally led them to a row situated behind the prosecutor's table. Sasha saw them come in and waved. She cast a curious glance at Ally, then smiled at Maggie. Maggie hadn't told her who she'd be there with, and she didn't know if Sasha knew who Ally was. But she didn't care. Soon this chapter would be closed.

They stood with everyone else when the judge entered, then sat again when he commanded it from the bench. When Carey's case was called, Maggie grasped Ally's hand. She forced herself to look at him as he followed the deputy into the room from the door leading to the courthouse's temporary detention area.

He immediately scanned the crowd, relief painting his expression when he locked on Ally. For a moment, Maggie saw the brother Ally described from when they were kids. His face looked softer than she remembered—younger. His love for Ally emanated from his eyes. When his gaze shifted to Maggie, she expected to see it harden. But she detected no hatred or resentment, only extreme sorrow. She didn't see an evil man, rather one who had gotten lost and so desperate. Despite knowing how he got here, she'd never been able to see him that way before. But there was no denying it in the face of the agony before her.

The deputy steered him behind a table, next to his attorney, and the moment was broken. He stood beside the public defender, his shoulders rounded and his head bowed. After some conversation between Sasha and the judge about the details of the plea, the judge turned to Carey. To his credit, Carey raised his chin and gave the judge the respectful attention he deserved.

"Mr. Rowe, has your attorney briefed you on the plea agreement just discussed here in this courtroom?"

"Yes, Your Honor."

"So, then, how do you plead?"

Cary glanced over his shoulder at Ally and gave a small nod, which Ally returned. Ally's fingers tightened around Maggie's when he turned back to the judge and said, "Guilty."

About the Author

Erin Dutton resides near Nashville, TN, with her wife, but will gladly jump at any opportunity to load the dogs up in the car or RV and travel. In 2007, she published her first book, *Sequestered Hearts*, and has kept writing since. She's a proud recipient of the 2011 Alice B. Readers Appreciation Medal for her body of work.

When not working or writing, she enjoys playing golf, photography, and spending time with friends and family.

Books Available From Bold Strokes Books

Daughter of No One by Sam Ledel. When their worlds are threatened, a princess and a village outcast must overcome their differences and embrace a budding attraction if they want to survive. (978-1-63555-427-4)

Fear of Falling by Georgia Beers. Singer Sophie James is ready to shake up her career, but her new manager, the gorgeous Dana Landon, has other ideas. (978-1-63555-443-4)

Playing with Fire by Lesley Davis. When Takira Lathan and Dante Groves meet at Takira's restaurant, love may find its way onto the menu. (978-1-63555-433-5)

Practice Makes Perfect by Carsen Taite. Meet law school friends Campbell, Abby, and Grace, law partners at Austin's premier boutique legal firm for young, hip entrepreneurs. Legal Affairs: one law firm, three best friends, three chances to fall in love. (978-1-63555-357-4)

The Last Seduction by Ronica Black. When you allow true love to elude you once and you desperately regret it, are you brave enough to grab it when it comes around again? (978-1-63555-211-9)

Wavering Convictions by Erin Dutton. After a traumatic event, Maggie has vowed to regain her strength and independence. So how can Ally be both the woman who makes her feel safe and a constant reminder of the person who took her security away? (978-1-63555-403-8)

A Bird of Sorrow by Shea Godfrey. As Darrius and her lover, Princess Jessa, gather their strength for the coming war, a mysterious spell will reveal the truth of an ancient love. (978-1-63555-009-2)

All the Worlds Between Us by Morgan Lee Miller. High school senior Quinn Hughes discovers that a broken friendship is actually a door propped open for an unexpected romance. (978-1-63555-457-1)

Falling by Kris Bryant. Falling in love isn't part of the plan, but will Shaylie Beck put her heart first and stick around, or tell the damaging truth? (978-1-63555-373-4)

An Intimate Deception by CJ Birch. Flynn County Sheriff Elle Ashley has spent her adult life atoning for her wild youth, but when she finds her ex, Jessie, murdered two weeks before the small town's biggest social event, she comes face-to-face with her past and all her well-kept secrets. (978-1-63555-417-5)

Cash and the Sorority Girl by Ashley Bartlett. Cash Braddock doesn't want to deal with morality, drugs, or people. Unfortunately, she's going to have to. (978-1-63555-310-9)

Secrets in a Small Town by Nicole Stiling. Deputy Chief Mackenzie Blake has one mission: find the person harassing Savannah Castillo and her daughter before they cause real harm. (978-1-63555-436-6)

Stormy Seas by Ali Vali. The high-octane follow-up to the best-selling action-romance *Blue Skies*. (978-1-63555-299-7)

The Road to Madison by Elle Spencer. Can two women who fell in love as girls overcome the hurt caused by the father who tore them apart? (978-1-63555-421-2)

Dangerous Curves by Larkin Rose. When love waits at the finish line, dangerous curves are a risk worth taking. (978-1-63555-353-6)

Love to the Rescue by Radclyffe. Can two people who share a past really be strangers? (978-1-62639-973-0)

Love's Portrait by Anna Larner. When museum curator Molly Goode and benefactor Georgina Wright uncover a portrait's secret, public and private truths are exposed, and their deepening love hangs in the balance. (978-1-63555-057-3)

Model Behavior by MJ Williamz. Can one woman's instability shatter a new couple's dreams of happiness? (978-1-63555-379-6)

Pretending in Paradise by M. Ullrich. When travelwisdom.com assigns PR specialist Caroline Beckett and travel blogger Emma Morgan to cover a hot new couples retreat, they're forced to fake a relationship to secure a reservation. (978-1-63555-399-4)

Recipe for Love by Aurora Rey. Hannah Little doesn't have much use for fancy chefs or fancy restaurants, but when New York City chef Drew Davis comes to town, their attraction just might be a recipe for love. (978-1-63555-367-3)

The House by Eden Darry. After a vicious assault, Sadie, Fin, and their family retreat to a house they think is the perfect place to start over, until they realize not all is as it seems. (978-1-63555-395-6)

Uninvited by Jane C. Esther. When Aerin McLeary's body becomes host for an alien intent on invading Earth, she must work with researcher Olivia Ando to uncover the truth and save humankind. (978-1-63555-282-9)

Comrade Cowgirl by Yolanda Wallace. When cattle rancher Laramie Bowman accepts a lucrative job offer far from home, will her heart end up getting lost in translation? (978-1-63555-375-8)

Double Vision by Ellie Hart. When her cell phone rings, Giselle Cutler answers it—and finds herself speaking to a dead woman. (978-1-63555-385-7)

Inheritors of Chaos by Barbara Ann Wright. As factions splinter and reunite, will anyone survive the final showdown between gods and mortals on an alien world? (978-1-63555-294-2)

Spinning Tales by Brey Willows. When the fairy tale begins to unravel and villains are on the loose, will Maggie and Kody be able to spin a new tale? (978-1-63555-314-7)

Love on Lavender Lane by Karis Walsh. Accompanied by the buzz of honeybees and the scent of lavender, Paige and Kassidy must find a way to compromise on their approach to business if they want to save Lavender Lane Farm—and find a way to make room for love along the way. (978-1-63555-286-7)

The Do-Over by Georgia Beers. Bella Hunt has made a good life for herself and put the past behind her. But when the bane of her high school existence shows up for Bella's class on conflict resolution, the last thing they expect is to fall in love. (978-1-63555-393-2)

BOLDSTROKESBOOKS.COM

Looking for your next great read?

Visit BOLDSTROKESBOOKS.COM
to browse our entire catalog of paperbacks, ebooks,
and audiobooks.

Want the first word on what's new?
Visit our website for event info,
author interviews, and blogs.

Subscribe to our free newsletter for sneak peeks,
new releases, plus first notice of promos
and daily bargains.

SIGN UP AT
BOLDSTROKESBOOKS.COM/signup

Bold Strokes Books is an award-winning publisher committed to quality and diversity in LGBTQ fiction.